WHAT READERS ARE SAYING ABOUT KAREN KINGSBURY'S BOOKS

Karen Kingsbury's books inspire me to be a stronger follower of Jesus Christ, to be a better wife, mother, sister, and friend. Thank you, Karen, for your faithfulness to the Lord's gentle whisper.

Tamara B.

It's as simple as this: God's heart comes off these pages — every line, every word. You can feel the love and redemption of Christ through every character's life in each book. The message is a message of hope, hope in the One who has saved us and reigns victorious!

Brenae D.

Karen's books are like a personal Bible study — there are so many situations that can be applied directly to the truths found in God's Word to help strengthen and encourage me.

Laura G.

I have read many of Karen's books, and I cry with every one. I feel like I actually know the people in the story, and my heart goes out to all of them when something happens!

Kathy N.

Novels are minivacations, and Karen Kingsbury's novels are my favorite destination.

Rachel S.

Karen Kingsbury's books are amazing! They are inspirational, encouraging, heart touching, and definitely life changing. Thank you, Karen, for sharing your gift with us.

Lisa M. P.

The best author in the country.

Mary H.

Karen's books are like chocolate — very addicting! You can't just eat one piece at a time, you have to eat the whole thing — you can't just read one chapter at a time, you have to read the whole book!

Sarah M.

Karen truly has a God-given talent. I have laughed, cried, and rejoiced with your characters as if they were real people! Please keep writing, Karen. I can't put your books down! God bless you!

Rebekah H.

The stories are fiction; their impact is real.

Debbie L. R.

It was my lucky day when a friend introduced me to Karen Kingsbury's books! A day without KK isn't complete …

Bette O. J.

My daughter and I "fight" to read Karen's books first. She has even said, "Mom, I'll do dishes. *You* go read the latest Karen Kingsbury book!"

Terry S.

Recently I made an effort to find *good* Christian writers, and I've hit the jackpot with Karen Kingsbury!

Linda

Karen Kingsbury books are like my best friends, they make me cry, laugh, and give me encouragement. God bless you, Karen, for using your talent for Him.

Tammy G.

Every time I read one of Karen's books I think, "It's the best one yet." Then the next one comes out and I think, "No, this is the best one."

April B. M.

Karen Kingbury's books are fantastic! She always makes me feel like I'm living the story along with the characters!

Courtney M. G.

Karen's books speak to the heart. They are timely, entertaining, but, more important, they speak God's love into hungry souls.

Debbie P. K.

Whenever I pick up a new KK book, two things are consistent: tissues and finishing the whole book in one day.

Nel L.

When I was in Iraq, Mrs. Kingsbury's books were like a cool breeze on a hot summer day, and they made the hard days a bit easier to bear. By the end of my tour, all the ladies in my tent were hooked!

Olivia G.

These books are the *best*! I have bought every one of them. I love getting my friends "hooked" on Karen Kingsbury!

Dana T. C.

Not only do Karen Kingsbury books make you laugh and make you cry, they will leave you begging for more. I stay awake all night when a new one comes out reading by flashlight while my family sleeps!

Hellen H.

Reading a Karen Kingsbury book is like watching a really good movie. I just can't get enough of her books.

Esther O.

The lady who orders books for our church library shakes her head and laughs when I tell her, "Okay, Karen Kingsbury has a new book out! I get first dibs when you get it!"

Jeannette M. B.

Each new Karen Kingsbury book is like a visit home. Nothing beats time with family and friends, which is just what Karen's characters are!

Erin M.

As someone who has struggled with health issues over the last two years, Karen's books have been such an encouragement to me. They remind me that God is with me, and will never leave me. Please keep writing. I need that reminder.

Carrie F.

Pick up a Karen Kingsbury book, and I guarantee you will never be the same again! Karen's books have a way of reaching the deepest parts of your soul and touching places of your heart that are longing for something more.

Becky S.

Karen Kingsbury's books make a way for God to get a hold of your heart and never let go!

Jessica E.

Karen Kingsbury really brings fiction to life, and I'm "longing" to read the next segment. Real men really do read KK!

Phil C.

God's love, mercy, and hope shines through every one of Karen Kingsbury's books. She has a passion for the Lord and it shows in every story she writes. She is amazing!

Kristi C. M.

It is hard for me to walk out of a bookstore without a Karen Kingsbury book in my possession. I am hooked.

Shilah N.

Karen Kingsbury is changing the world — one reader at a time.

Lauren W.

Karen writes straight from the heart and touches each of her readers with every new story! Love, loss, family, faith, all the struggles we each face every day come to life in the characters she creates.

Amber B.

Other Life-Changing Fiction™ by Karen Kingsbury

www.KarenKingsbury.com

KAREN
NEW YORK TIMES
BESTSELLING AUTHOR
KINGSBURY

THE BAXTER FAMILY

Coming Home

A Story of Undying Hope

ZONDERVAN®

ZONDERVAN.com/
AUTHORTRACKER
follow your favorite authors

We want to hear from you. Please send your comments about this book to us in care of zreview@zondervan.com. Thank you.

ZONDERVAN

Coming Home
Copyright © 2012 by Karen Kingsbury

This title is also available as a Zondervan ebook.
Visit www.zondervan.com/ebooks.

This title is also available in a Zondervan audio edition.
Visit www.zondervan.fm.

Requests for information should be addressed to:

Zondervan, *Grand Rapids, Michigan 49530*

Library of Congress Cataloging-in-Publication Data

Kingsbury, Karen.
    Coming home / Karen Kingsbury.
       p.   cm.
      ISBN 978-0-310-26698-3 (hardcover, jacketed)
      I. Title.
    PS3561.I4873C66—2012
    813'.54—dc23   2012014735

Published in association with the literary agency of Alive Communications, Inc., 7680 Goddard Street, Suite 200, Colorado Springs, CO 80920. www.alivecommunications.com

Cover photography: © Andre Jenny / Alamy
Interior design: Michelle Espinoza

Printed in the United States of America

12 13 14 15 16 17 18 /DCI/ 20 19 18 17 16 15 14 13 12 11 10 9 8 7 6 5 4 3 2 1

DEDICATION

To Donald, my Prince Charming . . .

ANOTHER YEAR BEHIND US, AND ALREADY Tyler has finished his first year at Liberty University, while Kelsey is now a married woman. I'll never forget watching you walk our sweet girl down the aisle. Hard to believe that precious wedding-planning season has come and gone. Isn't our Lord so faithful? Not just with our kids, but in leading our family where He wants us to be. Closing in on a year in Nashville, and it's so very clear that God wanted us here. Not just for my writing and to be near Christian movies and music — but for our kids, and even for us. I love how you've taken to this new season of being more active in my ministry, and helping our boys bridge the gap between being teenagers and becoming young men. And now that you're teaching again we are both right where God wants us. Thank you for being steady and strong and good and kind. Hold my hand and walk with me through the coming seasons — the graduations and growing up and getting older. All of it's possible with you by my side. Let's play and laugh and sing and dance. And together we'll watch our children take wing. The ride is breathtakingly wondrous. I pray it lasts far into our twilight years. Until then, I'll enjoy not always knowing where I end and you begin. I love you always and forever.

To Kyle, my newest son . . .

KYLE, YOU AND KELSEY ARE MARRIED now, and forevermore we will see you as our son, as the young man God planned for our

9

daughter, the one we prayed for and talked to God about and hoped for. Your heart is beautiful in every way, Kyle. How you cherish simple moments and the way you are kind beyond words. You see the good in people and situations and you find a way to give God the glory always. I will never forget your coming to me and Donald at different times and telling us that you wanted to support Kelsey and keep her safe — and ultimately that you wanted to love her all the days of your life. All of it is summed up in the way you do one simple action: The way you look at our precious Kelsey. It's a picture that will hang forever on the wall of my heart. You look at Kelsey as if nothing and no one else in all the world exists except her. In your eyes at that moment is the picture of what love looks like. Kyle, as God takes you from one stage to another — using that beautiful voice of yours to glorify Him and lead others to love Jesus — I pray that you always look at Kelsey the way you do today. We thank God for you, and we look forward to the beautiful seasons ahead. Love you always!

To Kelsey, my precious daughter ...

MY PRECIOUS DAUGHTER, YOU ARE MARRIED now. I think of the dozens of books where I've written about you in these front pages, how you have literally grown up in dedications. The days when you were in middle school and high school, college and engaged. All of it has been detailed in the dedications of my books. And now you are Kelsey Kupecky. Your wedding was the most beautiful day, a moment in time destined from the first thought of you and Kyle in the heart of God. Kyle is the guy we've prayed for since you were born. God created him to love you, Kelsey — and you to love him. He is perfect for you, an amazing man of God whose walk of faith is marked by kindness, integrity, determination, and passion. We love him as if we've known him forever. Now, as you two move into the future God has for you, as you seek to follow your dreams and shine brightly for Him in all you do, we will be here for you both. We will pray for you, believe in you, and support you however we best can. With Kyle's ministry of music and yours in acting, there are no limits to how God will use you both. I rejoice in what He is doing in your life, Kelsey. He has used your years of struggle to make you into the deeply rooted, faithful young woman you are today. Keep trusting God, keep putting Him first. I always knew this season would come — and now it is here. Enjoy every minute, sweetheart. You will always be the light of our family, the laughter in our hearts, the one-in-a-million girl who inspired an entire series. My precious Kelsey, I pray that God will bless you mightily in the years to come, and that you will always know how He used this time in your life to draw you close to Him and to prepare you for what's ahead. In the meantime, you'll be in my heart every moment. I love you, sweetheart.

To Tyler, my lasting song ...

IT'S HARD TO BELIEVE YOU'RE ALREADY finished with your first year of college, ready for the next season of challenges and adventures. I love that it's summer now, and once again you are home. Especially when having a home in Nashville is something new to you. Considering how quickly we made the move to the south, it's amazing you have any sense of home at all. But that will come, and you've handled the changes so well. Along the way you have grown into an amazing godly young man. Your blog, *Ty's Take*, is being followed by so many of my readers longing to know how God is working in your life while you're at college. What's incredible is how you have become such a great writer in the process. I know you are planning to make a ministry-related career out of singing for Jesus on stages from sea to sea. But don't be surprised if God also puts you at a computer keyboard where you'll write books for Him, too. Oh, and let's not forget your gift of directing. So many exciting times ahead, Ty. I can barely take it all in. I still believe with all my heart that God has you right where He wants you. Learning so much — about performing for Him and becoming the man He wants you to be. You are that rare guy with a most beautiful heart for God and others. Your dad and I are so proud of you, Ty. We're proud of your talent and your compassion for people and your place in our family. And we're proud you earned a scholarship to Liberty University. However your dreams unfold, we'll be in the front row cheering loudest as we watch them happen. Hold on to Jesus, son. Keep shining for Him! I love you.

To Sean, my happy sunshine ...

IT'S SUMMER, AND FOR THE FIRST time you get a whole off-season just to focus on basketball! That's a wonderful thing, but even more wonderful is the way you've improved as a student, Sean. You are growing up and listening to God's lead, and in the process you are taking your studies and your homework so much more seriously. God will bless you for how you're being faithful in the little things. He has such great plans for you, despite the fact that the move to Nashville wasn't altogether easy on you. We all left great friends behind in Washington, perhaps you more than the others. But you are open to communicating about your feelings, and you believe with us that the opportunities here are worth pursuing. You've always had the best attitude, and now — even when there are hard days — you've kept that great attitude. Be joyful, God tells us. And so in our family you give us a little better picture of how that looks. On top of that, I love how you've gotten more comfortable talking with me and Dad and Kelsey about your life. Stay that close to us, Sean. Remember, home is where your heart is always safe. Your dream of playing college sports — soccer or basketball — is alive and real. Keep working, keep pushing, keep believing. Go to bed every night knowing you did all you could to prepare yourself for the doors God will open in the days ahead. I pray that as you soar for the Lord, He will allow you to be a very bright light indeed. You're a precious gift, son. I love you. Keep smiling and keep seeking God's best.

To Josh, my tenderhearted perfectionist . . .

SOCCER WAS WHERE YOU STARTED WHEN you first came home from Haiti, and soccer is the game that God seems to be opening up for you — both when we were in Washington and here in Nashville. We prayed about what was next, whether you might continue to shine on the football field and the soccer field, or whether God might narrow your options to show you where He is leading. Now we all need to pray that as you continue to follow the Lord in your sports options, He will continue to lead you so that your steps are in keeping with His. This we know — there remains for you a very real possibility that you'll play competitive sports at the next level. But even with all your athleticism, I'm most proud of your spiritual and social growth this past year. You've grown in heart, maturity, kindness, quiet strength, and the realization that time at home is short. God is going to use you for great things, and I believe He will put you on a public platform to do it. Stay strong in Him, and listen to His quiet whispers so you'll know which direction to turn. I'm so proud of you, son. I'll forever be cheering on the sidelines. Keep God first in your life. I love you always.

To EJ, my chosen one . . .

EJ, I'M SO GLAD YOU KNOW just how much we love you and how deeply we believe in the great plans God has for you. With new opportunities spread out before you, I know you are a bit uncertain. But I see glimpses of determination and effort that tell me with Christ you can do anything, son. One day not too far off from here, you'll be applying to colleges, thinking about the career choices ahead of you and the path God might be leading you down. Wherever that path takes you, keep your eyes on Jesus and you'll always be as full of possibility as you are today. I expect great things from you, EJ, and I know the Lord expects that, too. I'm so glad you're in our family — always and forever. I'm praying you'll have a strong passion to use your gifts for God as you head into your junior year. Thanks for your giving heart, EJ. I love you more than you know.

To Austin, my miracle boy ...

AUSTIN, I CAN ONLY SAY I'M blown away by your effort this past school year. Leaving Washington and all your friends was not easy — especially for you, since you were our most social student at King's Way Christian. But rather than grumble and complain or waste time looking back, you simply moved ahead. From that first day when you stepped onto the football field, you have given one-hundred percent of your special heart to everything related to your new school. Of course in the process you've made friends and memories because you were willing to pour into this new experience. All of you boys have handled the move so well, but I see you seriously embracing it. Along the way you are becoming such a godly leader, determined to succeed for Him, standing taller — and not just because you've grown several inches lately. Austin, I love that you care enough to be and to do your best. It shows in your straight As and it shows in the way you treat your classmates. Of course it absolutely shows when you play any sport. Always remember what I've told you about that determination. Let it push you to be better, but never, ever let it discourage you. You're so good at life, Austin. Keep the passion and keep that beautiful faith of yours. Every single one of your dreams is within reach. Keep your eyes on Him, and we'll keep our eyes on you, our youngest son. There is nothing sweeter than cheering you boys on — and for you that happened from the time you were born, through your heart surgery until now. I thank God for you, for the miracle of your life. I love you, Austin.

And to God Almighty, the Author of Life, who has — for now — blessed me with these.

ACKNOWLEDGMENTS

NO BOOK COMES TOGETHER WITHOUT A GREAT AND TALENTED team of people making it happen. For that reason, a special thanks to my friends at Zondervan, who combined their efforts with a number of people who were passionate about Life-Changing Fiction™ to make *Coming Home* all it could be. A special thanks to my dedicated editor, Sue Brower, and to Don Gates and Alicia Mey, my marketing team. Thanks also to the creative staff and the sales force at Zondervan, who worked tirelessly to put this book in your hands.

A special thanks to my amazing agent, Rick Christian, president of Alive Communications. Rick, you've always believed only the best for me. When we talk about the highest possible goals, you see them as doable, reachable. You are a brilliant manager of my career, an incredible agent, and I thank God for you. But even with all you do for my ministry of writing, I am doubly grateful for your encouragement and prayers. Every time I finish a book, you send me a letter worth framing, and when something big happens, yours is the first call I receive. Thank you for that. But even more, the fact that you and Debbie are praying for me and my family keeps me confident every morning that God will continue to breathe life into the stories in my heart. Thank you for being so much more than a brilliant agent.

Also, thanks to my husband, who puts up with me on deadline and doesn't mind driving through Taco Bell after a football game if I've been editing all day. This wild ride wouldn't be possible without you, Donald. Your love keeps me writing; your prayers keep me believing that God is using this ministry of Life-Changing Fiction™. Also thanks for the hours you put in helping me. It's a full-time job, and I am grateful for your concern for my reader friends. Of course, thanks to my daughter and sons, who pull together — bringing me iced green tea and understanding my sometimes-crazy schedule. I love that you know you're still first, before any deadline.

Thank you also to my mom, Anne Kingsbury, and to my sisters, Tricia and Sue. Mom, you are amazing as my assistant — working day and night sorting through the e-mail from my readers. I appreciate you more than you'll ever know. Traveling with you these past years for Extraordinary Women, Women of Joy, and Women of Faith events has given us times together we will always treasure. The journey gets more exciting all the time!

Tricia, you are the best executive assistant I could ever hope to have. I appreciate your loyalty and honesty, the way you include me in every decision and the daily exciting changes. This ministry of Life-Changing Fiction™ has been so much more effective since you stepped in. Along the way, readers have more to help them in their faith, so much more than a story. Please know that I pray for God's blessings on you always, for your dedication to helping me in this season of writing, and for your wonderful son, Andrew. And aren't we having such a good time too? God works all things for good!

Sue, I believe you should've been a counselor! From your home far from mine, you get batches of reader letters every day, and you diligently answer them using God's wisdom and His Word. When readers get a response from "Karen's sister Susan," I hope they know how carefully you've prayed for them and for the responses you give. Thank you for truly loving what you do, Sue. You're gifted with people, and I'm blessed to have you aboard.

I also want to thank Kyle Kupecky, the newest addition to the Life-Changing Fiction™ staff and to our family. Time and again you exceed my expectations with business and financial matters, and in supervising our many donation programs. Thank you for putting your whole heart into your work at Life-Changing Fiction™. At the same time, I pray your music ministry becomes so widespread and far-reaching that you can one day step down and do only that. In the meantime, just know that I treasure having you as part of the team.

Kelsey, you also are an enormous part of this ministry, and I thank you for truly loving the reader friends God has brought into our lives. What a special season, when you and Kyle can be married and also work together doing ministry from our home office. God is so creative, so amazing. Keep working hard and believing in your dreams. Along the way, I love that you are a part of all God is doing through this special team.

Tyler, a special thanks to you for running the garage warehouse and making sure our storage needs are met, and that we always have books to give away! You're a hard worker — God will always reward that. Thanks also to my forever friends and family, the ones who have been there and continue to be there. Your love has been a tangible source of comfort, pulling us through the tough times and making us know how very blessed we are to have you in our lives.

And the greatest thanks to God. You put a story in my heart, and have a million other hearts in mind — something I could never do. I'm grateful to be a small part of Your plan! The gift is Yours. I pray I might use it for years to come in a way that will bring You honor and glory.

FOREVER IN FICTION

FOR A NUMBER OF YEARS NOW, I'VE HAD THE PRIVILEGE OF offering Forever in Fiction™ as an auction item at fund-raisers across the country. Many of my more recent books have had Forever in Fiction™ characters, characters inspired by real-life people.

In *Coming Home*, I bring you two Forever in Fiction™ characters. The first winners are Albert and Caroline Keck and their family, who won the Desert Christian Academy auction and chose to name their longtime friend Elizabeth Larsen to be Forever in Fiction™. The Keck family and Elizabeth Larsen have been friends for the past thirty-eight years.

Elizabeth is a beautiful seventy-six-year-old pastor's wife with blue eyes, blonde hair, and a tall, slender build. She has a love for people. Elizabeth is known throughout her community for her warm personality, hunger for God's Word, and her ability as an accomplished speaker.

Elizabeth has been married to Paul, a retired pastor, for forty-five years and together they raised two daughters — Kristi and her sister, Kathy, who at age twenty-seven was called to heaven. They have one granddaughter, Cassidy, who they love spending time with, and they love to vacation at Big Bear Lake and in Hawaii. Elizabeth also enjoys reading, watching sports, listening to music and keeping in touch with friends around the world. Elizabeth is a special visitor in the hospital waiting room in *Coming Home*. Her kind words of encouragement and compassion make a difference for the Baxter family.

Keck Family, I hope I've captured a glimpse of your amazing

friend, Elizabeth, and that you smile when you see her here in the story of *Coming Home*, where she will always be forever in fiction.

My second winners are Jules and Lori Griggs, who won Forever in Fiction™ at the Grace Brethren Booster Club Auction in Thousand Oaks. Jules and Lori chose to name their eleven-year-old son, Joey Griggs, as a character in *Coming Home*. Joey is a rough-and-tumble boy who loves riding quads, playing soccer, baseball, and basketball and never stops moving. Joey is an only child, but he loves spending time with his family in Hawaii or on RV trips. He is kind and compassionate, polite, and funny. In addition to sports, he recently found a love of performing, when he played the trumpet in his school's Christmas program. In *Coming Home,* Joey plays the friend of Devin Blake.

Jules and Lori, I hope you smile when you see your wonderful son in the pages of *Coming Home*, where he will be forever in fiction.

A special thanks to both of my auction winners for supporting your various ministries and for your belief in the power of story. I pray that the donations you made to your respective charities will go on to change lives, just as I pray lives will be changed by the impact of the message in *Coming Home*. May God bless you for your love and generosity.

For those of you who are not familiar with Forever in Fiction™, it is my way of involving you, the readers, in my stories, while raising money for charities. The winning bidder of a Forever in Fiction™ package has the right to have his or her name, or the name of a loved one, written into one of my novels.

To date, Forever in Fiction™ has raised more than $200,000 at charity auctions. Obviously, I am able to donate only a limited number of these each year. For that reason, I have set a fairly high minimum bid on this package so that the maximum funds are raised for charities. All money goes to the charity events. If you are interested in receiving a Forever in Fiction™ package for your auction, e-mail your request to *office@KarenKingsbury.com* with the words *Forever in Fiction* in the subject line.

In His Light,
Karen Kingsbury

THE BAXTER FAMILY

Coming Home

One

WHERE HAD THE YEARS GONE?

If Ashley Baxter Blake asked herself one question as she set about planning her father's surprise seventieth birthday it was that one. Where in the world had the years gone? Wasn't it just yesterday that she was flying off to Paris, determined to outrun the reach of her family, the bond of shared faith? Yesterday when she thought Landon Blake too safe and real love too predictable?

She walked across the kitchen of the old farmhouse, the one with the wraparound porch and half a dozen bedrooms framed by old country walls and surrounded by sprawling Indiana acreage. The home where she'd grown up. The Baxter house. Ashley pulled a mug from the cupboard and poured herself a cup of coffee. The comfortable smell of fresh-ground espresso beans and sweet cinnamon filled the air, surrounding her with a million memories.

It was the first Saturday in June, and she'd promised her son Cole she'd make cinnamon rolls to mark the finish of his sophomore year at Clear Creek High School. And of course to celebrate the mostly As he'd gotten on his finals. But for now the kids were still asleep and Landon was out back working on the rose garden. The one her mother had planted and cared for so well before her death.

Ashley looked out the window and surveyed the yard and the trees at the edge of their property. Like old friends from a thousand wonderful moments, the memories gathered. The way they were bound to gather as the details of her father's birthday party came together. Her parents had lived in this very house, after all. The laughter and voices of the five siblings still rang in the walls and from the windows. She took a sip of her coffee and she could see them again. Brooke and Kari and herself ... Erin and Luke. Running across the property or fishing at the pond with their father.

The surprise of their lives was that there weren't just five Baxter kids. There were six. Pictures of Dayne joined the others in her mind, the times when he first found their family and his place among them. A sigh came from the recesses of Ashley's heart. How faithful God had been over the years, how full of provision and beauty. And redemption.

Redemption above all.

Another sip of her coffee and Ashley couldn't help but smile. How many times had they prayed as a family in this very kitchen? How often had their father pulled out his old Bible to lend wisdom when all the world felt like it was falling apart, or when decisions seemed too difficult to make? Yes, theirs had been a beautiful life and always at the center there had been her father.

John Baxter.

He was more than an amazing dad. He was one of Bloomington's favorite people, a doctor at St. Anne's Hospital until a few years ago, and a leader at Clear Creek Community Church. His confidence and kindness spoke peace and truth into every situation. Even after their mom lost her battle to cancer eight years ago, their dad had been a pillar of strength. In the quiet of the early summer morning, Ashley felt the sadness again in her heart. The way she would always feel it when she thought about her mom. But it was hard to imagine how any of them might've survived that time if it hadn't been for their dad's faith. A faith he fanned into a flame for all of them.

She pictured her dad now — healthy and happy, married to

their mother's friend, Elaine, and excited about his retirement years. Most of the family was here in Bloomington, but Ashley's sister Erin and her husband, Sam, and their four girls lived in Texas again. Dayne, too, lived far away. He and his wife, Katy, and their two kids spent most of their time in Los Angeles at the beach house they had in Malibu.

Just last week the local family had met here at the old Baxter house for Sunday dinner and her dad had smiled big. "Elaine and I are planning on more travel this fall. Spend a little time in Texas watching the girls' soccer games. Maybe go to LA when Dayne makes his next movie." Her dad chuckled, his eyes dancing with life. "He says we can be extras. Can't pass up that offer."

Ashley took another few sips of her coffee and let the faithfulness of God settle in around the tender places of her soul. *You've been so good to us, Lord, giving us a love that defines family. And it all started with my parents.* She paused in the silent prayer and looked up at the blue sky over Bloomington. They'd had their days of sorrow certainly. Maybe more than most families. But even then God had made them closer, stronger. And always their father was at the center.

Thank You for him, Lord. Ashley smiled, warmed by the sun streaming through the window and the memories of the past thirteen years. She would forever be grateful for her parents' tenacious love and determination to see her through her rebellious years. For loving her when she returned from Paris and wanted nothing to do with them.

So much had happened since then, so many seasons. *What will the coming years look like, Lord? What brilliant moments of joy, what moments of growth, what times of heartache are ahead?* For a moment, just thinking about the possibility of unknown sorrows seized her heart and brought a rush of fear.

She exhaled, feeling her fears fade as quickly as they had come. Whatever the future held, she didn't need to be afraid.

Good and bad times were a part of life. As her dad always said, "This too shall pass." And through the years that had been true. Nothing stayed the same, except this: God's faithfulness, and the love they had for each other.

ASHLEY WATCHED LANDON BRUSH THE DIRT off his hands onto his jeans and walk up the path to the back door and into the kitchen. He still looked like the young firefighter she'd fallen in love with a decade before. He grinned when he saw her. "Aren't you the most beautiful girl in the world?" He had a smudge of dirt on his cheek, but his blue eyes were all she could see. He came to her and took her gently into his arms. "It's always the same feeling, Ash. Every time I see you." He whispered near the side of her face, holding her body close against his.

"What's that?" She looked into his soul, consumed with a love that had been tested by time. A love without limits. "What do you feel?"

"Like somewhere, sometime, at some point I must've done something right." He kissed her, stirring the always near passion between them. "Because in all His love and mercy, God Almighty chose to give me you."

She felt her smile start in her heart and fill her face. This time she initiated the kiss and after a minute or so they both drew back, breathless, as quiet laughter filled the slight spaces between them. The feel of his face against hers would always be one of Ashley's greatest pleasures. "You have it all wrong." She worked her hands up into his hair and he did the same. When she could speak again she looked into his eyes, straight through him to the parts of him where only she had access. "You're the gift, Landon. You always have been."

He looked at her for a long time, running his thumb lightly over her cheek. "Not sure how I'm supposed to finish in the garden now." He chuckled. Before he could say anything else, Devin's voice from upstairs interrupted them.

"Mom!" He was seven, and every bit the life of the family. "Are the cinnamon rolls ready?"

Ashley grinned at Landon and then moved a few feet away. "Almost. Is Cole up?"

"Nah, he's a lazybones." Devin ran down the stairs as fast as his feet could carry him. He popped into the kitchen, his blond hair tousled, eyes wide. "Want me to wake him up?"

For a moment Ashley held on to the picture of him, his legs longer than they'd been at Christmastime, his pajamas an inch or so too short. She needed to work the image into a painting some-how. For now she went to the oven and checked the pan inside. "He can sleep another ten minutes."

Devin sighed. "Nessa's up." He rolled his eyes. "Playing with her dollhouse. She doesn't wanna look for frogs with me today. She already told me."

Ashley shared a look with Landon as she stifled a giggle. "I bet Daddy'll look for frogs with you."

"Are you kidding?" Landon pushed the sleeves of his long-sleeve T-shirt up. "I was already out there this morning and frogs are everywhere. It's like the plagues of Egypt."

Devin ran to him and flung his arms around Landon's legs. "That's perfect!" He took a quick step back and held out his hand like a crossing guard stopping traffic. "I'll be right back!"

He ran off and Landon crossed the kitchen to meet her. "Even frogs won't take my mind off you."

"Mmm. You make loving easy." They kissed again, the sort of kiss that would stay with them through the morning. "I'm going to check on Janessa."

"Play with dolls, you mean?" Landon's eyes shone with the familiar teasing she'd come to love. "I know you. You can't resist."

"I am grateful God gave us a girl." She turned toward the

stairs. "And true, I might choose doll clothes over frogs." She punctuated the air with her pointer finger. "Not that I don't like frogs. I was an expert before you came along."

They both laughed. "Hey, before you go. You calling everyone today about the party?"

"I am. I'm still trying to talk Erin into coming. She lives a thousand miles away, so I get it." She paused. "I just know Dad would really like her here."

Landon hesitated. "So ... I have an idea ... about the party."

"Okay." She leaned against the counter and freshened up her coffee. "Today's an idea day for sure. I want more than a barbecue."

"Exactly." He folded his arms, thoughtful. "How about each of the six of you write him a letter? Put into words what your dad has meant to each of you." He shrugged, a smile playing on his lips. "You could read them that night. At the party."

"Hmmm." Ashley pictured the possibility. "We'll need extra tissues."

Landon laughed again. "Well, yeah ... but everyone needs a little emotion at a seventieth birthday party, right?"

Ashley liked it. Every one of the grown Baxter kids had a unique and special story. What better time to relive together the faithfulness of the Lord and let their father know how great a role he'd played in the stories of their lives. "Landon ... that's perfect. What a great idea!"

"You know ..." He plucked at a part of his T-shirt near his shoulder. "Every now and then I have a good one."

Devin came running down then and grabbed hold of Landon's hand. "Hurry! Before the rolls are ready. Maybe we can catch the big guy by the pond."

Landon and Ashley shared one more look as he ran off with their younger son. Ashley checked the oven once more and figured she still had eight or nine minutes. Long enough to spend a little time with Janessa and her dolls. She hurried up the stairs and found her daughter lost in a world of make-believe, sitting on her knees, her feet tucked beneath her as she talked to her Kelsey Baby doll. "You want the prettiest clothes, right?"

Janessa held the doll up and danced her around, giving her a high-pitched voice, even higher than her own. "Of course I do, Mommy."

"Okay, then." Janessa set her down and began sorting through dolly outfits.

Ashley watched for a minute from the doorway, unseen by her daughter. Janessa was four, and full of imagination, much like her brothers. But hers didn't take the shape of backyard adventures. Rather Janessa dreamed of dances and princesses and fashionable clothes. Ashley could only imagine how she'd be in high school.

"Hey, there." She stepped into the room and dropped slowly to the floor beside her daughter. "You getting Kelsey Baby ready for a big day?"

Janessa's eyes were the deepest blue, wide and full of innocence. "She's going to coffee with her mommy."

"Ohhh." Ashley nodded, as dramatic as her little girl. "What's she going to wear?"

"Well," Janessa pulled a gold lamé dress from the pile of clothes. "This dress and white shoes."

"I like it." Ashley ran her hand lightly down her daughter's long blonde hair. "You have such lovely taste."

Janessa sat a little straighter. "Thank you. Kelsey Baby says gold is the best because this is a really special coffee date."

The conversation continued, and again Ashley tried to memorize the moment. The sound of her daughter's voice, the feel of the carpet beneath them, the summer breeze through the cracked window, the shimmer of gold lamé. All the details that would fade with time, when Janessa was too old and busy for dolls on a Saturday morning.

Five minutes passed, and Ashley stood. "Time for cinnamon rolls."

Janessa gasped. "Kelsey Baby loves cinnamon rolls." She smiled at Ashley. "I hafta get her dressed first, okay?"

"Okay. I'll save you both a seat." Ashley grinned. By the time she reached the kitchen, Cole was up and sitting at the bar, the sports section sprawled out in front of him. He saw Ashley and smiled. "Morning, Mom. Thanks for baking."

"First Saturday of summer." She slipped on the oven mitts, pulled the pan out and set it on the tiled counter. "Wouldn't miss it."

Cole leaned his elbows on the counter and looked at her. "So I've been thinking." A comfortable silence settled between them for a long moment. "My birth dad. What was he like?"

Ashley tried not to react, even though everything in her felt like it had suddenly flipped upside down. "That's a random question."

"Yeah, I mean, I know who my dad is." He glanced out the window where they could see Landon and Devin. "But the other guy. Am I like him, or do I look like him?"

"Well." Her heart was in her throat, and she struggled at first to find an answer. "I didn't know him very long, Cole. Sadly." She hated the regret and sense of defeat that pushed in against her heart and soul. "He was an artist. A very good one."

"Hmmm. That's what I thought." Cole angled his head, pensive. "Maybe that's why I've been into photography lately."

Ashley didn't point out the fact that she, also, was an artist and that he easily could've gotten his creative bent from her. That wasn't what he needed to hear right now. She smiled at him. "That might be it."

"I mean, it's no big deal." He shrugged. "I was just thinking I should try to find out. You know, look up who he was just so I know."

"We can definitely do that sometime." She wondered if he could sense her discomfort.

"Yeah, maybe sometime." Cole knew that his biological father was dead. But Ashley had never told him that the man had died of AIDS complications. Eventually that information and the story of her short relationship with the man would have to surface. Ashley wasn't looking forward to it.

Janessa ran into the room, and the conversation shifted to Cole's summer baseball schedule. A moment later, Landon and Devin returned to the kitchen with news that Landon was right: more frogs were making their homes around the pond this year than ever before.

"It's frog paradise." Devin raised his fist in the air as he took the spot next to Cole at the bar. "And guess what? Frogs and cinnamon rolls are even double paradise. Plus Joey is coming over. He rode his bike up and now he's asking his mom, but he said it should be fine if we're looking for frogs."

Ashley smiled. Joey was a wonderful boy who lived next door. He loved every sort of sport, and on hot summer days he loved catching frogs with Devin. His parents, Jules and Lori, had come over a few times for iced tea on the back porch while the boys played. He was the sort of friend Ashley hoped would stay in Devin's life for a long time.

"Joey's the best friend ever, Mom, you know why?"

"Why?" Ashley laughed lightly at the intensity of Devin's tone.

"Because he taught me everything I know about riding quads and catching frogs."

Ashley laughed out loud this time. "That's why, huh? Quads and frogs?"

"Eww." Janessa held her Kelsey Baby close to her chest. "Girls don't like frogs." She looked at her doll. "Right, Kelsey Baby?" She paused. "She says she likes princes more than frogs."

"*How* old is she?" Landon whispered the question, laughing

under his breath as he helped Ashley serve the hot rolls. "You know what I think?" He directed the question to the kids. "I think this is going to be the best summer ever."

"Yes!" Cole took a second cinnamon roll from the platter. "I feel a home-run record coming on."

Ashley smiled. A million paintings wouldn't be enough to capture the joy of raising these kids and living this life. When they finished eating they scattered to the backyard and Janessa headed upstairs to change her doll's outfit again. Ashley took the opportunity to sit outside on the back porch and call her siblings. The idea of everyone writing a letter for their dad filled her heart with possibility. The idea that Erin and Dayne and their families might even come? He wouldn't expect this.

She smiled and had another idea. She could even make him a scrapbook. Collect photos from all six of them and re-create the beauty of the last decades. It could be organized by each of his kids in chronological order. Dayne, Brooke, Kari, Ashley, Erin, and Luke. She could even leave room for the letters — so that after they each read them at the party, he could insert them into the book. It would be the greatest scrapbook because their individual stories were so amazing. The things they had come through and the ways God had worked in each of their lives. Sometimes it was more than Ashley could believe.

The scrapbook could be a tremendous gift.

Ashley called Dayne first. Her oldest brother told her he and his family were definitely coming home for the party. "We'll probably fly in that morning and stay through the Fourth of July."

"Perfect." That was Ashley's hope. Their dad's birthday was at the end of June, but the annual picnic at the lake would be the perfect ending to the reunion. She worked her way through the list of her siblings. Each of them was thrilled with the idea of writing a letter for their dad. Erin was the only one who didn't answer, and leaving a message wouldn't be the same, especially when Erin wasn't sure yet if she and her family could make the two-day drive at the end of the month.

The patio overhang kept the direct sun off Ashley, but already the air was warm and humid. Landon had set up a batting cage for Cole at the back of their property where he was hitting one ball after another as they fired at him from the pitching machine. Landon and Devin had stopped looking for frogs, and instead they were collecting trimmings from the garden in an oversized plastic bag.

Ashley tried Erin's home number this time and after two rings this time she answered. "Ashley, hi!"

"You're home! I thought I was going to get your answering machine."

"Sorry. I saw your call come in. I was helping Amy with her sunscreen." She laughed. "We're going to the lake, so everyone's buzzing around getting ready. Amy's so fair skinned it takes ten minutes to make sure she's covered."

"Janessa's like that." Ashley settled back in her chair. She liked this, feeling closer to Erin, talking about their kids. For so many years the two of them rarely spoke; but lately they talked more often, and things were comfortable between them. "Tell me you're coming for Dad's birthday. Everyone else'll be here." She paused, allowing the smile in her voice. "Please?"

Erin laughed again. "It's Sam you need to talk to. He isn't sure he can get the time off work."

"Well ... you moved back more than a year ago, so that means he should have at least a few weeks, right?" Erin's family had lived in Bloomington for a while, but the recession made it hard for Sam to find a job locally and they had been forced to move back to Texas.

"Hmmm. You sound like me." The voices of Erin's girls filled the background. "Anyway, I'll talk to Sam again. I feel like he was starting to cave last time I brought it up."

"Perfect. I'll pray for a complete caving." Ashley explained about the letters for their dad.

"It sounds wonderful, Ashley — oh, it looks like we're ready to go." Erin must have covered the speaker because her voice was muffled as she told the girls to take the cooler out to the car. "Listen, I'll write the letter either way. But I want to be there. Really."

The call ended and Ashley scribbled the words, "Maybe. Hopeful." She went back inside, and called for Janessa. The little girl came running downstairs, still holding her doll. This time she was dressed in a red and white checkered gingham outfit. Ashley held out her hand as Janessa ran up to her. "Kelsey Baby looks ready for some outdoor time."

"She is." Janessa's eyes looked full of adventure. "She might even look at one of Devin's frogs."

"Let's see what they've caught." Holding hands, Ashley and Janessa walked out back to the boys. "It's a beautiful day."

"Because God drew it, Mommy. Right?"

Ashley smiled. "Yes, baby. God's the greatest artist of all."

No words were truer, today especially. His artwork was evident everywhere. From the blue sky overhead to the full rich green of the trees that surrounded their property to the new rosebuds on her mother's bushes to the faces of her family. Wherever she looked one truth remained.

The images from that summer day were simply breathtaking.

Two

ERIN SPREAD PEANUT BUTTER OVER A DOZEN PIECES OF BREAD. She could hardly wait to sit on the sand of Lake Travis. Something about the sun on her face and the water lapping on the nearby shore always took her back to the past and made her worry a little less about today.

And she definitely had reason to worry. Naomi Boggs, the social worker in charge of the adoption of three of her four girls, had called and left messages twice, both times with ominous news. The girls' birth mother — Candy Burns — was out of prison, and she wanted to see her daughters.

The idea was unthinkable, so Erin still hadn't called her back.

She willed herself to relax as she slipped the sandwiches into individual Ziploc bags. Visitations with Candy Burns? The woman had tried to sell her girls before she was convicted of second-degree murder in a drug deal gone bad. Erin had a feeling the woman wasn't rehabilitated, as she claimed, but rather looking for some sort of financial gain. Not that she had proof of this just yet, but Erin knew Candy and now she could only feel suspicious. More than that, she was terrified at the thought that the open adoption agreement they had with the girls' biological grandmother could somehow translate to regular visits with Candy.

Visitations weren't going to happen as long as Erin had anything to say about it.

Put it out of your mind, she told herself. *You can call her back on Monday.* God wouldn't let anything happen to her girls, not after all Erin and Sam went through to adopt them. She felt herself relax. Besides, her brother Luke was a lawyer. He'd help them.

She put the sandwiches in a brown grocery bag and slipped in a box of crackers and six apples. "Sam ... you ready?" She could hear him in the garage, probably packing the ice chest with the bottled water and sweet tea. The sound of the girls giggling upstairs told her they were nearly ready. They loved spending a summer day at the lake.

Erin took the bag of food to the garage where she found Sam. "Sandwiches are ready."

"Perfect." He grinned at her. Sam was a hard worker. This day off would be good for him. "How about the girls?"

"I'll check." Erin thought about Ashley's call as she hurried to the girls' room. It felt good to be wanted at her father's upcoming party. And it gave her something else to think about besides Candy.

She met the girls halfway up the stairs, and after a few more trips back into the house for towels and sunscreen they were on their way. Their favorite beach was thirty minutes down the highway and Erin was grateful that the girls fell into their own conversations as soon as they hit the road. A quick glance in the rearview mirror reminded Erin again how happy their girls were, how they naturally paired off — Clarissa and Chloe, sixteen and fourteen, and Amy Elizabeth and Heidi Jo, nine and eight. Her three blonde daughters, and her little brown-skinned Heidi Jo. Her youngest had a different birth mother, but the four were as close as any biological sisters. Almost like God had known the plan He had for the girls to be friends even in the midst of that messy year eight years ago when she and Sam adopted them.

A warm breeze came through the cracked window and Erin felt herself relax. She glanced at her husband and smiled. Sam looked happier than he'd been all week, ready for a family day on the water. If ever he was in the right mood to say yes to a trip to Bloomington it was today. She put her hand on his knee. "Ashley called when I was making lunch."

"Hmmm." Sam had his hand on the wheel, the other resting on the open window as they headed north on Market Road. He flashed her a crooked smile. "Your dad's birthday?"

"She had a great idea." Erin shifted in her seat so she could see him better. "Everyone's writing Dad a letter. Then we'll read them out loud when we're all together."

Sam laughed quietly and looked at the road ahead. "She doesn't give up, does she?"

"Not usually." Erin smiled at the tenacity of her sister.

"I mean, she seriously knows how to get her own way." Sam's tone was still kind, but his words came across harsh.

Erin watched him, discouraged. She didn't want to fight with him, but she hated moments like this. When it seemed Sam had something against her family. She lowered her voice so the girls couldn't hear her. "You like them, right? My family?" She tried not to sound angry or defensive. She didn't want anything to ruin the afternoon.

"Of course I like them." He gave her a strange look. "My parents have been dead for ten years, Erin. I mean, come on. The Baxters are all the family I have." He allowed a confused laugh. "You aren't serious."

"I don't know. I just wanted to make sure."

He waited a few seconds. "I mean, Erin, for most of the first years of our marriage you were the one who didn't like your family. Remember?"

His words caught her off guard and reminded her of the truth. He was right. If Sam had any doubts about spending time with the Baxters, she had planted them. She had always been close to her parents, but there were many years when she didn't feel close to her sisters. Years when they seemed to leave her out of their conversations and get-togethers. Things were better now, but she was wrong to blame Sam for his hesitation.

"You're right." She hesitated. "But it's different now."

"I know." He looked at her and their eyes held for a moment. "It's okay, Erin. You don't need a clever way to ask me."

She held her breath, not sure where he was headed with this.

He laughed again. "I was going to tell you and the girls today. I already put in for the time off."

"What?" Erin shrieked the word. "Sam, are you serious? We're going to Bloomington?"

"Yes." He looked in the rearview mirror. "Did you hear that, girls? We're going to Bloomington!"

"We are?" Clarissa's voice was the loudest. "Dad, you're the best!"

The girls hooted and hollered, celebrating the fact that once more they would be headed back to the town they loved most. The years they'd spent living in Bloomington, surrounded by cousins, couldn't compare to their experience in Austin. Even though they'd made friends in Texas, Indiana was home to them — as it was for Erin. Only Sam preferred Texas, but Erin understood. His career was here, after all.

The girls chatted a million miles an hour about the fun times ahead, and the anticipated thrill of being in Bloomington again.

"I guess you're the hero." Erin held Sam's hand again. "I know it's a long drive, but I'll help."

"It'll be fun. Seeing your dad … the surprise party. I really didn't want to miss it. I just wasn't sure about the time off. When I knew the situation, I didn't hesitate. I was going to tell you today. Even before Ashley called."

"Then it was meant to be!" Erin settled back into her seat and let the sun warm her face. She could hardly wait for the weeks of June to pass so they could hit the highway.

In the back the girls were singing a Group 1 Crew song at the top of their lungs, and Sam laughed louder than before. "I must be crazy ... agreeing to four summer days on the road with this group."

"Oh, come on, Dad!" Chloe's voice rose above the song. "You love road trips with us girls. All those bathroom breaks! It's paradise!"

"I'll be the judge of that." Sam took Erin's hand this time, and squeezed it gently. "I like seeing you this happy."

"It's a good feeling." Erin leaned closer, studying her husband, the fine lines around his eyes that had crept up in the worrying seasons. "Thank you, Sam. Really. You don't know what it means to me."

"Actually," he smiled at her, "I think I do."

She laughed lightly at his response, giddy for the reality only still making its way from her head to her heart. They were actually headed back to Bloomington. They needed to be careful with their money. But Ashley had said the whole family could stay at the Baxter house, so other than gas and groceries and one night's stay in a hotel coming and going, the trip would be fairly affordable.

They arrived at the beach ten minutes later and emptied the towels and rafts and picnic basket from the back of their van. The girls ran off to the water while Sam spread a blanket out on the sand not too far from the shore, and Erin called Ashley to tell her the good news.

Her sister answered almost immediately. "You can come!" Ashley's voice was high and hopeful.

"Wait." Erin laughed out loud. "How did you know?"

"What?" Ashley screamed. "You mean you can? I was only guessing. I mean, I've been praying Sam would say yes, and so I just assumed ... but still. Seriously, Erin? You can come?"

"Yes." Erin felt a slight catch in her voice. "Sam wasn't that hard of a sell. He just wanted to make sure he had the time off." She paused. "He wants to be there."

"I know." Ashley's apologetic tone came quickly. "I didn't mean anything against Sam. It's just, things had to work out for him. With his job and all."

Erin felt the joy fill her heart again. "Exactly." She and Ashley talked for another few minutes, and when the call was over she glanced at Sam. He was sprawled out on a towel nearby, the sun baking his back. Poor guy. He worked so hard lately, ten hour days most of the time. "You awake?"

No response. She watched his back rise and fall, sound asleep after just minutes on the beach. He needed a day like this, to lie in the sun and forget the pressures of work, the stress of trying to pay the bills.

She was about to close her eyes and enjoy a few minutes of the sun on her face when her cell phone rang. She glanced at the caller ID and saw that it was Naomi Boggs. Erin felt like all the sand on the beach had been dropped on her chest. She nearly ignored the call again, but then she found a new determination. She couldn't run from this forever. It was time to fight for her girls.

"Hi, this is Erin."

"Hello. This is Naomi Boggs, Department of Children's Services." The woman sounded weary. "I've been trying to reach you. Is this a good time?"

Not really, Erin wanted to say. She kept her eyes on the girls, splashing and playing in the water just ahead. "Yes. This is fine." She exhaled, feeling trapped. "Can you explain what's happening? With my girls' birth mother?"

"First, you need to know that I am an agent of the state ... which means I have to act on what the state deems best for the girls." She paused. "I don't always agree, but Candy does have a right to see the girls."

Erin felt a ray of hope. At least the social worker seemed to be on their side. Naomi provided the latest development in a succinct manner. In the open adoption agreement Erin and Sam had with Candy's mother, Lu, there was a clause that agreed the girls would also be allowed visits with Lu's extended family.

Memories of the contract hit Erin full force. She knew exactly the clause Naomi was referring to, because her brother Luke had warned them about it after reviewing the papers. But Erin and Sam had been so anxious to make the adoption final that they chose to believe there was nothing to worry about — especially with Candy serving twenty years to life in prison. The agreement was signed and Lu had come to see the girls only twice — both times in the first year. Erin provided the woman with a letter each year updating her on the girls — another clause in the contract. And year after year everything seemed fine.

Until now.

Erin tried to focus on the words coming from the social worker. "The clause absolutely gives Candy permission to attend the visits with her mother, Lu," Naomi was saying. "She's called nearly every day since she's been out of prison. Apparently Lu lost your contact information when your family moved to Bloomington. Now she — and her daughter — are desperate to reconnect with the girls."

Erin felt the fight rising within her. "Doesn't that seem strange to you?"

"It does." She sighed, the heaviness in her tone again. "The way Candy has worded some of her statements makes me feel like she has ulterior motives. But I can't be sure." She paused. "And the contract allows for it."

Erin tried to remain composed. Then another thought hit

her. Maybe Naomi didn't fully understand the history of the girls' birth mother. Naomi was new, so maybe this was the time to catch her up. "Would it help if you knew a little of the girls' history, Mrs. Boggs?"

"I have their file, and —"

"Have you read it?"

"I've looked over the —"

"Look, I'm not trying to be rude." Erin pinched the bridge of her nose, forcing herself to keep control of her emotions. "This isn't something you can merely look over. This is more than a case, Mrs. Boggs. These are my daughters, and their story is an important part of this."

Naomi hesitated. "I'm sorry. Please ... tell me."

Erin settled back into her beach chair again. She was grateful her girls were down the beach, out of earshot. She breathed in slowly and started at the beginning. "Candy Burns was a crack addict when she gave birth to her third daughter. At that point she was overwhelmed by the responsibility so she contacted the state and made plans to give the baby up."

The story was unbelievable, and Erin had to keep reminding herself she wasn't making up the details. Candy asked for financial help during the course of her pregnancy — which Erin and Sam provided. But before the baby was born she told Erin she couldn't give the baby up without a large sum of money. Erin and Sam reported her attempted extortion, and the adoption seemed to be off. But before the district attorney could file charges against Candy, she shot and killed a man during a drug deal.

"That's how we wound up with all three of Candy's daughters. They were age six, four, and newborn at the time."

"Again ... I'm sorry." The sound of turning pages came from Naomi's end of the call. "The story's all here. I guess ... I focused more on the murder."

"That's another thing." Erin felt the intensity in her voice. "Why is Candy out? Her sentence was twenty years to life."

"The courts reevaluated about three years ago and decided the penalty was too harsh. That, plus she had excellent behavior in prison. She took parenting and college courses. The model prisoner, from what it sounds like." Naomi went on to express her concerns, how Candy had mentioned a few times about working something out, coming to an understanding regarding the situation with the girls. "I'm not convinced that her motives are pure." Naomi's frustration sounded in her tone. "She's said a few questionable things. But nothing that would cause a judge to deny her the chance to see the girls."

The whole situation made Erin want to take the girls and hide somewhere on the other side of the world. "I'm not willing to let my daughters see Candy." Erin wanted to be clear. "I would have to have a personal conversation with her to see if she's changed. But my gut tells me she hasn't."

Naomi sighed. "Unfortunately, it won't be up to you. The courts have already deemed her a fit mother. And since the adoption agreement allows for Lu Burns's extended family to participate in the visits, we don't have a lot of options." She hesitated. "Sometime next week we need to work out a time for a first meeting. Initially the visits will be at our office."

Again Erin felt sick to her stomach. "I'll be contacting my lawyer, Mrs. Boggs. And then yes, we can talk next week."

The call ended and Erin tilted her face toward the sun. *Please, God ... help me protect my girls.* She would call Naomi on Monday and ask for more time. Maybe they could deal with the mess after their summer trip to Bloomington. That way she could talk with Luke in person. The possibility helped her relax a little more.

She looked at Sam, still sleeping on his towel beside her. Erin closed her eyes and for a moment she let herself go back, back to the beginning with Sam. She had always wanted the early marriage and houseful of kids and picket fence. To be like her parents, John and Elizabeth Baxter ... that's all she ever wanted.

But time and again God had different plans.

Love evaded her through college and not until she and Sam met at church did she finally find the one she'd been waiting for. The early days were marked with love and laughter, and they were home from their honeymoon just two months when they began looking at baby furniture. Erin hadn't expected a struggle when it came to having kids. Her mom had six kids, after all. And her siblings had no trouble bearing children.

Only Erin couldn't seem to get pregnant.

The failed attempts began taking a toll on their marriage — that and the fact that Sam worked himself to exhaustion. Erin kicked off her sandals and felt the gritty lake sand between her toes. It was her fault. Looking back, she'd been more concerned with having babies than making love last with her husband. She had even flirted with a guy she had no business talking to, and in time she had nearly allowed herself to walk away from her marriage as if it had never happened. In a last-ditch attempt to avoid a divorce — something that would've broken her parents' hearts — Erin did the only thing she could think to do. She asked that someone in women's ministry at their church might call her. Someone who could speak truth into her heart where her marriage was concerned. Erin had expected anonymity — but instead she was matched up with her own sister Kari.

After meeting with her sister, Erin found a strength in God she hadn't known before. She became strong enough to love Sam, and to build him up as a leader in their home, and she found the strength to build a relationship with her siblings. She was even strong enough to survive their mother's death from cancer a little while later. Eventually the babies came — not from her and

Sam, but from the Lord, through a social worker. All four of her daughters.

But most of all, as Kari's words of wisdom came to life and as Erin and Sam found the love they'd been missing, God brought them children. Not one or two babies, but four beautiful girls. All in one month.

Erin adjusted her sunglasses and watched her girls. The older ones paddled around on their rafts while the younger ones splashed at them as they trailed behind in their inner tubes. Erin stood and peeled off her shorts and T-shirt. She wrapped a towel around her one-piece suit, and headed for the water, dropping the towel only at the last minute. "Time to share your raft!"

The girls all cheered; and when Erin climbed on Clarissa's raft with her, Clarissa said, "You're the best mom ever!"

Erin giggled. "Just wait until I dunk you!"

They all laughed, and Erin was filled with love for these girls she knew to be the best kids ever. And she knew that after all they'd been through, she wasn't about to let Candy Burns ruin anything.

Three

THE FIRST WEEK OF JUNE FLEW BY IN A BLUR OF LITTLE LEAGUE games and dance classes. Not until Kari Baxter Taylor and her husband, Ryan, dropped off their three kids at her dad's house did she allow herself to get truly excited about his surprise party. Because one thing was certain — if the kids knew, they'd never be able to keep the secret. Jessie was thirteen that year, and as close as she was to her papa, she would almost certainly let some detail slip. But at eight and five years old, RJ and Annie would absolutely make the secret known.

After she'd hugged her dad and Elaine and thanked them for watching the kids, she and Ryan returned to their car. Ryan had written today's outing on the calendar two months ago. Kari's Date Day was all it said. And now that they were alone in the car, Ryan smiled at her. "Do you know what today is?"

"June 8?"

"More than that." He took her hands in his, and the look in his eyes melted her in a single heartbeat. "Thirteen years ago today I accepted the coaching position at Clear Creek High. The one that brought me back to Bloomington."

"That long?" Kari turned in her seat, her shoulder pressed into the soft leather of their Acura. They were still parked out front of her dad and Elaine's house. "My dad's turning seventy and you've been back in my life for thirteen years?" She uttered a bewildered laugh. "How did that happen?"

"Exactly." Ryan's eyes shone. He released her hands and

started the engine. "That's what today's about. Remembering how all this happened."

"Hmmm." Kari faced the front of the car again, but instead of the road ahead she could only see the trail of years, the adventure of faith and love they'd shared over time. "It's a tough story."

"It is. But it's like so many stories where God is the author. His fingerprints mark every chapter."

"True." Kari wondered if she was ready for this, for an afternoon of going back in time. "So where are you taking me?"

"Guess." He put one hand on her knee as he drove. "Where did we find out the truth all those years ago?"

Kari knew immediately. "Lake Monroe." She pictured the path around the lake, and the sandy beach where late one summer night the misunderstandings that had defined their past all fell away like sand through their fingers. She smiled at him. "Really? You're taking me there?"

"The picnic's in the back. I figured no one's love story holds a candle to ours. We have to remember it every once in a while or we'll forget." His eyes met hers again. "And we can never let that happen."

"No." She lifted her gaze to the bright blue June sky over Bloomington. "We need this."

"That's what I hoped you'd say." He kissed her hand and focused on the road. "So, tell me about Ashley ... She called this morning, right?"

"She did. Just more details about my dad's surprise party." Kari eased her fingers between his and let the feeling soothe her soul. "Everyone's on board with the letter writing for Dad."

"Beautiful." Ryan nodded slowly. "There won't be a dry eye in the room."

"It's true." Kari thought about her siblings, how each of their stories held the darkest pain and the most brilliant victories. "Dad was there while each of us found our way. He was always at the center, giving us a hug or a Bible verse or the words we needed."

"Even better that we're doing this today." Ryan sounded thoughtful. "I've always wanted to celebrate the eighth of June this way, but this is the first time I've acted on it." His smile was tinged with a greater depth. "God's timing is perfect."

At the next stoplight Ryan slipped a CD into the player. "I made this for today." He adjusted the volume so they could hear it better. "Some of the songs that helped me survive back then."

The first song was by Steven Curtis Chapman, a ballad called "His Strength Is Perfect." Ryan caught her eyes again as the familiar melody filled the car. "It was a classic that year. And it definitely got me through." He began to sing along. "He'll carry you … when you can't carry on."

"I love it." She ran her thumb alongside his hand. "I remember hearing it all the time that summer. Like God wanted us to get the message firmly in our hearts. Before we could think about what He was doing by bringing you back to Bloomington and the job at Clear Creek High."

They sang along for the rest of the drive to the lake, and Ryan parked in his favorite spot — the one near the private marina. They still kept a boat docked there, and they had plans to take the kids out on the lake tomorrow. As Ryan grabbed the picnic basket and a blanket from the back, Kari raised her eyebrows. "Are we taking the boat?"

"Not today. I want to walk the same path, find the same spot on the beach where we talked that night." He smiled, in no hurry. "If that's okay."

"It's perfect." She took the blanket from him and they set out shoulder to shoulder, taking their time as they reached the path and began making their way around the outer edge of the lake. "Where do we begin?"

"At that summer barbecue." He chuckled. "Feels like yester-day and a lifetime ago all at once." In no time they reached the spot, and Kari saw two beach chairs and a small table with a vase full of roses. Ryan placed his iPod in a portable speaker between the chairs. He took a miniature remote controller from his jeans pocket and tapped it. The same music from the CD in the car began to play.

"Ryan?" She looked at him, her mouth open. "When did you do this?"

"I used a flashlight." He laughed. "I couldn't let you know what I was up to. I left and came back before you woke up."

He set the picnic basket down near the table and took the blanket. When he'd spread it out in front of the chairs, he took her in his arms. For a long time they held on to each other and slow danced to the song.

People need the Lord ... people need the Lord.

Ryan framed her face with his hands, and worked his fingers into her hair. "You're so beautiful, Kari. You always have been." He kissed her and Kari remembered how very nearly this love didn't happen. How they could've missed it if God hadn't allowed the timing to be perfect.

Ryan led her to the chairs and when they were seated side by side, the morning lake spread out before them, he took a deep breath. "I was playing football out in the street with a bunch of eighth graders. It was the summer before I started high school."

Kari looked out at the water, but the images that danced before her eyes were from more than twenty years ago. "I remember you ran into the backyard for a burger and my dad introduced us."

"He wanted me to put a shirt on." Ryan laughed. "You were only twelve but I thought you were the most beautiful girl I'd ever seen."

Kari waited, letting the memory come to life again. "After you left to go back to your game, I remember looking down and thinking something was missing." She let her eyes find his again. "It was my heart. It belonged to only you from that point on."

"Mine was split between you and football." He chuckled. "But then you were only in middle school."

For the next two years Kari didn't see Ryan much. "I figured you forgot about me."

"I remember when you started at Clear Creek High. The guys were all talking about you." Ryan slid his chair closer so their bare arms touched. "You were the prettiest girl at school, even then."

"I felt skinny and young and awkward." She laughed. "I was shocked when I made the cheerleading squad."

He gave a low whistle. "My friends found out I was friends with you and they bugged me to set them up." His smile warmed the morning. "I never did."

"You kept your distance. I remember that." She shot a teasing look at him. "I figured you didn't like me."

The truth was she couldn't date until she was sixteen. So on her sixteenth birthday, a few weeks after Ryan graduated from Clear Creek, he showed up at her front door with roses. Roses much like the ones he'd brought for her today. "I figured maybe you liked me after all. It was the best day ever."

"I liked you. I always liked you." Ryan looked a bit guilty. "But I was headed off to play college football and you were only a junior in high school."

If Kari didn't know the rest of the story, it would have been easy to let the sadness from that time cloud her heart again. "When you didn't call, the date felt like the cruelest trick."

"I could've at least explained myself." Ryan looked into her eyes. "With how I treated you I couldn't believe you would talk to me again. But when my dad died, you were the one there for me."

During Christmas break of her senior year Ryan's father died of a sudden heart attack. From that point on, he and Kari were inseparable. A breeze from the lake washed over them and Kari was grateful for Ryan's nearness. "I understood. I was just as close with my dad." She gave him a sad smile. "I still am. I wanted to help you feel whole again."

"Even when I went back to OU, you were the one I leaned on."

Kari stared out at the lake. "Phone calls and letters and summer breaks — it's what I lived for that last year of high school." By Ryan's senior year in college, Kari was modeling and taking classes at Indiana University and Ryan was more involved in football than ever before. "When you were drafted by the Dallas Cowboys I prayed nothing would change." Kari leaned in closer to him. "But your life was moving so fast." Everyone wanted Ryan's attention and that summer after he graduated he didn't have time for much more than training.

"Football was everything." Regret sounded in Ryan's tone. "It was my fault we grew apart. My dreams of playing pro consumed me." His eyes pierced hers. "But nothing about my life was ever right without you." His tone fell. "Even if I did a terrible job showing you, I still loved you."

"I wasn't sure."

Ryan stood and poured them each a glass of iced tea. "And then I got hurt."

"Yes." Kari's stomach instantly turned to knots. She lifted her face and let the wind off the lake ease some of the heartache. "I still remember exactly where I was, what I was doing . . . how I felt when you got hit."

Ryan absently rubbed the back of his neck. "One minute I was running like the wind, faster than ever. I jumped into the air and snagged a bullet of a pass and then . . ." his voice trailed off.

"I was doing laundry, watching the game in bits and pieces."

She hadn't heard from him in weeks, and rumor had it he was seeing other girls. "I was at the back of the house when my dad yelled. He told me to come quick. That you were hurt!"

The images were as vivid now as they had been then. Ryan motionless, lying facedown on the ground. Medical personnel hovering around him, players clustered, silent and shocked, praying.

Out on the lake a speedboat passed by pulling a water-skier.

"I remember hitting the ground," Ryan waited till the boat was in the distance. "I couldn't feel anything but my face in the mud, the grass in my nose and mouth."

"You thought you were paralyzed, right?"

"I didn't think it; I knew it." He looked out at the lake. "In a fraction of a second I was finished. My whole life changed." He looked at her. "I couldn't breathe, couldn't fill my lungs. I begged God to let me live." He hesitated. "You know why?"

Tears filled her eyes and she shook her head.

"Because I wanted to see you again." He gently brought her hand to his lips and kissed it. "I only wanted you, Kari. That's all."

She sniffed and ran her fingers beneath her eyes. "It was my dad who came up with a plan. He knew I couldn't be apart from you so we set out for Dallas. Wherever they took you, whatever happened next I had to be there."

Ryan leaned over his knees. For a long time he rubbed his neck. "I hate this part."

"Me, too." Kari would always feel guilty for what happened next. They arrived at the hospital and found Ryan strapped to a bed in intensive care. Ryan was sedated but they were able to see him.

"My mom told you what happened."

"She did." His neck was broken, and his paralysis could be permanent. The only hope was an emergency neck surgery. If that went miraculously well, then he could regain motion. "I was ter-

rified, praying constantly." Kari remembered the sick feeling that
consumed her that day. She and her dad held hands while they
sat down the hall, beseeching God to heal Ryan's spine. Sometime
well after midnight they fell asleep on adjacent couches in a more
secluded section of the waiting room.

"I barely understood what was happening. But I knew you
were there."

Kari felt guilty again. Ryan's surgery lasted a few hours. When
it was over, Kari asked the nurses about seeing him. But the head
nurse shook her head. "Not now, dear. His girlfriend is with him."

"I didn't understand. I thought ..."

Ryan reached out and held her hand. "We agreed long ago on
this very spot that it wasn't your fault."

"I should have known you wouldn't have another girlfriend.
Not without talking to me."

But the nurse went on about how Ryan's mother was so happy
that the girl had come to the hospital, so grateful that she would
support him after his injury. Kari had walked away from the conversation too stunned to speak. She woke her father and told him
they needed to leave. If he was confused by her sudden and desperate need to leave the hospital, he didn't say so. He only looked
intently at her and then nodded. Kari had always known that the
trip to Dallas was more about what she needed and less about
Ryan. At least as far as her dad was concerned. Not until they
were halfway back to Bloomington did she find the words to tell
him the truth.

Ryan had someone else.

The missed moment hung in the air while the music played
softly in the background. His swelling went down a few days later
and he had complete feeling and motion once more.

"I was so confused." Kari fought the sadness overtaking her.

"I can imagine." Ryan groaned, a guttural sort of painful sound
that came from the recesses of his soul and a place that would

never quite move on from what happened that day. "Of course, the girl was you, Kari. My mom had been talking about you." He looked at her. "I had no idea why you left, what happened."

"And I didn't even answer your calls while you were recovering. All those months of physical therapy."

The entire misunderstanding was so epic, so life altering. Worse, while Ryan found his way back to the football field that spring, she met a grad student named Tim Jacobs. At Kari's college graduation party a few months later, she was talking to Tim when Ryan stopped by.

"I wanted to tell you I still loved you, that nothing had changed." His voice softened as he looked at her again.

"I wouldn't even look at you." Frustration pressed in around her. Ryan didn't stay long and after that night Kari and Tim were an item. They were married that summer while Ryan's career in the NFL took off.

"You will never know how it felt that day when my mom called and told me you'd gotten married." He sat straighter in his chair, as if even now it was hard to breathe with the weight of the memory. "I figured I'd never see you again."

Kari smiled. "It's hard to believe that was thirteen years ago today."

They stood and walked to the water's edge. He stared into her eyes, and after a long moment, he kissed her. Kissed her the way he had back then. Kissed her in a way she had never expected to be kissed by him again.

"I remember the first time I saw you after I moved back."

The sun was higher in the sky now, the early afternoon warm and beautiful. "At church. In the prayer room after the service."

"By then I knew about Tim's affair." He ran his fingers over her cheek. "I remember what you said that day in the prayer room. You said love was a decision. And God hated divorce."

"It's still true."

"Definitely." He took her hand. "Let's walk."

"Yes." She needed to move around, shake off the sadness of the past. They held hands as they strolled along the shore to the far end of the beach. "If he had lived, I would've stayed with him."

Everyone in Bloomington knew about Tim's murder. By then it was late fall and the high school football season was over. Ryan accepted a coaching position with the New York Giants, mostly so he could get away from Bloomington and the feelings he still had for Kari. The cool lake water felt good on Kari's feet. A tangible reminder that this was not that January and that she wasn't stuck back in the news of that awful day.

Hours after hearing of Tim's death, their daughter Jessie was born. "I woke up and someone was singing in my hospital room." She stopped and turned to him. "I thought it was my dad. But it was you."

Ryan was sitting at the foot of her bed, Jessie cradled in his arms.

"I think back on our story, the things we could've done differently." They returned to the beach chairs. He stopped and faced her. "Ways we could've avoided missing out on each other the first time around."

"It's one of those things I'll ask God as soon as I get to heaven." Kari touched her lips to his, and for a while they forgot about the past. Forgot everything but this single sweet moment, their feet in the sand and in all the world only the warmth of the summer day and the miracle of the love they shared.

They talked about the years since their wedding day and when they finally ran out of memories, Ryan let himself get lost in her eyes. "I love you with all my heart, Kari."

"I love you, too." She ran her fingers along his face, his jaw. "However many tomorrows we have left, they won't be enough."

They stayed awhile longer, listening to the music and laughing about the recent past. The whole way back, Kari was quiet.

Their story wasn't an easy one, but it had led them to this and so it was worth remembering. Every detail. In addition, today reminded her of the role her dad had played in her life. Now that she'd spent the day remembering, the letter would come more easily. Kari could hardly wait to get started.

She wondered if all of her siblings were spending a little time remembering today, in light of Ashley's assignment. After all, some of their stories didn't only involve heartache. They involved what could have been a permanent loss. The loss of a child. Certainly Ashley would have such a piece to her story — what with the baby she and Landon lost at birth. But even greater was the loss that nearly came one summer day ten years ago. That part of their family story was certain to appear in the letter written by their oldest sister, Brooke. Kari talked silently to God as they drove up at her dad's house once more. Because if anyone would need strength remembering the time when their dad's love mattered most it was Brooke.

Whose story had, in some ways, affected them all.

Four

LIFE WAS BUSY FOR BROOKE BAXTER WEST, AND THAT THIRD Saturday in June was no exception. She and her husband, Peter, ran a successful medical practice and on the weekends they took turns making rounds at St. Anne's Hospital. This was Peter's weekend, which meant Brooke was in charge of getting Maddie to soccer practice and Hayley to her dance class across town.

With everything else, Brooke still made time to drop in at the crisis pregnancy center she and Ashley opened several years ago. The schedule for all of them was so busy Brooke rarely took time to look back. It was all she could do to look ahead, both eyes on the road in front of them as they barreled through life.

But ever since this morning and Brooke's coffee date with Ashley, the past had been knocking at her heart. She'd put it off long enough. She needed to write the letter to her dad. Even so it wasn't until she walked into the dance studio with Hayley and took her spot at the back of the room with the other mothers that Brooke let it hit her the way it hadn't in far too long.

The fact that Hayley shouldn't even be here.

Sure, she walked a little slower than the other girls and in school she struggled more than Maddie. But she kept up. And here, in a class full of dancers, Hayley had no trouble fitting in, no problem dipping and spinning and dancing to the music. Grace and strength in motion.

It was the idea of writing a letter to her dad. That's what had done this. And even now she could picture writing the letter and attaching it to a color copy of the greatest gift her dad had ever given her. A torn page from a magazine containing one very simple image.

A pink bicycle.

Yes, if she was going to write her father a letter thanking him for all he'd been and done and provided over the years, if she was going to put into words what his love and acceptance and hope and belief had done for her since she was a young girl, there would be no avoiding the terrible summer a decade ago.

Until that year, everything about Brooke's life had gone like clockwork. Whatever she dreamed of doing, she did. Hard work and good timing played into it, but as Brooke obtained her medical degree and as she fell in love with fellow intern Peter West, she didn't give God credit for her success. The Lord had blessed her with intelligence and drive, but she'd found a way to make things happen on her own.

While the rest of her family attended church, she and Peter bought vegetables at the farmer's market and hung out with friends on Sundays. In the depths of her heart she actually felt sorry for her family, relying on an archaic faith.

She and Peter might not have had a perfect marriage back then, but their fights were nothing other people didn't go through.

Brooke settled into the hard-back chair at the corner of the room. The music began.

"Okay, everyone, this is hip-hop. It'll be a little more up-tempo."

Hayley found her place in the front row and when the music started she bounced to the beat, watching the instructor. Brooke felt the memories gathering like so many storm clouds. Her father, of course, had suggested Brooke and Peter get counseling at Clear Creek Community Church, but Brooke had pulled herself through medical school. Certainly she could work things out with Peter.

How ridiculous I was back then, Lord. She let the statement swing from the rafters of her mind for a few seconds. *Prideful and arrogant. I'm so sorry ... I'll always be sorry for my heart the way it was. Before the accident.*

My daughter ... your sins are forgiven. They are as far removed from Me as the east is from the west.

Brooke breathed more deeply, the certainty of her restoration underlined once more with the reassuring whispers. Without the faith they'd found that long ago summer, the fear of letting her girls grow up, of watching them do something as simple as drive away for a trip to the mall — would practically paralyze Brooke. But after watching God work the miracle in their lives He'd worked back then, Brooke knew the truth.

God was in control. She had nothing to fear. No matter what happened next or how the outcome played in their lives, whatever triumph or tragedy might take place, God loved them. Nothing could ever change that.

"Okay, that's how it's done." The dance instructor signaled for his assistant to stop the music. "Let's break it down. We'll take it in counts of eight."

The look of concentration on Hayley's face was in itself a miracle. Even though she didn't like to, Brooke could still remember when her younger daughter's face was only blank and lifeless. As if the parts of her mind and brain that made her uniquely Hayley were gone forever.

It happened at a children's birthday party. A swim party.

Maddie was six that summer and she could swim like a fish. But Hayley needed a life jacket. Brooke had put sunscreen on the girls that afternoon, and she'd fastened Hayley's life jacket. But on the way inside the party, her pager went off. Brooke was on call and she was needed at the hospital. Her last words to Peter were the same ones that haunted her to this day. The words she had to put out of her mind often.

"Keep her life jacket on, Peter. She has to wear it. Even if she complains."

Peter had nodded absently and taken the girls by their hands. Then the three of them jogged up the steps to the party and Brooke headed to St. Anne's. The call that day turned out to be nothing serious, and every minute Brooke regretted not being with her family.

The details of what happened next were pieced together by Peter and the moms at the party. Apparently, the first few hours went along without a hitch. But then the kids moved inside for cake and presents and Hayley demanded her life jacket be taken off. The group — around twenty kids and another ten siblings — along with half a dozen mothers filled the kitchen for the happy birthday song. When it was over, Peter told Maddie to keep an eye on Hayley while he and a few dads caught the end of a heated game between the Yankees and the Braves.

Peter never could quite account for how much time passed, but after an inning or so Maddie appeared at his side wondering where Hayley was. She and her little friends had looked but had not been able to find her. Brooke would regret till the day she died the fact that she hadn't been there. When she rewrote the afternoon in her mind — the way she had done a thousand times — always she was there. And when the cake was finished, she would find Hayley's life jacket and snap it back on the child. Never mind her fussing about it.

Instead, while Brooke tended to her patient, Peter flew off the recliner and scrambled down the back stairs, racing out onto the patio only to see the most terrible sight, a sight he still said would never quite leave him. Three-year-old Hayley was lifeless at the bottom of the pool.

Peter shouted for someone to call 9 – 1 – 1 and then he dove into the water, fully clothed, his shoes still on. The whole way down he could only picture every wonderful memory with his little girl, fighting through the brick wall of futility. With a strength fueled by crazy adrenaline, Peter propelled Hayley to the surface and pushed her up onto the cement deck.

Not until the paramedics were rushing through the house and spilling onto the back patio did Hayley cough up even the slightest bit of water. She was still blue, still lifeless when they took over CPR from Peter and got her onto a stretcher.

It was about that time Brooke rounded the corner and saw the emergency vehicles. With an instinct that was beyond maternal, Brooke slammed the car into park and raced for the front door, convinced beyond any doubt that the problem was Hayley, that somehow the unthinkable had happened.

She hadn't worn her life jacket.

Brooke was halfway to the door when the paramedics hurried out carrying the stretcher. One of them held an oxygen mask over Hayley's little face, her pale blonde hair matted around her cheeks, her body motionless and blue.

"Five, six, seven, eight." The music kicked into high gear and the girls responded with the moves they'd learned just minutes earlier. Hayley stayed right with the beat, her eyes bright with exhilaration.

Remembering her accident was so much better at a moment like this, when proof of her miracle was so dramatically evident. It made breathing possible.

Doctors declared Hayley blind and brain damaged. They said she'd never run or walk or maybe even feed herself. Brooke and her father had always been close. The fact that Brooke had grown up to be a doctor like him gave them a bond nothing could touch. But she never felt a heart connection with her father until after Hayley drowned.

Up until then, her dad saw God in every patient and case,

every aspect of his work as a doctor. After the accident, it wasn't that her dad lost faith. Rather, he saw no room for miracles. Her prognosis was that severe.

"When I pray," he had told her a week after the accident, "I find myself asking God to maybe just take her home. So she can run and play and be free." He had tears in his eyes. "I just hate seeing her like this."

As Brooke sat day and night at Hayley's hospital bedside, running her hand over her daughter's tan forehead, and stroking her beautiful hair, she had considered such a prayer also. If there was to be no healing — and medical wisdom said there wouldn't be — then why pray for her survival? Heaven would be far gentler an outcome than living trapped in a body that no longer functioned, a brain that no longer responded to laughter and touch and the love of her family.

Later, Brooke would learn that her father had already chosen the birthday present he wanted to get Hayley when she turned four. A bright pink bicycle with training wheels. He had found a picture of the bike in a magazine and ripped it out to show the rest of the family. The perfect gift for little Hayley. But again, after the accident her dad put the magazine page away in a drawer, his dreams for an active Hayley drowned right there beside her.

Brooke brushed discretely at her tears. The other mothers were on their iPads or cell phones. She didn't want to make a scene. It wasn't normal to burst into tears during dance practice. But it was impossible not to feel the overwhelming joy at what happened next that summer.

Gradually, Hayley began to come back to them. Against all odds, she regained her sight. Then over the next few days she could move her arms and legs. It took time, but eventually she could recognize Brooke and Peter and Maddie.

One evening Brooke's dad showed up at the hospital and

hugged her for a long time. Then he gave her something he had only pulled from his dresser drawer that day.

The magazine picture of the pretty pink bike.

"The Bible says to pray believing. But after Hayley's accident I didn't believe. I doubted." He hesitated. "I'll never stop believing in miracles again."

Her dad went out that day and bought the pink bicycle. He kept it in his garage, praying and believing, and a few years later when Hayley was well enough he gave it to her.

In the early months after Hayley's accident, Peter couldn't see past his guilt. It didn't take long before Peter began taking pain pills. When Brooke found out about her husband's addiction, it was almost too late. All of which found her father right in the middle of the situation — praying for Peter, counseling the two of them, and most of all doing what he hadn't done at first in Hayley's situation.

Believing.

Now she and Peter were happier than ever. Their girls were active and healthy and only longtime friends and family remembered the desperate condition Hayley had been in after her accident. And the miracle she'd been granted.

Write a letter to her father? Her mentor and friend? The one she'd sought to be like since she was a little girl? Tears gathered in Brooke's eyes again just thinking about the things she could say. And the things she would never find a way to put into words. Her father was everything to her. The best doctor in Bloomington, a pillar of faith in the community, and the only one who had given her exactly what she needed when all of life felt like it was ending.

The picture of a pink two-wheeled bicycle.

All things considered, her letter would be easy to write. The hardest part was admitting her dad was actually seventy years old, and that despite his great health and the active lifestyle he maintained, the calendar told them what they couldn't ignore.

He was getting older.

Writing him a letter would be an exercise in joy, taking time to put onto paper her feelings for her father. She thought about her siblings, how some of their letters would be harder to write than others, and suddenly one face came to mind. Brooke cringed. There would be no way for her younger brother Luke to write the letter without covering the details of that horrible time in his life. A time when their dad chased after him and prayed for him and refused to give up on him. Hayley had taught them all to believe, and they did. But back then Luke tested their faith once again. During a time when they all referred to their younger brother as the son who had gone astray.

Luke Baxter — the prodigal.

Five

Mandisa's *What If We Were Real* was playing so loud the cupboards shook as Erin rushed around looking for the last suitcase. She'd tell the girls to turn it down, but she loved every song on the album and Sam was working late. Instead she sang along as she dashed down the stairs.

"Clarissa!" She had to shout to be heard over the music. "Do you have the blue suitcase?"

"What?" Clarissa stopped singing just long enough to stick her head out of the downstairs bedroom she shared with Chloe.

"The blue suitcase!" Erin pushed her hair out of her eyes and stopped at the girls' bedroom door, breathless. Chloe was standing in the middle of a pile of clothes, playing the air guitar and singing her heart out. "Chloe!" Erin laughed as she cupped her hand around her mouth. "The blue suitcase?"

"Yes!" Chloe's eyes lit up. She turned down the music in a hurry and laughed. "Sorry. It's under my bed." In a burst of motion she grabbed it and handed it to Erin. "Me and Clarissa are already packed."

"Perfect." She looped her arm around Chloe's neck and kissed her head. Then she did the same to Clarissa. "I'll use this for the little girls." She hesitated as she reached the door. "You can put the music back on. It makes the work go faster."

They all laughed and Clarissa grinned at her. "You're the best kind of 'cool mom.'"

"Yeah," Chloe giggled. "Not *too* cool. Like, you're still a mom. But you take us for Starbucks every weekend." She smiled big.

"Plus you can sing and dance and you even let us play the music super loud."

"Of course." Erin winked at them. "Especially when Dad's gone."

Again their laughter filled the room and Clarissa resumed the music. Erin hurried upstairs with the blue suitcase and stopped at the laundry room. The house was a split level, with one bedroom on the main floor, and two upstairs along with the laundry room. It was smaller than any house they'd lived in before, but it was within their means. Something she and Sam felt strongly about after his time off work and the debt they needed to chisel away at.

Erin surveyed the remaining laundry. She had two more loads before they could be fully packed. It was a little after eight and they were leaving at sunup tomorrow so she needed to make use of every hour. Even then she wouldn't sleep easily, not when she was this excited. In just two days she'd be with her family again! The calendar days had turned slowly since Sam first agreed to make the drive to Bloomington, but Erin had long since stopped trying to will away time, not for any reason whatsoever.

Even a Baxter family reunion.

Especially since she was able to delay dealing with Candy Burns and the visitation process. Apparently Candy had a few unresolved issues related to her release, so they agreed with Naomi to put off the matter until after the trip to Bloomington. Erin had talked to her brother Luke, and though family law wasn't his specialty, he promised to talk with her about the situation this week.

And so June had been a lovely month, filled with trips to the community pool and the whole family helping out with a week of Vacation Bible School and early morning walks with her older girls — who were getting more into fitness. Erin had loved those times especially — before Sam left for work, at an hour when he could watch the younger girls. On their morning walks, the girls' hearts were wide open, and conversation came easily. They talked about school and mission work and the beauty of adoption and the plans God had for them.

Erin smiled as she sorted through the dark and light tops in the laundry bin. The music from downstairs still filled the room, and it provided a movie soundtrack-type background for memories of yesterday's walk.

Clarissa had started the conversation. "There's no boys in our neighborhood. Anyone ever notice that?"

"Just little boys. Like Heidi Jo and Amy's age." Chloe shared a disappointed look with her sister. "Like how are we supposed to find friends to hang out with?"

Erin let them talk, but after a minute their concerns seemed to need a resolution. "You have your homeschool friends."

"True." Clarissa was always more chatty than Chloe. "But we just got back to Texas a year ago. Everyone's been friends for a long time. Like, their summer groups are already set."

"In the movies there's always like a summer love, the boy across the street or the high school lifeguard at the local pool." Chloe's expression turned dreamy. "That would make summer so much fun."

"But first you have to meet guys." Clarissa managed a defeated laugh. "Doesn't look like that's going to happen."

Erin kept up the pace, walking shoulder to shoulder with her girls. "I remember feeling like that."

"Really?"

"Yes." Erin was breathless in a good way. "Guys didn't notice me until I was in my twenties." She shrugged. "Your dad was really the first guy."

Chloe made a face. "Didn't you wish you'd dated more?"

"No." Erin smiled. They had headed up a hilly section of the neighborhood and all of them pushed hard. "I just wish I'd met him sooner."

At the top of the hill Clarissa turned uncertain eyes in her direction. "How do we know that guy's out there? Like, the guy God has for us."

Erin had waited a few seconds, letting Clarissa's question simmer. "Well … if God has a plan for you to get married someday, then I'm certain he's out there somewhere. He probably won't be sixteen years younger than you."

Clarissa and Chloe laughed out loud at that. "I never saw it that way." Clarissa looked up at the sky as they kept walking. "So he could be looking at this very same sky."

"Exactly." Erin appreciated their sweetness, their innocence. "You could even keep journals. Write to him. Someday your letters could mean a great deal."

"Hmmm." Chloe looked more thoughtful than usual. "What if we don't get married, Mom? What then? Like, God can still have great plans for us even if we're single?"

"Of course." Erin had been proud of Chloe for asking such a question. So many girls grew up believing the only way to be happy or in God's will was to be married.

After that they talked about several girls who had been in the news lately for their commitment to mission work overseas or for single-handedly running an orphanage or working in nursing. All of them never married.

"The purpose of life isn't to get married. It's to live for Jesus … telling people about Him and sharing His love." Erin was grateful for the conversation. "Yes, marriage is wonderful. Raising children is wonderful." She grinned at each of her girls. "But our purpose is to serve and love others and to shine brightly for God. No matter what."

The girls became quiet for a while. As they hit their turning point in the walk, Clarissa looked at her. "I like that, Mom. It takes the pressure off. Whatever God has ahead for us everything's going to be okay."

"Because He loves us." Chloe held up her hands and made a darling face. "And we love Him."

"Right." Erin figured she would remember the conversation between the girls forever. "We can trust Him with the plans He has for our lives."

And now, a day later and despite all she had to do with packing up the car and finishing the laundry, she wasn't surprised that the conversation was still fresh. It wasn't easy raising girls in today's culture. So much was expected of them at such a young age. All around them the culture celebrated girls wearing revealing clothing and rebelling against authority. Pop stars sang about every sort of wild lifestyle and yet somehow they needed to raise their daughters to be pure and honoring to God.

Erin pulled a load of hot jeans from the dryer. As she did, Amy Elizabeth darted down the hall singing much the same way Clarissa and Chloe were singing downstairs. Up here the volume wasn't quite so loud, and Amy stopped short when she saw Erin. "Mom, do you think I should bring my pink shorts and my blue ones?"

"Good question." Erin lowered a pair of jeans. "It's supposed to be warm, and we'll be there a whole week."

"But I'm bringing four other pairs already — the ones with the flowers and the white ones, and the two we bought last week."

Erin gave the dilemma the proper amount of thought. "I'd say if you want to bring the pink pair and the blue pair, you should. They're small and there's room in the suitcase."

Amy clapped her hands and her face lit up. "Yay! That's what I hoped you'd say." With that she resumed singing at the top of her lungs and skipped down the hallway toward the room she shared with Heidi Jo. Erin laughed quietly. The little girls were so sweet, so happy. It took very little to make their day.

As she finished the laundry she thought again about the situation with Candy, and her last conversation with Naomi. "We can delay this, but it won't go away," the social worker had told her. "The visits will have to happen."

God, if I'm right about Candy Burns, please show me ... I can't imagine letting the girls spend time with her. Please ... help us. She had to remember what she'd told her girls on their walk yesterday. God was in control. Certainly if it came to scheduling visits, they'd take place at a county facility with supervision. Even then she didn't want anything to change the happy natures of her girls. They were so easygoing, so comfortable with themselves and their lives. Erin and Sam wanted to be honest with them, so already they knew about the possibility of having to see their birth mother, and none of them wanted to go. Clarissa and Chloe had even pulled the age card.

"No one can make us see her, right, Mom?" Clarissa had spoken for the two of them yesterday night at dinner. "We decided we're too old. We don't want to see her."

The vacation to Bloomington would be good for many reasons, but certainly one was the fact that they could postpone dealing with the issue of Candy. Erin liked the idea of talking to Luke. They would figure out a plan and deal with the situation when they got back. In the meantime the girls wouldn't have to worry about it, at least for another week.

Erin did another load of laundry, transferring the whites into the dryer and starting the final load of shirts and shorts. For a time she had thought she'd try to get a job when they returned to Texas, but when she and Sam looked at it more closely the idea never made much sense. The girls would have to enroll at the local public school — and even though Erin had heard great things about the school system in Austin, she truly enjoyed homeschooling them. They all enjoyed it. That and the time it took to run the house would've made even a part-time job all but impossible.

Another hour passed, and Sam came through the door. He

looked tired, but his eyes told her he was excited. Erin met him and hugged him for a long time. "So late, darling."

"I know." Sam sighed and set his briefcase down. "The entire IT department worked overtime. The new system is nothing but trouble."

"I'm sorry." She rubbed her thumbs into the muscles at the base of his neck, doing her best to ease the tension there. "And now in ten hours we're hitting the road."

"Mmm." He lowered his head, enjoying the impromptu back rub. "That feels wonderful."

Erin continued the massage, but she wanted to know if he was still up to the drive. "We're still leaving at eight, right?"

"We are." He took a long breath and straightened a little. "I'm going to brush my teeth and hit the bed." Before he headed upstairs, he kissed her. "It's going to be a great visit. I really think so."

A light feeling lifted Erin's heart. Sam had no siblings and his parents were gone. Of course he was looking forward to the reunion. "That makes me happy."

Sam chuckled and patted her shoulder. As he started toward the stairs he stopped short. "Are the girls asleep?"

"Not yet." She allowed a bit of laughter. The music was off now, but the memory of it lingered. "We had a little Mandisa concert until just a few minutes ago."

"Sounds like fun." He hesitated, his eyes warm. "Sorry I missed it."

"It was." She grinned. "I'm sure they'll bring her CD for the ride."

"Between that and Starbucks I'll definitely need some guy time when we get to Bloomington." He laughed again and peered down the hallway. "Let's pray with the girls, get them settled down."

"Perfect." Erin moved to the base of the stairs. "Clarissa, Chloe, we're going to pray."

From the distance, she heard Clarissa respond. "Coming!"

They gathered in the younger girls' room, the way they often did for nighttime prayers. Sam sat on the edge of Heidi Jo's bed with Clarissa beside him, holding tight to his arm. Across from them Erin and Amy and Chloe cuddled together, their heads bowed.

Sam led the prayer. "Father, we come to You grateful. Thankful for our family and the love we share, and so glad for the trip we're about to take. Lord, You know all things, and You know the plans You have for us. Please use us as a light to others this week, and help us keep You at the center of all we do." He hesitated, his voice more serious than usual. "Please let Clarissa and Chloe and Heidi Jo and Amy Elizabeth know how much we love them, and let them know how special they are. In all the world, there could never be four more precious daughters. We love You, Lord. In Jesus' name, amen."

A chorus of amens followed, and Erin and Sam gave the girls hugs and kisses. When they reached Amy Elizabeth, their littlest daughter had tears in her eyes. Happy tears. "That was the sweetest thing, what you prayed, Daddy."

"Well, thank you little miss." He swept her into his arms and swung her around. "It's just the truth. That's all." He set her down and they talked for a few minutes about what the girls had packed.

"All right, lights out." Sam and Erin and the older girls headed for the door. "Try to get some sleep."

He said it in a way that made Heidi Jo and Amy start giggling. As if the idea of even trying to sleep when they were so excited was almost certainly out of the question. They left the younger girls' bedroom with Clarissa and Chloe, and the older girls headed for their bedroom. Chloe — always a sunbeam — stopped and turned back to them, her face lit up. "You know why we're the best daughters?" She grinned bigger. "'Cause you are the best parents." Her smile softened. "I can't imagine my life without you."

Clarissa nodded and put her arm around her sister's neck. "It's true."

The girls said good night once more and when they were in their room Erin eased her arms around Sam's waist. "Ever feel like we couldn't possibly be more blessed?"

He met her eyes and looked at her, straight to the depths of her heart. "All the time." He kissed her forehead. "See you in bed."

"Okay. I won't be up much longer. Just have to answer a few emails." She didn't say that one of them was — yet again — from Naomi Boggs. This time asking whether they would prefer the visits with the girls and their biological family to take place at a park or at the social services facility. Erin had ignored it. They'd been given permission to wait until after the trip to Bloomington. She would answer it then.

Erin felt the tension in her shoulders. With all her heart she wished they lived in Bloomington. Not only because she was finally feeling close to her sisters, but because it would put a thousand miles between them and Candy Burns. For now, though, she'd done what she could do. Begging the social worker for help so they could somehow avoid even one single visit with the girls' birth mother. Erin drew a deep breath and tried to move past the matter. She would enjoy her time with her family and believe God would work out the rest. It was like she told her girls.

They could trust the love of God — even in this.

Six

LUKE STEPPED ON A PLANE IN NEW YORK CITY'S LA GUARDIA Airport just after lunch and not until he was buckled into his first-class seat did he remember again Ashley's message. He and his wife Reagan had spent the last few days visiting her family in Manhattan. Reagan had already returned home to Indiana with their kids, but Luke had work in the city. He was returning on a red-eye late Thursday night because of his dad's birthday party. Not for the world would he and his family have missed seeing his father's reaction when he walked into Ashley's house on Saturday. Luke had no idea how his dad could be seventy, but he agreed with Ashley. His father deserved a letter. Luke just wasn't sure where to begin.

He leaned back and stretched out his legs. He was six foot three, about the same as Dayne, his older brother. The brother he hadn't known about until ten years ago. Dayne had been the Brandon Paul of his day, the most popular young actor around. Today Brandon was Luke's client, but more than a decade ago Luke had only connected with Dayne because of the law firm.

He couldn't imagine one of his kids not knowing about the others until they were adults. He and Reagan's three were very close — the way Dayne would've been with all of them if only they'd had the chance to grow up together.

Luke looked out the window of the plane. That year Tommy was eleven and Malin was seven. Little Johnny was three and getting into everything. The kids kept Reagan busy, but even so she was the most amazing mom, the woman he would love till the day he died. It was hard to believe there was ever a time when they had toyed with the idea of ending things.

His thoughts swirled and the letter loomed. He was almost out of time if he was going to take Ashley's advice and write it. He smiled at the thought of his spunky sister. Of all his siblings, Luke had been closest to Ashley. She'd been the one who had figured out about Dayne before any of the others. And when Luke walked away from everyone he loved, she was the one who rolled up her sleeves and came after him.

But not without the worn-out knees of his father, who had prayed night and day, crying out to God that Luke would return. He stared out the window and for a minute he watched the bag handlers, watched them grab hold of what must have been a fifty-pound suitcase and heave it from a cart into the belly of the plane. There was a sameness about their lives that sometimes made Luke envious. They could punch a clock and get the job done, leave it at the end of a shift and not think about bags again until the next morning.

Not so with legal work. People's lives rested on the cases he did and didn't win.

He pulled a pad of paper and a pen from his backpack. He had time on this flight. The bottom line was this: He wouldn't be who or what he was today if it hadn't been for his dad. The man was turning seventy. There could be no time like now to let him know for sure, in writing, how he felt.

Dear Dad, Luke let his pen fly over the paper. *This letter might be hard to write because in order to tell you everything I need to say, I have to go back. And that's a trip that has never been easy for me. But I'm about to hang suspended in the air between New York City and Indianapolis, and I've always had the clearest thoughts at thirty thousand feet.*

He paused and thought about the early years, how close he and his dad had been. If anything, Luke had lived with an unrealistic view of what it was to be a Christian man. He saw his father as perfect, and so he had expected perfection of himself and everyone else. Luke didn't notice takeoff or whether there was turbulence on the way up to their cruising altitude. His pen found smooth air regardless. *I guess I thought I was a pretty good kid. Like I had it all figured out. I knew I wouldn't make the big mistakes and in no time I'd have a life just like you. The easy Christian life. I smile now, thinking about how little I knew.*

The first cracks in Luke's idyllic life came when Ashley left high school and moved to Paris. Luke was outraged that his sister would do such a thing and he spoke harshly about her whenever her name came up. "What if she gets in trouble?" His tone was always gruff back then. "I have a feeling she will because lately she's — "

"Luke." His father had called him out on his attitude. "That's enough. We love Ashley, which means we need to be kind. If you're worried, pray for her."

Luke's pen moved across the page with ease. *I thought you were crazy. Like you should've been mad at her the way I was. And when she came back from Paris pregnant, I knew I was right. Which was really the beginning of the end for me. Something else you knew long before I did.*

His dad had warned him a number of times that his pride would hurt him in the end. "There're no perfect people, Luke," he would tell him. "Be careful."

Instead, Luke harbored a grudge against Ashley. He blamed her for tainting their family's image and reputation and he avoided her — especially when she came around looking for babysitting from his parents. About that time Luke fell hard for Reagan, a tall blonde athlete at Indiana University, a girl whose strong faith and clean living attracted him.

From the beginning they agreed that they shouldn't spend time alone. Neither of them had ever dated seriously, and after a few weeks when Luke kissed her good night it was a first for both of them. Back then he thought staying pure was a matter of will, something he could simply decide to do. But on September 10, 2001, everything he thought to be true and good about himself changed forever. On a night he would never forget, he and Reagan started off watching the Giants on Monday Night Football and ended up breaking every promise about purity they'd ever made.

Luke stopped writing and looked out the window at the endless blue, at the sky's distant floor of cotton-ball clouds. One detail about that night would haunt him always. Reagan's father had called when the game was over. His call went to voice mail because neither of them wanted to stop. In the message her father had been excited about the game. He talked about hoping to see her soon. At the time, Reagan had insisted that they didn't need to stop, didn't need to take the call. She could call him back in the morning. But in the morning, while Reagan and Luke were in separate classes stunned by the guilt and regret of their choices the night before, terrorists attacked New York City. Reagan's dad worked at the top of the World Trade Center, and before she had time to call him or tell him good-bye, he was gone.

Reagan wouldn't talk to Luke after that. She sat in her apartment too shocked to cry or speak or move. As soon as she could, she flew home to New York City, and after that she wouldn't take Luke's calls. Luke was devastated, of course. His entire world forever changed in a day. Several times Luke thought about going to New York, finding Reagan and demanding she talk to him. He was sorry for what had happened the night before 9 – 11, sorry he hadn't been stronger. But he still loved her. The silence between them could do nothing to make things right.

Reagan's complete severance of their relationship sent Luke into a tailspin that almost killed him. Later that fall he took up with a radical girl from one of his classes at IU, and not long after he moved in with her. Luke found his place on the letter again.

I've never seen you like that before or since, Dad. You were relentless. Like you would've walked over fire or broken glass or laid down your life to get me home again. You told me I'd believed a lie, and you were right. I can't calculate the sort of grief I caused you that year — mocking our faith, living with a girl I barely knew, and throwing out everything I previously believed to be true and right.

Through it all you never, ever gave up on me.

Again Luke stopped and this time he rested his head against the back of the airplane seat. It was still another hour at least before they landed, long enough to remember how much his family loved him. Not only his dad, but Ashley. The sister he had persecuted the most. The one he had judged and thought ill-equipped to be a Baxter. If it weren't for Ashley and their dad, everything about Luke's life as it was today would be different. The thought was horrifying.

Because what Luke didn't know when she left Indiana for New York City that fall was that Reagan had been pregnant. The following May she gave birth to a baby boy and named him Tommy, after her father, but even then she made no attempt to find Luke. In her mind they'd done the unforgivable. And because of their sin, she'd missed the chance to talk to her dad for the last time. It was more than Reagan could bear, and she assigned it all to her relationship with Luke.

The whole while, Landon Blake was in New York City working as a firefighter, but not until Ashley went to the City to see him did she spot Reagan and the baby. Which was how Ashley became the liaison between Reagan and Luke and facilitator of their eventual reunion. Even then it wasn't until his family's annual Fourth of July picnic that Luke fully returned. By then God had taught Luke much about pride and humility. No one had sunk further and faster than he had, so never again would he have room to judge. People fell. They sinned and made mistakes and acted out crazy decisions that went against everything they knew to be true.

And even then there was room for redemption.

Once more Luke returned to the letter. *I'll always remember the way your arms felt around me that day. I had it in my mind somehow that I was too dirty, too messed up to come home. I was worse than all my siblings combined. Yet there you were, tears on your face, holding me like I'd never done anything wrong. Then and now, you showed me what love looks like, what it means to forgive and extend grace to people.*

His dad's wisdom and love had come into play again and again over the years. *Your advice always worked, Dad. When Reagan and I have struggled, your words have brought us back to love again. I don't know what I would've done without you.*

Luke wrapped up his letter and smiled. It took two whole pages, which was okay. Ashley hadn't given him a limit. He could have easily written more. His dad had been the first to encourage them to adopt from China, and the first there to celebrate when he and Reagan brought Malin home. And when they adopted again—this time from a local agency—no one had been more supportive of their decision than his father. The fact that the baby turned out to be the son of Andi Ellison—friend of Bailey Flanigan—was an amazing reality that still boggled Luke's mind. But he would always hold in his heart the joy on his dad's face when they told him what they were going to name their newborn adopted son. John Baxter. Little Johnny.

The plane was about to land and he'd said what he needed to say. Good thing, since the party was tomorrow. If his letter had been difficult in places he could hardly imagine the letter some of his siblings had to write. And in that moment he felt a deep sadness for one of the six of them. The one who had missed the most growing up. The brother they knew nothing about until a decade ago.

Dayne Matthews.

Seven

JOHN BAXTER HAD A FEELING SOMETHING WAS UP. HIS SEVENTI-
eth birthday was approaching, and on this early Friday morning as he finished his devotions in Galatians, chapter 5, and put
down his pen after journaling about the fruit of the Holy Spirit, he
couldn't help but smile at the way Ashley had been acting. She'd
invited him and Elaine over for a barbecue on Saturday — a few
days before his actual birthday. But she must've asked him three
times this past week whether he was indeed coming, and verify-
ing the time and insisting they didn't need to bring anything.

If John knew his daughter, she was planning some sort of
surprise party. At least for the local members of the family. John
closed his journal and his Bible and checked the time. Often at
this early hour he would get a call from Erin. She woke up earlier
than most of them, the only way she could find time with the
Lord, she would say. No matter who might be at the barbecue
Saturday, he would miss the fact that Erin couldn't be there. She'd
already told him that she couldn't make it out to Bloomington
this summer. Finances were too tight, and Sam couldn't get the
time off work.

John unplugged his cell phone from the charger and found
Erin's number. He had gotten good at texting. It was the favorite
means of communication for most of the grandkids, and even for
his grown sons and daughters. At this hour it was the best way to
see if Erin was awake without actually waking her. He tapped out
a quick message.

I read Galatians this morning, like you suggested last time we talked. Such a great book. Today's reading was about the fruit of the Spirit. I read the list ... love, joy, peace, patience, kindness, goodness, thoughtfulness, and self-control ... and all I could think about was you kids when you were little. The atmosphere of our home. So grateful we had God guiding us through the years. You awake?

Elaine was already up making coffee in the kitchen. By the time John made the bed, his phone began to ring. John hesitated, enjoying his new ringtone. "Great Is Thy Faithfulness." A hymn that had meant so much to him and to the Baxter family over the years. He smiled when he saw Erin's picture in the screen. He picked up the phone and clicked the Talk button. "Hi, honey. How's your morning?"

"Great so far." She sounded a little distant, like it was windy wherever she was. "Isn't Galatians amazing? I'm on Ephesians now. So much the Lord is teaching me."

"I love that."

"Me, too." Again she sounded like she was in the middle of something. "How's the weather in Bloomington?"

"Sunny and cool now ... but it'll heat up later." He laughed a little. "Supposed to be in the nineties tomorrow."

"Hmm. I miss it." There was the sound of the girls' voices and at least a few giggles.

"What's going on over there?" John loved the way Erin parented. Her kids were so happy, so sure of the way they were loved.

"Oh ... just a little morning cleaning." She paused and more laughter filled the phone line. "Right, girls?"

They all seemed to say yes at the same time. John laughed, picturing them. "Tell them I said hi."

"I will." She hesitated again. "Your papa says hi!"

"Hi, Papa!" He could hear Clarissa's voice the loudest. But then that was nothing new. The girl was a spark plug for sure. And growing up way too fast.

"I wish you could be here tomorrow. We should've flown you and the girls in, since Sam couldn't get the time off."

"That's right ... your birthday's this week. Seventy, right?"

"The calendar says so, but I don't feel like it. Elaine and I have been bike riding along with our regular walking. I feel half that."

"Good, Dad. I'm so glad you take care of yourself." The laughter left her voice. "I wish I could be there, too. But it isn't only Sam. The girls have swim team this week, and Heidi Jo has soccer." A loud bit of laughter sounded in the background. "Are you having a birthday party? I haven't heard any plans."

"Not really." John suddenly wondered if he'd imagined the whole thing. If Erin didn't know about it, then maybe it wasn't happening. "Ashley and Landon are having us over for a barbecue tomorrow. I guess I kind of thought ... more of the family might show up."

"I wish we were there." Her tone was more serious than before. "Keep praying for Sam to get a job in Bloomington or Indianapolis. And pray for the girls and this whole thing with Candy." The worry was strong in her voice. She had kept him up-to-date about Candy's release from prison and the woman's interest in visitation rights. "We'd all rather be there than here."

"I will." John sat on the bench at the foot of his bed and looked out the window. The small tract home where he and Elaine lived was much smaller than the Baxter house, where he and Elizabeth had raised their family. But the view from the master bedroom looked out over a field and half a dozen horses. It made him feel like they were still in the country. He pictured his youngest daughter, busy with her family. "Hey, Erin ... I want you to know something."

"What's that?" The girls were still giggling hard enough to be heard.

"I'm very, very proud of you. Supporting Sam's decision to move back to Texas ... doing everything you can to help your family get on track financially. And being such a great mom to those girls." He smiled, even as tears gathered in his eyes. "I miss you all so much, but you're doing the right thing. Maybe we can Skype sometime this weekend."

"That'd be perfect."

"Anyway, that's it. Just wanted you to know how much I love you."

"Aww, Dad ... I love you, too. I wish we could all be there for your birthday. Really. I'm who I am today because of you, because of the faith and love you and Mom taught me."

John's heart swelled. "Thanks, honey. That means more than you know."

After a minute, the call ended and John sauntered to his closet and the box on the top shelf. It was where he kept everything from Elizabeth. Her favorite sweater, her special earrings and the things the kids had made her over the decades. Pictures of her, and a scrapbook of the letters she'd written to them. He pulled it down and set it on a dresser top at the far end of the closet. From inside he pulled out a framed photo, one he had always loved. It showed her when she was in her midthirties, surrounded by the five kids, her face glowing with joy and laughter.

Of all the girls, Erin looked most like her. And of all the girls, Erin had been closest to her. It was like the others all found their place socially and academically a little more quickly than Erin had. She was smart enough — she had a degree in education and she'd taught kindergarten before adopting the girls. But growing up she was always happiest with Elizabeth.

The reality of his approaching birthday hit him. Seventy years. Even though his precious Elizabeth had been gone for nearly ten of those, the time with her would forever stand as the greatest part of his life. Loving Elizabeth, raising their kids together. Yes, he loved Elaine and he treasured the time God had given him with his second wife. She was kind and considerate and she loved his family as if they were her own. But nothing could compare to the days with his first love. He never tried to pretend otherwise.

John stared at the photo and remembered again the grief and heartache when Elizabeth was diagnosed with breast cancer a second time. She'd battled it and won when the kids were younger, and she'd been free of the disease long enough that they all thought she was cured for good. But cancer was an unrelenting monster, pursuing every healthy cell and looking for an opportunity. Once it found one a second time with Elizabeth, its course was swift and deadly.

They all took her loss hard. Only the letters she'd written to them over the years and the faithfulness of God Almighty got them through it. Especially for poor Erin. Her siblings had all lost their mother, and the most important woman in their lives.

But Erin had lost her best friend.

When he began his courtship with Elaine, when it looked more and more like he might marry her and spend his remaining years with her rather than alone, Erin had been among the grown kids most affected. One time she pulled John aside with tears in her eyes.

"Dad, it's not that I don't want you to be happy. You know that, right?"

"I do, honey." He stroked her hair, understanding her pain. "Of course."

"It's just that …" a quiet sob slipped from her throat. "I don't want us to forget Mom. And I'm afraid … if Elaine's here all the time we won't be able to talk about her. Like it'll be awkward."

John had spent the next half hour explaining that nothing of the sort would happen. "Elaine was one of your mother's closest friends. She wants you to talk about your mom, honey. It'll never feel strange or awkward, I promise you."

The conversation seemed to help Erin get through the next few months and the reality of John's remarriage. And like he promised, Elizabeth came up often after that and even still today. Elaine remained deeply sensitive to all the Baxter family had lost when they lost Elizabeth, and she enjoyed talking about the memories of when she was alive.

Yes, God had worked through all the details, helping him hold on to his love for Elizabeth even while loving Elaine. John ran his thumb over the picture of Elizabeth and he remembered a sermon he'd heard once about love. The preacher had stated that there were several types of love. An all-encompassing love for mankind, and a romantic love, and a more surface love for all things enjoyable. But John disagreed. In his experience there were as many kinds of love as there were people. Love between two hearts, two souls was never the same from one person to the next.

And so it was still true that he would never love anyone the way he had loved Elizabeth. They had been through most of life together, after all. The fall they'd gone through before they were married, and Elizabeth's unplanned pregnancy. The awful decision on her parents' part to send her away and insist that she give up her baby up for adoption — the way that sort of situation was handled back in those days. Their longing for their firstborn son all the years while they raised their family, and their determination to not talk about him sometimes for whole years in a row. The way they'd been advised by the counselor at the hospital not to talk about him.

John was still grateful beyond anything he could put into words that Elizabeth's prayer had been answered, that in her final hours she'd had the chance to meet Dayne and see that he knew about her. The heavenly reunion between them all one day would be sweeter than anything any of them could imagine.

John slipped the photo back into the box and returned it to the top shelf. There would be more time for remembering in the days to come. He needed that, and Elaine understood it. Especially in light of this birthday.

Before he left the bedroom he prayed, talked to God like he

did every single day at this time. There in his closet he slowly dropped to his knees. Something about the feel of the floor beneath his knees reminded him of his place before the Lord, the relative smallness and insignificance of anything he might face in comparison to the grandeur and love of God.

Father, You know my youngest daughter, Erin, and You love her. She misses family so much, Lord. Please help Sam find permanent work here in Indiana so we might all be together. And please protect those girls from their birth mother, if she's still a risk. If she is, please expose her, Lord. John forced himself not to feel anxious about the situation. God would go before them, the way He always had. He continued his prayer. *Father, if Erin could be here this week, she would. We all know that. But a permanent reunion could only come through a miracle, Father. That's what I'm asking for. The best birthday present ever would be to know that Erin could be surrounded by family once more.* He went on to pray for each of his adult kids, for their spouses and children and for the Lord to bless them in their talents and time, for Him to help them with whatever challenges they faced in this season.

When he finished praying, he stood, his heart full. However much he loved his family, however grateful he was for the way they walked with God and shared with their families the love they'd been raised with, John was most comforted by this single thought. The Lord loved them even more than he did. Whether it was a job situation or a health crisis or a tragedy of some sort, God had always seen them through. And that was the comfort he'd learned to live in now that he was almost seventy years old. There was nothing to worry about where his family was concerned.

God had everything in control.

ERIN HAD STIFLED HER LAUGHTER THROUGHOUT the conversation, and now that the call was over she and the girls and Sam all laughed out loud at the surprise they were about to play on her dad.

"He has no idea." Sam gave the girls a thumbs-up from the driver's seat and waited while the others found their places. "This is going to be fun."

"I almost lost it a few times." Erin buckled herself into the passenger seat and looked back at the girls. She waggled her finger at them. "You four couldn't stop laughing. I still don't know how I got through the conversation."

"It was so funny," Heidi Jo clapped her hands. She and Amy Elizabeth sat together in the middle seat with Clarissa and Chloe in the back, their usual seats. "You were telling Papa we wish we could be there and the whole time we were packing the car."

"I thought for sure he'd hear us laughing," Clarissa shook her head. "Mom, I was like, so loud."

"It wasn't just you!" Erin laughed again. "Your sisters were laughing, too. I guarantee he heard us. That's why I had to tell him you were cleaning."

"Which, by the way, did you girls have time to clean?"

Erin was still turned around, looking at their girls. Chloe winced. "It's better than last night."

"Ours is clean, Mommy." Heidi Jo smiled, her brown eyes taking up what looked like half her face. "I promise."

"Yeah, but Mom helps you." Chloe tapped her younger sister lightly on the head a few times. "Don't forget that."

Again they laughed, all of them despite the lack of sleep and the long drive ahead.

"Okay, are we ready?" Sam looked back at the girls and then at Erin.

Only then did she gasp. "The computer. I forgot to turn it off."

"You don't have to turn it off, babe." Sam raised his eyebrow. "I'm an IT guy, remember?"

"Yeah, but I want to. We might get lightning this week." She opened the door and hurried out. "I'll be right back."

Sam pointed to the front door. "Hurry."

She ran three steps toward the house and then turned around and flew back to the car. "I need the keys. Please." Her words ran together as she held out her hand.

Sam laughed as he killed the engine and handed her the key ring. "Still hurry."

"Yes." She flashed Sam a nervous look and darted toward the house. "Sorry. I'll be right back."

Inside, Erin ran to the computer. She was about to shut it down when she saw the private Facebook message. Facebook was the last page she had opened late yesterday, looking to see if Ashley had sent out more details about the surprise party.

But her sister had waited until this morning. *Finally*, she thought to herself. If there were details she needed, better now than not at all. She clicked the icon and her private messages opened up on a new page. As they did, Erin felt the blood leave her face. The new message wasn't from Ashley.

It was from Candy Burns.

Erin felt suddenly sick. Her eyes raced over the message once and then a second time. But something strange and unexpected happened as she read Candy's message a third time. Erin's horror turned to hope. The message said this:

Dear Erin, as you know I'm out of prison and I'm a changed woman. I really do think I'd make a good mother now. But I'm also open to a deal. My expenses are very high and I don't have a job. If the deal is right, I'm sure I could move on, start a new life, if you know what I mean. In the right situation, I could have other kids. I hate to mess up your happy family. Let me know your thoughts. Candy B.

Erin sat back hard in the computer chair. This was it! The proof she needed. The hope inside her built until she laughed out loud. The woman must've been back on crack to write those words, to incriminate herself.

She didn't have time to copy and paste the message into a text for Naomi, the girls' social worker. So she decided to take care of it from the road. Her phone had a Facebook app, even though she had never used it. Either that or the matter could wait until they got back from Indiana.

With a few quick clicks Erin shut down the computer and hurried back out to the car. Sam grinned at her as she took her seat. "Ready for lightning?"

"Ready." She would tell him about Candy's message later. For now she turned and gave the girls a thumbs-up. "Ready for Mandisa?"

"Yes!" All four of them shouted the word at once, and then they all fell into another round of laughter.

She slipped in the CD and, as the music played and the girls sang out loud, Erin couldn't get Candy's message out of her mind. While Sam drove through town and as he got onto the highway, she couldn't stop thinking about the woman's words, the clear extortion once again hinted at between the words. Yes, some women could find rehabilitation and redemption in prison, some could go on to be wonderful mothers, Erin had no doubt.

But she had met Candy in person, and the cold indifference the woman had felt about her daughters back then was not something that could be easily changed through a program or a class. Only an act of God could've turned Candy into a redeemed woman. And from what Naomi had said, "religion wasn't part of Candy's progress in prison."

Even Naomi doubted Candy's intentions — because of things she'd said in a number of conversations. But still Naomi had no choice but to recommend the visits because there was no actual proof that Candy's motives were suspect.

Until now.

Suddenly Erin couldn't keep the information to herself another minute. She wasn't sure how to use the Facebook app, so she pulled out her phone and called up Naomi's contact information. Then she tapped out a text.

Look, something urgent has come up. I can prove to you that Candy only wants money out of this. I'll call you when we get back to Texas. This can wait until then.

There were times when Erin had mixed feelings about taking a trip back to Bloomington, times when she hadn't been sure about the way her siblings felt about her, and whether they even cared if she and her family were part of the get-together. But she felt nothing like that this time. This might even be the best reunion they'd ever had.

As if God Himself agreed with her, Erin called up her Bible Promise app and the verse for today was Psalm 13:6. She read it silently with an even greater hope than before. *I will sing the Lord's praise, for He has been good to me.* Indeed, Erin planned to sing with her family all the way to Bloomington. Because yes, the Lord had been good to them. So very good. The fifth song on the album was starting.

"Mom, can you turn it up a little?" The question came from Clarissa.

Erin gave Sam a questioning look. "Is that okay?"

He winked at her. "You can play it as loud as you want." He looked in the rearview mirror. "As long as everyone sings." He turned up the volume as the music started to play. "This is my favorite kind of concert."

And like that they were all singing and Erin pushed away thoughts of Candy. They would drive halfway today and finish tomorrow. Ashley had asked them to be at her house by five o'clock, since their dad was supposed to be there at five thirty. She smiled as she leaned back into her seat and faced the road ahead.

It would be the greatest surprise ever.

Eight

DAYNE CHECKED HIS WATCH AS HE HEADED DOWN THE STAIRS OF their Malibu home. Ten a.m. Still plenty of time for a walk with Katy. He hurried around the corner and into the kitchen. The kids had been up at six, and just now Dayne had tucked them in for a quick nap. They'd need it, since they wouldn't likely sleep on the flight to Indiana later that afternoon.

Once Sophie and Egan were down for their naps, Dayne found his wife and her aunt in the dining room having coffee.

"Foggy morning." He peered out the patio door at the beach. "Typical for this time of year."

"It's still beautiful. In fact, I was just saying I might never leave." Peggy Wayne was ten years younger than Katy's mother — who had passed away a few years ago from complications of diabetes. Katy hadn't been very close to her aunt, but her mother's funeral had stirred new interest in the family. Aunt Peggy had been out to see them twice in the past year — a blessing for all of them.

"When you're finished ... could we take a walk?"

"Sure." Katy's look told him she knew he had a lot on his mind. She took a final sip of her coffee. "I was done. Just chatting." Katy stood and kissed her aunt on the cheek. "You'll listen for the kids?"

"Yes, yes." She waved her hand, shooing Katy away. "You two go run off. If I lived on a beach I'd only be inside to eat and sleep."

Dayne smiled. The woman was refreshing, a spunky grandmotherly type and someone he believed would be part of his family for all time. He and Katy grabbed hats and headed down their back stairs. With the fog, the shoreline was nearly empty.

They walked across the sand to the shore and Dayne put his arm around her shoulders. "I like her."

"Me, too." Katy grinned at him. "I think she's adopted us. With her never having married, we're sort of the only family she has." For a few seconds she was quiet. "I guess if anyone knows about finding family later in life it's you."

Dayne squinted at the gray horizon. "I've put off writing that letter. This morning it's all I can think about."

"I wondered if you found time."

"I had time. I guess I couldn't figure out how to put my feelings on paper." He looked at her and slowed his pace. "The fact that he's turning seventy. It makes me realize how many years I missed."

"Hmm." Katy looked straight ahead, as if she were seeing images from the past same as he'd been seeing them all day. "I hadn't thought about that."

"It's why I wanted to walk." He tightened his hold on her, loving the way her body fit against his. "I thought maybe if I talked about the last ten years I'd find a way to write about it." He was quiet for several steps, the morning sand cool on his feet. "It's still hard to believe. How we found each other."

Katy slipped her arm around his waist. "If you hadn't found the Baxter family, you wouldn't have found me."

"Exactly." They were closer to the surf now and they kept their steps slow and measured. As if the winds of yesterday were too strong to walk quickly against.

"Why don't you tell me the story again, how you found out you were adopted." She smiled at him. "It's been a while."

He stopped for a moment and kissed her lips, a kiss marked with deep passion and a grateful kind of love. She always knew exactly what he needed. Even now. "Okay." He let the story line up in his heart once more. "Of course, I didn't know I was adopted until after my first parents died. You remember that, right?"

"I do." She seemed in no hurry. "I guess I want to hear your feelings on all of it. Pretend like you've never told me before."

They started walking again and Dayne breathed in the wet salty air. She was right. The only way to tell the story was to start at the beginning. He told her again how his parents had adopted him but then moved him to Indonesia to preach the gospel. Dayne was raised in a boarding school for missionary kids, a fact he resented with every passing hour when he was a kid. "I felt like I was competing with God. Like He was my enemy and I was losing." He lowered his gaze to the sand for a few seconds. "I fought for my parents' time right up until the moment they were killed."

The plane crash happened without warning; the small Cessna dropped from the sky and broke apart in a ball of fire on the jungle floor. Rescue workers found very little of his parents' remains. At the time, Dayne was eighteen without siblings or any family. A small settlement from his parents' estate allowed him to enroll at UCLA and move to Los Angeles — as far from his parents' mission field as possible. He moved into a dorm and in the first few weeks he found a talent agent. Before he'd been in town a month, he had a decent part in a movie.

A year later he landed the lead role in a film that broke records at box offices, and like that Dayne Matthews was a household name. The next Brad Pitt, people called him. He was wanted by every casting agent and desired by every woman in Hollywood. Early on, the fame and wealth led to wild nights and crazy opportunities, choices Dayne embraced despite everything his parents and his upbringing had taught him.

"I thought I was still battling God, only this time ... this time I was going to win." The memories of those days made his stomach hurt. "I was such a mess."

"You were out of control, no doubt." Katy's look told him she felt sorry for him. "I'm sorry you had to go through that. Every-one thought you'd have a tragic ending — like so many celebrities."

"I lived life one party to the next. If I hadn't found you ..." He let his voice trail off. "I don't know if I'd be here."

Katy stared out at the ocean, the past clearly weighing on her, too. She had been running Christian Kids Theater back then, liv-ing in Bloomington and content to stay there. She stopped and looked at him. "Back then never in a million years would I have believed we'd meet, let alone wind up like this." She put her arms around his neck and kissed him, clinging to him in a way that soothed his doubts. However broken his past, God had used the heartache to bring him to her.

"One morning — I don't really remember why — I went to my parents' storage unit." Dayne had rented the space to hold their belongings after the crash. "I looked through the boxes — almost as if I wanted some kind of hint, some way to understand myself."

There, in a dusty old box, he found a picture of a beautiful brunette, an old photo cracked and faded by the years. Dayne had stared at the picture for a long while, trying to figure out who the woman was and why her picture was stuck inside a box of her mother's things. After a minute he shrugged and set the framed photo back in the box and moved on to his parents' other belongings.

"And a few weeks later you were in your lawyer's office and you saw Luke?"

"Yes. But I didn't see him first. But in the first ten minutes three people told me I looked like this Luke Baxter." By then Luke had worked at the LA office for a while and he'd been hearing how much he looked like Dayne. He ran his fingers down Katy's shoulders. "No one actually meant that it was possible. Me and Luke Baxter? Related? It was too crazy even to suggest."

But one afternoon Dayne was meeting with Luke in his office

when for a moment the young lawyer had to step out and take a phone call. In his absence Dayne glanced at the framed pictures on Luke's desk. One showed an extended family, what looked like a host of siblings and their spouses along with a bevy of children and an older couple. But the other picture was far more dated. It showed a young man and woman, maybe in their early twenties.

"I gasped out loud, because I knew." Dayne walked a little slower, the memories strong. "The woman was the same one I'd seen in the box of my mother's things. I was positive."

"What did you think?" Katy still looked surprised, as if she were only hearing the story for the first time.

"I didn't think I was adopted. I had no idea about that. I wondered if maybe the woman was a friend of my mom's, somehow. I couldn't wait to get back to the storage unit."

When he did, he took the photo from the frame and looked at the back. The message written there rocked Dayne's world. After that he could only surmise that somehow his parents hadn't told him the truth and that maybe — just maybe — he was adopted. But that quickly led him to the next obvious possibility. If he was adopted and the guy at the law firm looked just like him ... and if the lawyer had a framed picture of a woman who seemed to possibly be Dayne's birth mother, then didn't that mean —

"It sort of hit me all at once, like being pulled into a riptide. Fighting it would only make it more impossible to find my way back to the shore."

"Aww, sweetheart." She stopped and faced him, searching his eyes. "I'm sorry."

"It's okay." He pulled her into a close hug and for a long moment they swayed. "I didn't have anyone I could be angry at, but I didn't have God, either. No real way to navigate my feelings or make sense of them. My parents should have told me."

She eased back and put her hand gently alongside his face. "I was praying for you."

"You didn't know me." Gradually the meaning in her words dawned on him. "Wow ... you're right."

"Yep." She kissed him again, more lightly this time. "I prayed for the guy I would marry." She raised her brow, her eyes bright with a sweet sort of teasing. "I had no idea I was praying for the Dayne Matthews. I probably would've prayed harder."

They both laughed at that. Dayne took her hand and they headed north along the beach again. "But still," her tone grew more serious, "I was praying. It's amazing to think how God was answering those prayers when neither of us even knew it."

"It makes sense." He chuckled, the miracle of his life fully alive inside him the way it hadn't been for a long time. "I mean, how else could I explain what happened after that?"

Katy smiled, but she didn't say anything. She didn't need to. They both knew the next part of his story. Dayne lifted his face to the foggy sky. He needed this, a chance to realize the gift God had given him when he saw his mother's photo in the law firm that afternoon. The timing had been so completely divine.

Once Dayne read the back of the photo he did the only thing he knew to do. He was Dayne Matthews, so he could hardly call up Luke Baxter and tell him he suspected they might be brothers. What if the guy went to the press or demanded money? Anything was possible. Instead he hired a private investigator and gave him simple instructions. Find out everything about the Baxters, and, most of all, find out if the mother had given up a baby boy when she was younger.

The news came back more quickly than Dayne expected, but it wasn't all good. Yes, Elizabeth Baxter was his biological mother, and her husband, John, was his birth father. The family was good and true and wholesome, raised in a strong faith and with a strong love for each other. The sort of family Dayne had longed for all his life.

But in his research the PI had found out something else. Elizabeth was dying of breast cancer with maybe only a week or so to live.

The next morning Dayne flew into Indianapolis and drove a rental car to the hospital in Bloomington. As he was about to step out of his car he spotted all of them, the entire Baxter family leaving the hospital. They were emotional, clearly. Several of them had arms around each other's shoulders and their heads were bowed, the moment serious. Dayne guessed they were headed out for a meal, a chance to get away from the hospital for a little while. As they came closer he saw Luke and then the others, girls who had to be his sisters. He hesitated, wondering if he should introduce himself, wondering if they'd recognize him from the movies or if they'd think he was some crazy imposter.

But as he started to get out of the car he heard the sound he'd come to know better than his own heartbeat. The sound of cameras clicking.

Dayne remembered his frustration. "I shut the door. I figured the paparazzi could take pictures of me sitting in a car in a hospital parking lot. But if I approached the Baxters, they would want to know why." And just like that everything real and good and private about his birth family would be gone forever. They would be scrutinized and photographed and made to be an object of public curiosity.

So Dayne stayed in his car.

After a few minutes he drove to the front of the hospital, parked illegally and hurried inside, baseball cap pulled low over his face. The paparazzi knew better than to follow him into a hospital. And for the next hour he had the only time he would ever have with his birth mother.

"I was desperate to meet her." Dayne felt the sadness again. He'd missed so much by not knowing about his family in his early years. "And the cool thing is she was expecting me. I think she'd been praying for me, that she would meet me. That's what she said, anyway."

"That was the same day ... the first time you saw me."

"I was a wreck by then."

He sighed and stopped walking. For a long while he stared out at the Pacific and simply felt. Felt the sand beneath his toes and the ocean breeze on his skin. Felt the love of the only woman he'd ever wanted, the girl he had fallen for from that very first long ago moment. God was so good, letting him find Elizabeth Baxter ... even when he only had the privilege of knowing her for an hour.

"She didn't get that I was famous." Dayne chuckled but the sound was more sad than funny. "Which was so great. Because she was proud of me anyway. She was so sick she was borderline lucid. But still she talked to me like she'd known me all my life."

"In a way she had. Through prayer, anyway." Katy eased her hands around his waist and leaned on his shoulder. "It wasn't her choice to give you up."

"I wish I would've known her with my dad. I have a feeling they were beautiful together."

"Definitely. Look at the family they created."

Dayne let that settle in for another long moment. "We can start walking back. The kids will be up soon." He put his arm around her again and kissed the top of her head. "I love you. Thanks for listening."

"It's important. Remembering." She smiled up at him. They walked a little faster than before, more aware of the time. "It's not like we do this often. It's been years."

She was right. Dayne rarely brought any of this up, mainly because it felt better to believe he'd always been part of the Baxter family. "When I left the hospital all I could think was I should've grown up there, in Bloomington. Then I see this old community theater and a sign on the marquis, *Charlie Brown the Musical*." He hesitated, feeling the way he'd felt that day. "I knew if she hadn't given me up I would've done theater in that building. My whole life might've been different."

Dayne couldn't resist, so he parked and snuck in through the back door. He slipped into the back row and watched the production. "You came up on stage at the end of the show and it was like the complete picture. Because I knew I would've dated you. There would never have been anyone for me but you."

"My choreographer told me you'd been there." She laughed. "We all thought she was crazy."

The encounter started a pursuit of Katy, one that Dayne kept up until he proposed to her a few years later. Along the way he and Katy dealt with stalkers and attacks in the gossip rags. Ultimately, Dayne had to wrestle with the one thing that truly figured to keep them apart.

His lack of faith.

But a trip to Mexico to visit his missionary friend from boarding school changed everything. After the miracle of that trip, Dayne didn't see God as the enemy.

The breeze had died down, and the sun was breaking through the fog. He smiled at her. "Remember what I did after that?"

"How could I forget?" She put her head on his chest and they stayed that way for a minute. "I came home from CKT rehearsal the next day and there were flowers waiting for me." She looked up at him, deep into his eyes. "The card said, 'I once was lost but now am found.' After that I knew."

"What did you know?" His voice was soft, barely louder than the sound of the breaking surf.

"I knew you loved me."

He kissed her, unaware of anything around him but her. Always her. "With all my life, Katy."

They had met up again after that and started a conversation, how things might work out and whether she could live his life or not. But then he was in the most awful car accident, a head-on collision on Pacific Coast Highway caused by pursuing paparazzi. He had almost died, and even after surviving the initial trauma, he faced months of rehab. Katy had gone to LA to push him, to insist that he never give up.

And to tell him she loved him, too.

When he came back to Bloomington after his recovery time, he found that the Baxters and the Flanigans and so many others in Bloomington had completely renovated the old house on the edge of the lake, the one Dayne planned to fix up before the accident.

"Wasn't that the most amazing thing, pulling into the driveway and seeing half the town there?" They still faced each other. Katy was the one person he had shared all this with. His entire history since he found out he was a Baxter. "It was like an incredible episode of a home makeover show."

"I couldn't believe how much work they'd done."

Dayne grinned. "Let's walk. I keep getting distracted."

"It's a pretty great story."

"It is." He laughed and took hold of her hand. "I couldn't have made it up, that's for sure."

After that it was only a matter of time before Dayne proposed to her. He was so thrilled to have his new relationship with the Baxters, so excited about his wedding plans that he'd moved into the lake house and for a while he thought he'd be content in Bloomington.

But the chance to make movies for God beckoned him every day. When Keith Ellison called from LA asking him to partner in a faith-film venture, Dayne talked it over with Katy and the two made the decision. They would live and work in LA as long as God might use them there.

"The hardest thing about leaving Bloomington?" Dayne

looked up at the sky, but he felt the wetness in his eyes. "Knowing that I'd see my dad less." He paused, his thoughts and emotions swirling together. "I'd just found him ... you know?"

"I'm glad we go back often."

"We do." He didn't want to feel guilty. This wasn't about whether they'd made the right decision. "I just miss him. I lost a lot in the whole deal. Missing out on being a Baxter all those years." He stood a little straighter as they reached their back steps. "And now he's seventy."

"You know what that means." Katy hugged him once more, running her hands along his arms and back.

"What?"

"It means you need to find an hour to put that whole story in a letter. Before tomorrow."

For the first time that month, the letter felt possible. "You're right. That's exactly what I'm going to do." He could hardly wait to get to Bloomington, to spend a week celebrating his father's seventy years with the greatest family ever. Dayne might not have had as many years with John Baxter as the others, but this much was sure.

They were the best years of his life.

Nine

THE MORNING OF HER FATHER'S SURPRISE PARTY, ASHLEY DID something that might've surprised her brothers and sisters.

She drove to the cemetery.

There were certain days Ashley made a point of going, and this was one of them. Long before she made plans to throw a surprise party for her dad this final Saturday in June, she knew she'd spend time in the early morning hours at the cemetery. Now, at just before seven in the morning, she quietly kissed Landon's cheek as he slept and she slipped on a lightweight Nike jacket. The kids were asleep, too, and would be for another hour at least.

She left the house without making a sound and she kept the radio off while she drove. The cemetery was on the outskirts of Bloomington, in a pretty patch of land lush with green grass and the occasional trees and shrubs. Ashley narrowed her gaze on the road ahead and thought about her decision to make this trip. Her mother and baby daughter were not at the cemetery. She knew that much.

But something about going to the place where they were buried created in Ashley a reflective feeling, an almost sacred moment where she could remember vividly once more the beauty of those two lives and the depth of how she missed them. The cemetery was a place where Ashley's soul found a quiet it didn't easily find at other times.

She pulled into the parking lot and easily found her way down the winding paved sidewalk through the cemetery to the place where they were buried, the two of them side by side. Her mother's larger tombstone, and Sarah's smaller one. She liked to think that God had allowed Sarah to be born with anencephaly because her dear grandmother — Ashley's mom — would've wanted a grandchild with her in heaven. Ashley sat on the bench adjacent to the graves.

Her mother had lived long enough to see her get married. Ashley would always be grateful for that. She looked up at the blue sky overhead, at the full branches of the oak tree not far from where she sat. Landon had gone to New York City after 9 – 11 to look for his firefighter buddy, Jalen. It took months before his body was found in the pile at Ground Zero, and only then did Landon come home.

Ashley could picture that moment like a painting in her mind, the way she would always picture it. She'd been working on a piece of art, her paints and easel set up outside what had then been her parents' house. The one she and Landon shared with their kids now. She hadn't known he was coming, and suddenly he was there. His hands on her shoulders, and the whisper of his voice in her ears.

"You have the most beautiful hair." His words found their way straight to her heart. "Has anyone ever told you that?"

She had turned around and found him standing there, his face weathered, his shoulders sunken. As if the experience in New York had all but killed him. And with that they were together, together in a way that nothing and no one could ever separate again. The wedding plans happened quickly but the whole time her mom was fighting for her life. Ashley prayed along with the rest of the family, but her prayer was more personal.

That God would allow her mom to live long enough to see her get married. In all His mercy, the Lord answered her prayer. One particular memory presented itself that early morning. The moment Ashley tried on her wedding dress in her mother's bedroom. Her mom was too weak to leave the house, but that day she stood and came to Ashley. For several minutes she helped button up the back of the gown and she fawned over the train and helped adjust it so she could take in the whole of the sight of Ashley.

"I'm not sure if there's ever been a more beautiful bride." Her face shone with happiness, and for the first time in weeks she looked almost well again.

Ashley had let the words find permanent lodging in her heart. Her mom had certainly said the same words to her sisters over the years and to Reagan when she and Luke married. But in that moment she felt like truly the most beautiful bride ever.

Tears filled Ashley's eyes in the cool morning light, and she blinked them back. Maybe it was just that she had needed to hear the words more than her sisters needed them. After all, she was the Baxter girl who had gone off to Paris and made foolish decisions, the one who had probably hurt their mother the most. The reconciliation and redemption Ashley felt, standing before her mother in her wedding gown, was something she would hold on to until her final heartbeat.

"Oh, Mom ..." Ashley breathed the words out loud. "I still miss you so much." She looked down at the tombstone, at her mother's name and the few words they were able to etch into the marker. "We're throwing Dad a surprise party. You probably know, but I wanted to tell you. I can't believe he's turning seventy."

She let her eyes fall on the smaller stone.

"Sarah ... you were such a special baby. God must be using you for a very great purpose in heaven."

Ashley smiled through her tears. There was no way to calculate the things little Sarah had taught her. When she was born, they all filled the hospital room. Everyone in the Baxter family, all of them holding hands and singing songs of praise. Celebrating life as if there was no sign of impending death.

They passed little Sarah around the room, taking turns holding her and loving her and singing quiet songs of praise to God on her behalf. When Sarah was returned once more to Ashley's arms, they sang the hymn that had come to mean so much to them over the years.

"Great Is Thy Faithfulness."

Cole had done something then, something that he still talked to Ashley about. He had given her a drawing he'd done, a picture of Ashley's mother holding baby Sarah, the two of them in a beautiful land. A land Cole told her was heaven. "I saw the two of them, so I drew it," he told her.

No artwork before or since could compare to that single illustration and what it meant to Ashley in the hour before Sarah's death. From that point on, Ashley was at peace, certain that her baby girl would be fine. Until they met again she would be loved and cared for and safe — not only with Jesus.

But by Ashley's mother.

At the time, Ashley still struggled with her father's decision to remarry, and of all her sisters she and Erin were probably the most distant with her dad's new wife. But Sarah's birth changed all that. Elaine came to the hospital with a small pink outfit for the baby. Clothes that gave Ashley a very clear message.

Sarah's life mattered. It was meant to be celebrated before it could be mourned.

From that day on, Ashley felt a fiercely protective love for Elaine.

Ashley finished up by praying, asking God for His blessing on her father's birthday party. That it would be a time of sweet laughter and remembering. When she was finished, Ashley stood and filled her lungs with the morning air. She still had a lot to do to get ready for today. She'd spent enough time in the cemetery, remembering and thanking God.

Now it was time to get back to the living.

THE BARBECUE WAS OPEN AND LANDON was struggling with the grate, trying to clean it and adjust it closer to the fire. Ashley watched him from the kitchen window and after a minute he walked through the back patio door and held up the scrub brush. "This isn't cutting it." Grime from the barbecue practically covered his arms. "Remind me again why we didn't clean this thing after the Labor Day barbecue last year?"

She couldn't help but laugh. "Can I take a picture? Please? You look like an ad for an industrial cleaner."

He raised an eyebrow in her direction. "Do I have grease on my face, too?"

"Well," she winced, "let's just say the whites of your eyes look very bright."

Laughter came over him, too. "Any suggestions?"

She looked under the sink and found a different scrubber. It wasn't as bristled, but it promised dramatic results. "Here." She handed it to him. "Maybe clean off before you use it."

He took her advice and went to the sink. A few minutes of hot soapy water and a handful of paper towels later and he looked like himself again. "Now I won't scare the children." He chuckled. "How long before I need to start the barbecue?"

Ashley looked at the clock on the microwave. It was just after four. "As long as it's hot by four-thirty. I have the tray of meat ready." She turned to him again. "I thought it'd be better to have the burgers and hotdogs ready before everyone gets here. That way we can all be together and you won't be stuck outside cooking."

"I like it." He held the new scrubber up in the air. "Here I go. Wish me luck."

He walked back outside and Ashley held tight to the feeling inside her. Something about her dad's big birthday, or maybe her earlier visit to the cemetery made her more nostalgic than usual.

Knowing that her dad was seventy years old was a stark reminder to all of them. Time didn't stand still, even for the greatest of love.

Even for the Baxter family.

Landon felt better these days, his lungs healthier than they'd been when he was fighting fires. His new job — helping out with drug intervention in the schools — was every bit as rewarding and the improvement in his lungs made doctors hopeful that Landon's life expectancy might not be affected by his disease. A disease he'd most likely gotten as a result of his work at Ground Zero.

All of which was why Ashley sometimes watched Landon a little longer, holding on to the sight of him. There was no telling how long any of them had, after all. Always better to treasure the moment. Life had taught her that if nothing else.

She pulled up a bar stool at the kitchen counter and called each of her siblings, just to make sure they were on track for five o'clock. Dayne and Katy had landed at the Indianapolis airport late last night and they'd driven to Luke and Reagan's. The two families would caravan to Bloomington. Dayne guessed they'd be a little early. The same was true for Brooke, although Peter had rounds at the hospital and wouldn't be able to come till later. "He tried everything he could to get it rearranged." She sounded frustrated. "He'll meet up with us around seven. He said to save him a burger."

"We will. Tell him not to worry." Ashley was amazed that only Peter couldn't make the initial surprise. "With all our different schedules, it's amazing so many of us can be together. Dad's going to flip."

Brooke's tone lightened. "I know. I've been counting down the days." Her smile came through the phone line. "The girls, too. They love their papa so much."

"All the kids are that way. They have the greatest grandpa in the world, and they know it."

"Exactly."

Next Ashley called Kari. Her family also was running early. "We've been looking forward to this for so long."

"Us, too." Ashley double-checked that Kari was bringing the potato salad. It was a recipe the Baxters had gotten from the Flanigans, but it took a lot of work. It was the one thing Ashley knew she wouldn't have time for.

"Made it last night." Kari sighed. "Made me think of Mom. She always made everything from scratch."

Ashley told her how she'd gone to the cemetery that morning and how their mom had been on her heart, too. "I still miss her so much."

"She should be there today." Kari's voice was soft. "Nothing against Elaine."

"She will be. Remember the letter she wrote to us? She'd be there in Jessie's smile and Cole's laughter and Hayley's determination?" She paused. "She'll be there."

"You're right." Peace filled Kari's tone. "See you in a bit. Love you."

"Love you." Ashley hung up and dialed Erin.

Only their youngest sister was a wild card on whether they'd all be there at five o'clock. Unexpected traffic could delay them and Heidi Jo sometimes suffered from motion sickness. Yesterday was one of those times. She hadn't slept well, so they had stopped at a grocery store for crackers to calm her stomach before they got on the road this morning. They were running maybe half an hour late last time Ashley talked to her.

Her sister answered on the first ring. "Good news!" The girls were singing to Jeremy Camp in the background. "We made up the lost time!" Erin sounded thrilled. "We should roll into your house right around five. Definitely before Dad and Elaine get there."

"Yay!" Ashley could already picture the surprise. Especially with Erin there. Over the last week, their dad might've come to expect something was going on. Ashley had probably said more than she should have. Made too many phone calls checking on his timing for the barbecue. But there was no way he expected Erin and Sam and the girls to be there. "Okay, well, drive safe. See you in a few."

"See you. Love you, Ash."

The song in the background was Jeremy Camp's *I Still Believe*. Ashley could make out the words better now. She raised her voice so Erin could hear her. "Love you, too." She was touched that even when they were going to see each other so soon Erin made a point to say she loved her. It made her grateful they were going to have a whole week together.

When she was finished making the calls, Ashley checked the guest room. Cole and Devin had made it their project, but Ashley hadn't looked in on it since they finished. She stood in the door-way and smiled. The bed was made, and everything was neat and tidy. On the table sat a vase with several long-stemmed roses. The boys must've clipped them from the garden out back. The one Ashley's mother had planted so many years ago.

She made a point to thank the boys later. The thoughtful touch of their mother's roses at the bedside was sure to be appreciated by Erin. Ashley was proud of her sons for thinking of it. Sam and Erin would sleep here, the older girls on the sofas in the TV room and the little ones on cots in Devin's room. They'd be snug for the week, but it would be great fun. It was all Janessa could talk about, the idea of having girl cousins in the house.

Ashley was about to head outside and check on Landon when she caught the smell of the barbecue. The new scrubber must've worked. Ashley laughed quietly, remembering the way Landon had looked covered in grease. Someone had once told her that proof of a healthy marriage was how often a couple laughed together. If that was the case, then she and Landon must be doing well.

A quick trip to the kitchen for a few trays of meat and the barbecue was underway. Cole brought out the buns and he and Devin worked alongside Landon to get the dinner cooked. Ashley returned to the kitchen to take the salads and fixings from the fridge and arrange them on the counter. Janessa helped by finding the paper plates and cups and in minutes the kitchen was ready. She checked the time on her phone and felt the excitement well up inside her. It was ten till five.

Her family would start arriving any minute.

Ten

MARTY COHEN COULDN'T KEEP HIS EYES OPEN.

He only needed to reach Indianapolis before he could finally take a break, finally rest his eyes. That was something most people didn't understand — the toll truck driving took on a person. He blinked three times and used every muscle in his face to open his eyes wide. Wider than usual so that maybe enough light streaming through the windshield might startle him into a state of alertness.

Deep breaths, Marty. Take deep breaths.

He hadn't been making his runs as fast as usual. Blame it on his age — he'd be fifty-four in the fall — or on the years he'd spent in the driver's seat. But whatever the reason, he needed more sleep than usual. The long runs weren't easy like before.

He glanced at the photo on his dashboard, his wife and two sons and their wives. The picture next to it was of his three grand-babies. Two little girls and a boy. The boy wasn't quite a year yet. Maybe they were the reason. Marty didn't enjoy being on the road the way he once had. He'd rather be home with his family — all of them in New Mexico now, just outside Las Cruces.

Frustration simmered deep inside him because he couldn't quit. He and Margie needed the money, and after this many years, Marty knew nothing else. Only trucking. He leaned hard over the wheel and hit the button on the door to bring the window down. His truck was nice. Something he and the wife were still paying off. A tricked-out exterior and the inside air-conditioned for hot summer runs like this one. His bed was nice, too. A bunk over the driver's seat.

But last night he hadn't slept well. The ticking clock didn't help. Somehow knowing that sleep was limited always made getting rest that much more difficult. With every few breaths he could almost feel the clock taunting him, reminding him that the hours of possible sleep were shrinking fast.

"Come on, Marty. You gotta do this." He slapped his face. Hard. First one cheek then the other. The trick worked, at least at first. He sat up straighter and gripped the wheel with both hands. Only then did he notice that the traffic on 58 East was heavier than usual.

Where have I been for the past few minutes? A sense of grave alarm worked its way through him. How could he have been driving without really seeing the road? And what did that say about his safety for the stretch between here and Indianapolis? If he were smart, he'd pull over and get some sleep. Never mind that it was only five o'clock and too early to call it a night, and never mind that the markets in Indianapolis were expecting his delivery tonight.

He was carrying potatoes, after all. How important was that compared to safety?

Marty turned up the radio. Country music, that's what he needed. He made the transition from 58 East to Highway 37 North. He'd pass Bloomington in a few minutes and then he'd have only an hour till the city. He couldn't stop. Couldn't risk another write-up from his boss. The man's warning played again in his mind, even as his eyes grew heavy again. "Cohen, you're losing time." He had called him into the office in Las Cruces and slid a document across the desk. "I've gotta write you up. Time is money in trucking."

"Yes, sir. I'll do better."

Now Marty's promise played in his mind, whispering to him,

shouting at him. He turned up the radio and breathed in deep. Elvis was singing, "Love Me Tender." A little Elvis. Yes, that's what he needed. The singer's music took him back to the early days with Margie, back when they first fell in love. *Love me tender, love me sweet ... never let me go ...* But as the song played, sleep grabbed at him, pulled at him like an unrelenting captor.

No ... I can't fall asleep. I can't ...

He didn't believe in God, never had. But his sleepiness terrified him so much he almost considered praying. Almost. "Get a grip, Marty. You can do this." He had no choice, really. He needed another few tricks, a few more ways to keep his mind alert through this last hour. Then he could drop his load and sleep twelve hours straight. If he could get through the next hour he'd be golden.

His eyelids dipped and dragged and for a full two seconds he closed his eyes. But as his head nodded forward he felt himself jerk back awake. What was he doing? He couldn't fall asleep. His eighteen-wheeler wouldn't handle a jerk of the wheel.

It could easily roll and cause a major pileup. The thought made him sick to his stomach, but even still his eyelids grew heavy again. Not until he heard the sound of a horn blaring did he realize he'd drifted into the fast lane. He made a quick adjustment and felt his load protest, felt the way the truck nearly didn't survive the move.

This was insane. He needed to stop and get coffee. A strong cup of iced coffee. Yes, that would do the trick. He glanced at his phone, at the app that told him what gas stations and convenience stores and coffee shops were at the next few exits. He spotted one five miles up the road, the last exit for Bloomington. A Starbucks just off the freeway. He might even get two drinks. No chance he'd fall asleep then.

If he could only last five more miles.

Elvis was lulling him to sleep. He leaned forward to change

the channel but at the same time he spotted construction signs in the far distance. Stop and go traffic would be even worse. He needed coffee before the delay.

He blinked, but his eyelids weighed a ton. What was he doing? Suddenly he remembered. He was changing the channel, trying to find anyone but Elvis, anything to keep him from slipping into a dream state. But he couldn't remember how to work the radio, couldn't find the strength to lift his right hand.

Was he sick? Having a stroke? Marty squeezed his fingers and felt a full range of sensation. It wasn't a stroke. But then why was he so tired? He couldn't keep his thoughts together, could barely remember what he was doing or where he was going or why he was sitting behind the wheel of a semitruck.

Potatoes, right? Something about potatoes. He lifted his brow, using every bit of his strength to open his eyes. But at the same time he felt a dream wash over him. He and his sweet Margie when they were only college freshmen, the way she looked that night at the county fair, the smell of her perfume. A feeling like a warm river swept him away, taking him with it and whisking him to a place where he no longer felt worried or troubled or anxious about anything. A place that beckoned to him the way it did every night, and suddenly he realized what the feeling was.

The feeling was sleep.

ERIN HADN'T COUNTED ON THE TRAFFIC. The city of Bloomington officials had for years discussed the possibility of widening Highway 37, but always the idea was tabled. Not until she saw construction signs ahead did she remember that last year at this time the city voted to finally move ahead with the plans.

"Uggh," she groaned. The girls were finished singing for now, and they talked quietly among themselves, beyond excited to reach Ashley's house. Erin squinted at the traffic ahead. "This'll make us late for sure."

"Not for sure." Sam positioned himself in the slow lane. "If it gets too bad I'll get off and take surface streets." He patted her hand. "We know the shortcuts."

"True." They could get off at the next exit a mile or so down the road and find a faster way to the house. If they could only make it through this last mile.

"Are we almost there?" The question came from Amy Elizabeth. "I can't wait to see Papa."

"Me, too, honey." Erin glanced over her shoulder and smiled at the girls. "You've handled the trip so well. All of you. We only have a few more miles." She looked ahead again. There were brake lights everywhere. "It's a complete standstill."

"Maybe you should call." Sam's expression was slightly concerned. "Just so they're not worried." He checked his watch. "I mean, we'll be there by five-fifteen if I had to guess. But by then we could arrive at the same time as your dad. Ashley might want to call and delay him somehow."

"Good idea." Erin liked the plan. "It'll all work out."

She had no sooner said the words when they came to a complete stop. She picked up her cell phone and checked her text messages. No response yet from Naomi Boggs, the girls' social worker. She tapped the screen a few times and was about to dial Ashley when the air was cut in half by the deafening sound of Sam's desperate shout. "Nooo!"

For the life of her she couldn't imagine why he'd be shouting. They were stopped, after all. It wasn't like someone was cutting them off or creating a dangerous situation. But his shout filled her heart and mind and soul. A shout of warning and danger and horrific bone-chilling fear. His shout became words, a handful of words that consumed Erin and reminded her of a lifetime of joy and pain and sorrow. All in as much time as it took her to breathe in, as much time as it took her to brace herself.

"Nooo!" He screamed this time. "Dear God, help us!"

The girls began to scream, too, and the moment felt suddenly surreal and in slow motion. It occurred to Erin that she should turn around, that whatever the problem it must've been coming from behind them. But she didn't want to look, didn't want to see the certain expressions of terror on the faces of her daughters. "Jesus ... please!" She added her voice to the mix and at the same time she felt the hit. Felt their van crumple like paper beneath the force of it, felt them smash into the car in front of them.

They were being hit by something enormous. Not like a typical accident, no. This was much different. The sound of screeching, twisting metal and the shattering of glass, the sudden cacophony of horrific sounds and blurred images and the sensation of complete devastation was the same as if they'd been hit by a train. The pain was fast and complete, consuming her mind and soul and sucking the life from her. But even more than that was the noise.

The deafening noise.

Erin felt the blood draining from her body, felt herself drifting away until finally, mercifully there was nothing but black.

Nothing at all.

Eleven

ASHLEY WATCHED KARI AND RYAN AND THEIR KIDS PULL INTO the driveway.

"Kari's here!" She watched Landon bring in another tray of burgers.

"Have Ryan come on back. He can take over for Cole and Devin for the last tray of hotdogs."

"We don't mind." Cole had accompanied Landon inside. "It's fun." He looked back at Devin, straggling into the house. "Right. Dev? We can help Dad."

"Sure." He grinned, excited to be doing man work, as he liked to call it. "We got this."

Ashley hurried out to the parking area near the garage just as Kari and Ryan stepped out of the car. Kari opened the back door and helped Jessie and RJ and Annie out.

"I've been looking forward to this." RJ pumped his fists a few times and ran off toward the front steps. He stopped short and looked back, concerned. "Dad ... do you need help?"

"No, son." Ryan laughed. "You're fine. Go on in."

Ashley offered to take the vat of potato salad, but Ryan had it before she could help. He nodded with his chin to the backseat. "There's another bowl in the back. Much smaller. Maybe get that one if you don't mind."

"Not at all." Ashley found the bowl and helped shut the car doors while Kari grabbed a flat of water bottles.

"I thought these would help." She grinned at Ashley. "Is everyone on time?"

"They said they were." Just then she saw Luke's and Dayne's cars pull into the driveway. "We still have about ten minutes."

"Good." Kari looked relieved. "Dad's going to be so surprised."

Ryan was a few steps ahead as they walked up the front steps. "Where's Erin?"

"She's close. She said they made up time somewhere. Should be here in a few minutes." Ashley couldn't believe they'd pulled this off. Getting all their families together at the same time was an amazing accomplishment.

"Did you hear the sirens?" Ryan stopped at the front door and looked back. "Sounded like a big wreck on the highway."

"No." Ashley felt a sinking feeling. "When did you hear them?"

"The whole ride here, practically." Kari's smile faded. "Sounded really serious."

"It could delay Erin and Sam." Ryan opened the front door with his shoulder. The potato salad dish he was carrying was the size of an ice chest. "I'm sure she'll call if she gets held up."

Yes, Ashley told herself. Whatever had happened on the highway or near it, Erin and Sam would certainly call if it delayed them. "They could always take surface streets. Plus there's all that construction on the highway." Ashley could've kicked herself. Why hadn't she warned Erin and Sam about the construction? Even on weekends the county's efforts to widen the road could cause delays up to half an hour.

They walked in and by the time they set the salads on the counter and exchanged hugs the others joined them. Luke and Reagan walked through the door first. Johnny was in Reagan's arms — even though he was nearly three he looked sleepy and he had his head on Reagan's shoulder. Tommy and Malin were wide awake. "Let the cousin party begin," Tommy shouted. "This'll be the best week of summer.

Ashley was grateful for the way the kids got along, but she was drawn to the look of concern on Luke's face. She walked up and took a watermelon from him. She set it on the counter and faced him. "What's wrong?"

"The sirens." He looked at Reagan and then over his shoulder at Dayne. "So many sirens, huh?"

"And ambulances." Dayne's face was masked in concern. "When's Dad supposed to be here?"

Katy was behind him with baby Egan in her arms and Sophie beside her. "Maybe we should call him, make sure he's okay."

Ashley's mind began to spin. Landon came up and put his arm around her shoulders. He whispered close to her. "It's okay. It's not him."

"Yeah." She blinked a few times and tried to avert the panic closing in on her. "Could you call him?"

"Sure. It probably has something to do with the construction. A fender bender, maybe." He pulled his cell phone from his pocket as the other adults waited. Then he tapped the face of his phone a few times and put it to his ear. After a handful of seconds he grinned. "Hey, John ... Landon. Just wanted to make sure you and Elaine were running on time. The burgers are ready."

Landon smiled big and gave the group a thumbs-up. "Okay, then. We'll see you in fifteen." He hesitated. "Okay. All right. Drive safely."

He tapped the phone again. "He's fine. They're on time."

"Good." Luke looked more relieved than the others. "It was just a lot of sirens."

"Anyway ..." Dayne had a case of water, too. "This is a party ... enough talk of sirens." He grinned at the others and walked around the room hugging Ashley and Landon and Kari and Ryan. "It's been too long. What? Three months?"

"Since Bailey and Brandon's wedding, so yep. Three months."

Kari walked over to the sleeping Egan. "He's huge. Look at him!" She reached out and took the sleeping baby from Katy. "He's almost one, right?"

"Yes," Katy laughed. "And he weighs as much as a two-year-old."

Dayne puffed out his chest, his eyes bright with teasing. "Gonna be tall like his dad."

"Or taller still, like his uncle." Luke laughed and gave Dayne a lighthearted punch in the arm. He peered at the baby. "Right, little Egan?"

Ashley felt herself relax, but she still didn't feel quite at ease. She wouldn't until she knew everyone in her family was safe. The group spread out into the kitchen just as Brooke arrived. She had Maddie and Hayley with her, but like the others her first concern was the sirens. "An ambulance raced past me and a few seconds later another one." She brought iced tea, and after she set the jug down she crossed her arms and faced the others. "Where's Erin?"

"Almost here." Ashley was quick to answer. She had to be, right? She'd been running pretty much on time, which meant if anything she'd be stuck in traffic from the construction or whatever accident was causing the trouble.

"I turned on the radio. I guess it was a pileup on the highway."

"Probably a bunch of sprained necks." Dayne took a few grapes from the plate Ashley had set out. "Never good. But the construction keeps things too slow for it to be very serious."

They all nodded and several conversations broke out among them. Kari and Dayne and Katy ... Ryan and Luke and Reagan. Meanwhile the kids ran out back checking out the frogs around the pond. After a few minutes, everything felt perfectly normal, all concern about sirens and ambulances gone.

Except for Ashley.

She could feel her heart racing. A feeling of doom had settled over her at the first mention of the sirens, and like sap she couldn't shake it, couldn't brush it off. With everyone talking, she slipped away to her bedroom unnoticed. Her hands trembled as she dialed Erin's number.

The phone rang once, twice, three times and then it went to voicemail. "Hey, Erin. It's me. Ash." She tried to still her shaking hands. "Listen, we're all here and Dad's pretty much on his way. Let me know if you're running late or stuck in traffic. I can still call him and try to buy a little time. Okay." She hesitated. "Call me back. Love you."

She'd kept her voice to a whisper because the last thing she wanted was to alarm the others. Especially when Landon and Dayne were no doubt right. Of all the hundreds and thousands of cars out and about in Bloomington that sunny Saturday June afternoon, the odds that the accident involved Erin and Sam were unbelievably slim.

Still . . .

She stared at her phone, willing it to ring. When it didn't, she had no choice but to join the others. Cole was just running into the house from the backyard. "Mom, can I get water bottles for everyone? It's burning up out there."

"Of course." Ashley's mouth felt dry. She wondered if she were the only one of her siblings battling a tsunami of fear and if she was crazy for letting herself feel this way. She walked toward the kitchen with Cole beside her. What was it he wanted? She reached the stack of plastic cups. "Iced tea?" She smiled at him.

"Mom . . . are you okay?" Cole leaned in, studying her eyes. "You don't look good."

"I'm fine." She didn't want the others to hear him. With all her energy she mustered the most normal smile she could find. "You didn't want tea?"

"I asked for water bottles." He still sounded worried about her. "For all the cousins."

"Right." *Get it together, Ashley. Don't act crazy.* She managed a pinched laugh. "I must be distracted."

"Yeah," Cole didn't look convinced. "I guess so." He patted her back. "If you're sick, you need to tell someone."

"No, really." She hugged him, appreciating his concern. "I'm fine, Cole. I am." She led him to one of the cases of water. "Take the whole thing outside." She found a Sharpie pen in the drawer nearby. "Have everyone write their names on their bottles. Otherwise I'll throw away ten of them half-full later tonight."

"Okay." He looked relieved. "Now you sound like yourself."

Good, Ashley thought. If she sounded normal, then things must be normal. She watched Cole leave and then she joined up with her siblings and their spouses at the old farm table, the one where they'd eaten a million meals growing up. Everything was fine. It was a beautiful day, and in a few minutes their dad was going to have the surprise of his life. The week was going to be one wonderful memory after another culminating in their Fourth of July picnic at the lake. Of course everything was fine. Like Dayne had said, what could happen when traffic on the highway was never more than a crawl lately? She felt her heartbeat slow back to normal, and though she couldn't quite shake her fear, she was able to join the conversation, able to put her irrational thoughts aside. The others were right.

What could possibly go wrong on a day like this?

But the group had no sooner sat down to catch up and wait for Erin and their dad to arrive when Landon got a call from a buddy at the fire department. Landon took the call away from the table but when he returned his face looked ashen. He sat down slowly and looked at the others.

"They might need me. He wants me to keep my phone on." He looked at Dayne and Ryan, and seemed to avoid the eyes of the girls at the table. "The accident was pretty bad. A semitruck rear-ended a family in an SUV. He was going full speed and the family was at a complete stop, stuck in traffic. There are at least fifteen vehicles involved, and they're still sorting through the injuries." He ran his hand along the back of his head. "Must be awful."

"Will you need to go?" Dayne's expression was far more serious than it had been earlier. "You're the best paramedic in town."

"I've been away from triage for a while." Landon bit his lip and still seemed to avoid looking at Ashley. "They know we're having a family party. He said they'll only call me if they run out of people to help."

Ashley knew her husband. He had to be fighting the urge to head for the highway and help, whether they called him in or not. His desire to protect and serve was that strong. She rubbed his back, trying to focus her attention on him and not these new details of the horrific accident playing out a few miles away. It was easy to pour her attention into Landon, easy to think about how he might be feeling.

Because suddenly and completely the fear she'd known was gone. It had disappeared as quickly as it had taken Landon to say three simple letters. And though many people would be dealing with a bad phone call today, the Baxter family members would not be among those. Because Erin and Sam didn't drive an SUV.

They drove a van.

Twelve

JOHN STEERED HIS SEDAN TOWARD THE COUNTRY ROAD THAT would lead him to the old Baxter house, the place where Ashley and Landon and their family lived. If he'd had a suspicion that his daughter was up to something before, he was almost certain now.

"It was the phone call. That was the tipping point." He smiled at Elaine. "Landon never calls to see if we're going to be on time for dinner. It's always sort of an open invitation kind of thing."

"Maybe he really didn't want the dinner to get cold." Elaine reached for his hand, her expression warm. "I don't want you to be disappointed."

They were almost out of town when a speeding ambulance came up from behind. John pulled over and let the vehicle pass, its sirens blaring, lights flashing. John hesitated before pulling back into traffic. "Whoever's involved in that emergency, Lord, help them now. Please . . ."

"Amen." Elaine frowned as she stared at the ambulance. "There's been a lot of sirens today."

"I heard them when we were getting in the car." He was retired now, but a day like this with several accidents or a major incident would've required all emergency room doctors to report to duty. "I hope it's nothing serious."

Elaine nodded, and as John pulled back into traffic she helped find their way back to the previous conversation. "So you really think there'll be more than Ashley and Landon there?"

"Definitely." He chuckled, his concern over the sirens and the ambulance easing. "Ashley can't trick me. She thinks she can, but I've been around a few years longer than her."

Elaine laughed and the sound was like music in the car. "I think that's the point."

"I mean, if it's just Ashley and Landon, that's fine." He kept his eyes on the road. "But I have a feeling."

Elaine leaned back in her seat and watched him. "You're very handsome for a seventy-year-old."

"Thank you. I think." He made a face. "Let's not say the number so often. I feel older every time I hear it."

Again Elaine laughed. "Okay. Let's talk about something else." She thought for a minute. "Tell me about your childhood, what your life was like."

John breathed deep. She was such a good friend, so easy to talk to. "It was lonely, actually. I was a baby when my dad was killed in World War II, so I was raised by my mom. An only child."

"Which is why you always wanted a big family."

"Exactly." He loved this, that he could talk about the past with Elaine. She had no jealousy in her, no reason to avoid the years when Elizabeth was at the center of his life. Those decades mattered to him, in a different way than this season in his life mattered. He was entitled to make memories and remember and cherish both. At least that's the way Elaine saw it, and for that John would always be thankful.

"Elizabeth felt the same way. Right from the beginning we talked about having a big family." He hesitated, the memories fresh and raw once more. "When she got pregnant we both knew the mistake we'd made. We asked God to forgive us, but we didn't for a minute think we wouldn't keep our baby."

Instead, her parents sent her away and he was unable to have contact with her. There were no cell phones, no way to get a message to her except by driving the six hundred miles to see her in person — which he did twice during her pregnancy.

How great was God to allow them to find Dayne again all those years after Elizabeth had been forced to give him up? "One after another the kids came, but always there was one missing. Even when we didn't talk about it with each other we felt his loss." He smiled at Elaine. "I'll be forever grateful that she got to meet him before she died."

"It was her prayer for so long."

"Yes." John turned onto the familiar street and slowed a little. "Don't want to be too early." He grinned at her. "In case there's a houseful."

"John!" Elaine laughed, but her expression was a little concerned. "What if it's just them? You can't be disappointed."

"I'm just teasing." He chuckled and rolled down the window, letting the sweet country air fill the car. "Ashley's always up to something. I like trying to second-guess her."

They pulled into the driveway and almost immediately John sat up straighter in his seat. "Ahh-haa! I knew it." He pointed at the parking area. "Unless Cole's having some sort of backyard party, looks like we might have a few visitors."

He easily recognized Luke's SUV and Kari and Ryan's car. Brooke's four-door was there, too. "Ashley can't fool me." His tone softened and he felt his heart fill with appreciation. "I love that girl. So thoughtful. I think she'll spend the rest of her life trying to make up for the years she lost in Paris. Making sure everyone in the family knows how much she loves them."

They parked their car but before John could step out his cell phone rang. Whoever it was, they were calling from St. Anne's. He still had the number programmed into his phone. He lowered his brow and cast Elaine a confused look. "Hello?"

"John, this is Phil at St. Anne's. I'm in the ER." Phil was an intern when John first began thinking of retiring. His voice sounded strained, panicked even. "You need to get down here."

He shifted, his heart rate speeding up. "You need more doctors?" The accident must've been worse than they imagined. "What happened?"

"No." The man mumbled a few cusswords under his breath. "John, it's your daughter. The car she and her family were in ... it was hit by a truck half an hour ago. It's not good. Get down here right away."

"Are you sure?" He did a count of the cars parked adjacent to his. There had to be a mistake. Everyone was here. "I think they're all at Ashley's house."

"No, John. This is very serious. Please ... get here now."

"Okay." He could barely draw a breath, barely feel himself ending the call and looking at Elaine. Even then he couldn't bring himself to say the words.

"John ..." she reached for his hand, her eyes suddenly wide. "What is it? What happened?"

He stared at the parked cars and another thought hit him. One of the guys could've brought the family car, and maybe it was Kari — in their second car. Or maybe Peter was here, but Brooke and the girls were in their SUV. He swallowed, trying to find his voice. "That was Phil from St. Anne's. He said ..." Something about putting words to the horrific news made it real. Or at least possibly real. There had to be some sort of mistake.

"Tell me." Elaine sounded as panicked as John's doctor friend. "What happened?"

"Phil ... Phil says it was one of my girls and her family. In the accident." He unbuckled his seat belt. "He said to get down to the hospital right away." He shook his head, more determined than ever.

"Dear God, no." Elaine closed her eyes for several seconds. She looked pale when she opened them. He could see the plan

forming in her mind before she spoke it. "We need to get inside."
Her words were slow and deliberate. As if she could only fight the
terrifying possibilities by focusing on the practicality. "We need
to see who's here. That's the only way ..."

John nodded, because he couldn't speak, didn't dare let himself believe that Phil was right and they needed to get to the hospital. But Elaine had a point. The only way to know was to get
inside. He slid his keys into his pocket and motioned for Elaine
to follow him. Before he stepped out, he hung his head. What was
he thinking, heading into the horrific unknown without praying?
Even if it wasn't his daughter, someone's family had been very
seriously injured.

"Pray with me, Elaine. Please." He took her hand and squeezed
it while he began. "Father, You know my racing heart. You know
my fear. Lord, this reality belongs to someone. Someone's daughter, someone's family. I come before You begging You that today
the cup not be mine. That You would help us make the walk to
Ashley's front door and that once inside Ashley and Kari and
Brooke and Luke and their families would all be accounted for."
He exhaled and heard the raspiness in his breathing. "Whatever
we find in the next few minutes, we can't walk through it without
You. Please, Father ... hold us up. Thank You for whatever You
have for us today. Because whatever it is, we believe You are with
us. In the powerful name of Jesus, amen."

"Amen."

John opened his eyes. Elaine looked almost green with worry.
He slid his feet out of the car. "I don't want to go inside."

"We have to."

She was right, of course. They didn't have time to waste,
because if one of his daughters and her family was indeed at the
ER, he needed to get there immediately. The two of them walked
up the front steps, their arms around each other. As they reached
the door, John barely knocked before someone flung it open.

"Surprise!" The foyer was full of his kids and grandkids, and John caught his breath. In the horror since the phone call he'd completely forgotten about his birthday. But even as they surrounded him and hugged him and even as he went through the motions of reacting to their surprise, John could only do one thing.

Count his kids.

Kari and Ryan and their children — accounted for. Brooke and Maddie and Hayley, all there. Ashley and Landon and their three, present. Luke and Reagan and Johnny, Tommy and Malin — all a part of the happy crowd hugging on him and kissing his cheeks and wishing him a happy birthday. Even Dayne and Katy and Sophie and baby Egan were there, and in the recesses of his mind John was stunned that his older son would've flown in for his birthday party.

Gradually he felt himself exhale, and beside him he felt Elaine do the same thing. They were all here. Erin was in Texas and his other sons and daughters were here with him. Phil had been wrong after all. It took several minutes — minutes that felt like hours — for his nerves to settle and for the group to migrate to the kitchen. Only then did his family quiet down, and only then did concern flash in the eyes of Dayne and Ashley and Brooke. The others were busy getting the kids situated, readying the kitchen for dinner.

"Dad," Dayne was the first to speak. "You don't look good. You feeling okay?"

"Yeah." Brooke tried to laugh, but it sounded forced. "You're supposed to be smiling. You look faint."

The conversation drew the attention of the others and John tried to smile, tried to dissuade them from asking further questions. The possibility was too awful to even talk about. Especially now that he could relax, now that everyone was accounted for.

"Seriously, Dad." Ashley looked more worried than the others. "Did something happen? You really don't look good."

Elaine held his hand, still beside him. She looked up and met his eyes. "Tell them, John."

"Tell us what?" Dayne was quick to pick up on the interchange.

The room fell quieter than before. John cleared his throat. He hated repeating what Phil had told him. It was too horrible. But he had no choice now. "When we first pulled up I got a call from the hospital, from a doctor friend in the ER." John reached for a glass of water and took a quick sip. His throat was still so dry he could barely form words. "He told me my daughter and her family had been hit by a truck on the highway."

"He said to get down to the hospital right away." Elaine's face was still pale, the near reality still clearly chilling for her as well.

Across the kitchen, Ashley crossed her arms tightly in front of her and leaned into Landon. The others seemed to react to the news, also. John felt slightly confused by their response. "We had to come inside so we could make sure everyone was here." He pushed himself to smile. "And you all are."

There was a long pause and Ashley looked from Kari to Landon. But it was Dayne who spoke first. "Dad ... Erin's on her way. She and Sam ..." he hesitated and looked at Luke and then Brooke. "They should've been here by now."

If someone had dropped the floor from beneath him, John couldn't have felt himself falling harder, faster. He leaned on the counter and hung his head. It couldn't be Erin and Sam. It wasn't possible, right? He had begged God to spare him from something like this.

"John." Elaine was beside him, her arm around him. "Honey, are you okay?"

Before he could look up, Brooke's cell phone rang. She had it in her hand, as if somehow she was expecting the call. All eyes in the room turned to her, even while the kids played outside unaware of the possible tragedy unraveling in the kitchen. Brooke held the phone to her ear. "Hello?"

Whoever was on the other line and whatever they said, it happened fast. Brooke looked suddenly ashen and she mumbled only a few words before hanging up. When she did, tears welled in her eyes and her voice was a strange mix of a tortured whisper, and the most guttural shriek. "That was Peter." She pressed her fist into her middle and seemed to try to catch her breath. Kari and Ryan came up on either side of her and held her up. She shook her head, desperate to get the words out. When she looked up the truth was as clear as air. Even before she said the words. "It's Erin. We ... we need to hurry."

A plan came together immediately, but everything about it felt like some strange surreal dream. All his life as a doctor in the emergency room, John had wondered about the most severe accidents. The ones where the tragedy was widespread. A group of four teenage boys who all drowned when they fell through thin ice ten winters ago ... or a carload of teenagers all killed when they tried to pass an RV on a country road late one fall night.

How did anyone handle such a thing?

Not that the Baxter family hadn't suffered its fair share of tragedies. Landon's near fatal injury in the house fire thirteen years ago and Hayley's near drowning. Ashley's baby Sarah and certainly losing Elizabeth to cancer.

But the magnitude of today's news threatened to overshadow them all. John's body flipped into function mode, a self-defense mechanism he'd learned long ago working in the emergency room. The adults called the kids into the house, and they explained the situation. Aunt Erin and Uncle Sam had been in a car accident. The older kids — Cole and Jessie and Maddie — all wanted to go to the hospital. Elaine and Reagan offered to stay with the others.

"Is someone hurt?" Devin's eyes were big and full of tears. He walked around the group of adults — all of them trying to figure out who would ride with whom and whether they should bring anything to the hospital. Devin tugged on Ashley's T-shirt. "Mommy, is someone hurt?"

"Yes, baby." Ashley pulled him close as if she desperately needed the reassurance of his hug. She kissed his blond head. "I think someone's hurt."

Devin shook his head, reacting to the news before any of the adults dared to allow themselves to consider the gravity of the situation. The utter devastating gravity of it. Devin started to cry. "No, Mommy. I don't want anyone to be hurt. Please ... we have to pray for them."

John's tears came then. Because of all things in a room full of people who loved Jesus more than life, it had been the child among them who had reminded them of the first order of business. The absolute desperate need to come together in prayer. "Devin's right. We need to pray." The world had turned upside down, but as soon as he made the statement about praying he felt gravity kick in once more, felt the world right itself. He held his arms out and took hold of Elaine's hand on one side and Devin's on the other. The circle came together quickly and through the heartbreaking sounds of tears and sobs from Devin and Hayley and RJ and Tommy.

Landon took charge of the moment. "Father God, we don't know what's happened today, but our sister — " his voice caught and he struggled for several seconds. The kids were trying to stifle their tears, but the sound made it hard for all of them. Dayne cleared his throat. "Our sister Erin and her family have been in an accident. Lord, please hold them in Your arms and breathe healing into their bodies. Sustain us through the coming minutes and hours." Tears filled his own voice. "Don't let us walk this path alone, Father. Please. In Jesus' name, amen."

And with that they grabbed purses and water bottles and car

keys and headed out the front door, each of them hurrying, feeling the desperate urgency.

The whole while, all John could think was why hadn't Erin told him? They had talked yesterday morning, after all. She'd said she was helping the girls with a cleaning project. John rode with Dayne and Katy, grateful for the ride. He could only sustain the left-brained doctor mode for so long. Especially if the news was bad — and he had the worst feeling that it was. That whatever had happened, this would be a day they would remember the rest of their lives.

You should have told me, Erin, he thought to himself. He might've talked her out of it, convinced her that they should save Sam's vacation time for Christmas, that it would be too great a burden on their family to make the two-day trip all for his birthday. But even as John formed the argument in his mind, he realized he was wrong. If Erin told him she was on her way to see him, he would've celebrated every minute until she arrived.

That was the worst of it. John sat in the front passenger seat while Katy and Luke offered to take the backseat. He didn't argue. He felt torn between flinging the door open and running to the hospital on foot so he might get there faster or throwing up out the window. Neither choice was really an option so on the drive to the hospital he kept his head in his hands. Erin never should've come. She should've been back in Texas with her husband and girls. Safe and whole. They could've talked on Skype that night. Even as Dayne picked up speed on the country road, John still didn't want to believe it. Was it possible there was still a mistake? That she'd been telling the truth yesterday and had stayed home?

His irrational thoughts left him exhausted. The worst of it was that this trip had been for him, to celebrate his birthday. Erin and Sam weren't doing anything dangerous or crazy. They were trying to honor him the only way they knew how.

By coming home.

Thirteen

BROOKE RODE TO THE HOSPITAL WITH KARI AND RYAN, AND BY the time they climbed into the car she was back on her cell phone trying to find any information anyone would give her. But the details were sketchy, the prognoses for Erin and Sam and the girls too scrambled to make sense of. The only message Brooke couldn't miss was the obvious one.

They needed to hurry.

She was about to make yet another call, this one to Peter, when she realized that beside her in the car, thirteen-year-old Jessie and Maddie were softly crying. Brooke slowly stopped the call and lowered her phone. What was she doing? The anxious phone calls would only trouble her niece more. She put her hand on Jessie's knee and then on Maddie's. "They have the best doctors working on them."

In the front seat Ryan was driving, Kari seated beside him. They held hands but neither of them said a word. What could they say? Instead of more phone calls, Brooke did what the rest of them in the car, what Landon and Ashley and Cole in the car in front of them, and Dayne and Katy and Luke and her dad in the car behind them were doing.

She prayed.

God ... this can't be happening. Let there be a mistake, please ... let them be fine. Just a few stitches or a broken bone. Nothing serious, please, God.

The prayer continued without a break until finally they pulled into the St. Anne's parking lot. Brooke couldn't help but notice several ambulances still parked outside the entrance to the emergency room. *You're a doctor, Brooke ... you can handle this.* She reminded herself between urgent prayers. But as she did she wondered how the rest of her family would handle whatever was next.

What she had learned — what she hadn't shared — was that Erin and Sam's van had been stopped in traffic when they were rear-ended by an eighteen-wheeler. According to witnesses the driver never hit his brakes. The impact crushed her sister's van and shot it into the cars in both lanes in front of them. In all, nearly twenty cars suffered some sort of damage, and the ER was full of injured people.

The truck driver wasn't one of them. He had died at the scene.

But what she didn't know — what she hadn't been able to get from anyone, even Peter — was how serious the injuries were for Erin and Sam and the girls. In the distant analytical areas of Brooke's brain, she knew that something was gravely wrong. Because of course Peter knew. The whole ER would've known if there were serious injuries caused by the accident. Very serious.

If Peter hadn't told her, it was because he didn't want her to know until she got to the hospital. They walked across the parking lot, arms around each other in groups of twos and threes, all of them headed into the ER. Their dad looked like he might pass out, but still he took the lead. This had been his hospital, after all. The place where he'd worked for more than three decades. Whatever news was coming, he clearly wanted to be the first to hear it. Erin was his daughter, so it only made sense.

Brooke stayed close behind, believing somehow that her medical knowledge might help. But inside she wanted to be like Kari and Katy who hung near the back of the group, almost as if they would've liked to have turned around and run the other way.

Because once they knew the details, there would be no turning back.

Their father walked up to the counter, but before he reached it a nurse spotted them. Her face looked grave and she spoke loud enough for them to hear. "John ... everyone ... I'm going to take you to one of the family rooms. Doctor Clancy will speak with you there."

Dr. Clancy? Phil Clancy? Brooke's head began to spin. In the family room? This wasn't good. Phil should be working to save her family, not meeting with them in the family room. People only went to the family room when ... when ...

Jessie was crying quietly, along with Kari and Katy and Maddie and Cole. They kept their voices down, and wiped at their eyes as quickly as their tears came. But this much was clear. Everyone knew now that the situation was serious. Even the kids could tell. The nurse joined them in the waiting area and led them through a series of doors to a private room. "I'm sorry." Her face was drawn, and Brooke noticed that her hands were shaking. "Dr. Clancy will be right in."

There were enough seats for all of them, and most of them dropped to one of the chairs or sofas. Their father prayed out loud, putting words to the things they were feeling. "This doesn't look good, God. We are Your children, and we love You. We trust You even here, right now. We can't get through this without You. Please ... help us."

His prayer was absolutely needed. Brooke's heart raced along at triple time. She wanted to burst through the door and run to the various ER examination rooms until she'd found Erin and her family. What was happening just a few doors and walls away? Maybe her sister needed her. She closed her eyes and tried to remember her father's prayer. That God would help them through it. Brooke wanted to believe the Lord was with them, but she had never felt more alone in all her life.

She opened her eyes and looked around the room. Dayne

had one arm around Katy and the other around their dad. Beside them, Luke, Ashley, Landon, and Cole huddled together in a semicircle of four chairs. Brooke held hands with Maddie on one side and Kari on the other, and next to her was Ryan and their daughter, Jessie.

She wasn't sure how much longer she could sit here. The room felt like it was running out of air.

"I'm going to go check on — " She didn't have time to finish her sentence.

The door opened and Phil Clancy walked in, his face a mask of what could only be described as grief. A grief doctors tried to prevent every day they reported for duty. Brooke hung her head. When she made the decision to become a doctor, she did it because in some ways it gave her a sense of control she wouldn't otherwise have. Through knowledge and the practice of medicine she had learned how to affect the health of her patients. In some cases she had even been able to save lives. The knowledge that she could help in a situation that might otherwise be helpless was something Brooke loved most about being a doctor.

But here ... as they waited for Dr. Clancy to give them the news, there was absolutely nothing Brooke could do. She closed her eyes and waited.

"The accident was very bad. I'm so sorry, John ... Brooke ... the rest of you." He shut the door behind him and sat in one of the remaining open chairs.

Brooke looked up and found that everyone else had their eyes on the doctor. Only her father would know how very grave the situation must be in order for the news to come to them this way. In less than a few seconds, while Phil gathered his thoughts and seemed to struggle for a way to say whatever he had to tell them, Brooke looked at her father and noticed something. For all the ways he had taken care of himself and surprised people with his actual age, in this moment he looked like he'd aged ten years in an hour. He sat up a little more, still leaning against Katy. "Are they all alive? Can you tell us that?"

The doctor's hesitation told them that the worst possibility was now a reality. Brooke held her breath while he continued. Around the room Kari put her hand to her mouth and Ashley began to shake her head. Jessie cried out and buried her head in Ryan's shoulder.

Brooke wanted to ask them all to be quiet. Dr. Clancy wasn't finished, and he needed to get the words out, needed to tell them exactly what they were dealing with.

"I'm sorry." Phil looked from John to the others, finally meeting Brooke's gaze. "We'll need your help identifying the girls." He paused. "One of them is gone."

"No!" Kari cried out first. "Please ... no. Dear God ... why?" She seemed to realize the doctor wasn't finished, so she hung her head, her hand over her mouth again. Around the room all of them began to cry, doing everything in their power to listen, to grasp whatever else the doctor might say.

Dr. Clancy sighed and waited a few seconds. "Two of the girls are on life support. We've done everything we can for them. One of the younger girls has a broken arm and some internal bleeding, but her injuries don't seem life threatening."

"What about Erin and Sam? What about my daughter?" Their father's voice was strained and raspy.

"They're in surgery. We're trying to save them."

And like that they had the news. Ashley cried out next. "No ... please, God! She stood up and faced the wall of the family room, burying her head in the crook of her elbow. "Why? God ... tell me why?"

Cole began to cry harder, and Landon wrapped his arms around the boy. Kari was crying, too, uttering a series of *no*s and *why*s and across from her Katy stood and went to Ashley. The two of them sobbed, holding each other up. Dayne was about to move to his wife, at least it looked that way, but then their dad began to sway. He looked pale and sweaty. He leaned back and rested his head against the wall. When he tried to talk his voice was a slur of mumbles.

"Someone help him!" Luke shouted, his tone angrier than he probably meant it. "He's passing out!"

Brooke stood and went to him. Where was Peter? He had to know they were here. She needed him now more than ever. She put her hand on her father's shoulder. "Dad, take deep breaths. Put your head between your knees. Come on." She helped her father lower his head and then she turned to Dr. Clancy. "Phil, can you get him a cold cloth and some smelling salts?"

"Absolutely."

Dayne sat in the chair beside their father, and now he used all his strength to keep him from falling to the ground. "He's out."

"He'll be okay." Brooke was surprised at the calm in her voice. The news was still dancing just outside the distant perimeter of reality, but as the doctor hurried off for the cold cloth and smelling salts, Brooke had no choice but to play it again in her mind. One of the girls was gone. Two were on life support. Erin and Sam were in surgery, their situation critical. Then she remembered the other aspect of Dr. Clancy's news. The girls needed identifying. She ran her hand over the back of her father's head. "It's okay, Dad, breathe deep."

Around the room the others were still reacting, still breaking down and crying. Ashley remained against the wall, hitting it softly with her open hand. Landon and Cole embraced her from either side, but still Ashley cried out. "Why, God? Don't take them, please ... God, we need You!"

Katy had moved back to the chair beside Jessie and Maddie, who was crying alone while Brooke tended to their dad. Brooke looked over her shoulder at her sister-in-law. "Thank you." Again she was amazed at how controlled she sounded. The news was exploding through her heart like a shrapnel from a hand grenade. But someone had to keep it together. The nightmare had only just begun. They had to handle this the way the Baxter family always handled hard times. They had no choice.

Even still she wished Peter would show up. He must've been tending to one of his patients on another floor. Something serious, otherwise he would be here. She had to believe that.

"Is he okay?" Luke was still standing beside Brooke, watching their dad, his brow knit together in fear.

"He'll be fine." Brooke whispered low near their dad's face. "Breathe deep, Dad. It's all right." She looked back at Luke. "It's the shock. It caused him to faint."

No relief came over Luke, no change in his tension. "Are you sure? It could be his heart."

"It's not." Brooke wasn't sure of course, but she was convinced of one thing. God would only give them what they could handle. Even today.

Dr. Clancy returned and he handed Brooke a cool cloth, which she put on the back of her father's neck. At the same time, Phil snapped open the salts and waved them beneath her dad's nose. He moved his head from side to side a few times and then gradually he brought his head up again. "What ... what's happening?"

His words were still slurred, but his face had more color. Dayne went to Katy, and Luke took his place on the sofa beside their dad. He had his arm around him now. On the far side of the room, Dayne wrapped Katy in his arms. Kari and Ryan and Jessie huddled together, and Cole sat with Maddie now, the two of them holding hands and whispering what sounded like a fervent prayer.

Gradually their dad was coming to, and as he did he seemed to remember. His startled eyes glanced around the room. "What are you ... why ...?" His question trailed off and a sadness filled his face. He brought his hand to his eyes. "Erin . . . not Erin. Please, God." He leaned into Luke and started to weep. It was that sight more than anything since Dr. Clancy gave them the news that made Brooke's eyes well up. Their father — John Baxter — one of the strongest men in all of Bloomington was weeping for what had happened.

Even while he gave way to his sorrow, Phil Clancy motioned to Brooke. She gave the wet cloth to Luke. "Keep it on his neck." She spoke softly. "Just in case."

Luke nodded. "Thank you." The words held a deeper meaning, and Brooke understood. None of them knew what to do. God was using Brooke's strength — however imperfect — to sustain all of them for the moment. She followed Dr. Clancy into the hall.

"I'm sorry again." Phil hung his head and rubbed his temples. "It's one of the worst accidents this town has ever seen."

Brooke had an idea where this was going. She looked around Dr. Clancy. "Have you seen Peter?"

"There was an emergency in pediatric oncology. He might be awhile." Phil sounded emotionally exhausted. "He told me to tell you he's sorry." The man looked straight at Brooke. "We need the identity of the girls. Your dad . . . I don't want to ask him. Not in his condition."

This was what Brooke had feared and not wanted to voice. Even to herself. That with the rest of the family so upset in the other room, the task of identifying the girls would fall to her. *Dear God, I don't know if I can do it. I'm not strong.*

My strength is perfect in your weakness, My daughter. You are not alone . . . I will go with you.

The words of the Lord spoke straight to Brooke's heart. For all her years of praying, she'd only heard an almost audible response from God on a couple occasions. The fact that He'd speak to her now allowed her to take a steadying breath. She nodded in Dr. Clancy's direction. "Now?"

"Yes. I hate this. But the coroner has been called. Brooke, I need the identity of the child who ..." He didn't finish his sentence.

She nodded, the words of the Lord running through her mind again. *My strength is perfect in your weakness.* She felt her heart beat steady within her. "Take me to her."

Brooke tried to imagine how she would feel if these were her kids she was about to identify, and in the time it took her to blink her eyes she was walking this same hallway, coming to see Hayley after her drowning accident. She blinked again and tried to stay focused. The hospital staff seemed unwilling to look at them as they passed by. It was hospital protocol — give the family of victims the courtesy of seeing their badly hurt or dead relatives without the hospital staff staring.

The walk seemed to take forever, but finally Phil turned right into a room at the end of the hallway and Brooke followed. On the table, looking like she was only sleeping, was Heidi Jo. The nurses had cleaned her up because as Brooke came closer, she could see the way Heidi Jo's head had been damaged. Clearly her death had been instant. Brooke didn't realize she was crying until she saw her tears land on the cool white sheets surrounding the eight-year-old. Pretty brown-skinned Heidi Jo. Brooke soothed the child's long brown hair and leaned in close, holding her one last time.

More sad than anything else was this simple truth: Erin and Sam hadn't gotten to say good-bye. They were both fighting for their own lives, too hurt to even be aware that Heidi Jo was gone. Brooke wiped the back of her hand across one cheek and then the other. She remembered Dr. Clancy and she turned to him. "Heidi Jo." She looked at the precious girl again. "This is Heidi Jo. She's eight."

It was enough information for the coroner to find her birth certificate in Texas. Something they would have to do before a death report could be created. *You promised me strength, Lord.*

Brooke leaned against the gurney and closed her eyes for a second. How was anyone ever ready for this sort of news? For the job of identifying the body of a beloved niece?

Deep within her she felt it, actually felt it. A strength that didn't come from herself, one that only could've been the Lord with her. No other way she was standing here in this moment. She took a final look at the little girl. The child was in heaven now. All that remained was the proof she had existed. The shell of who she had once been. She stepped back from Heidi Jo's body.

"I need to see the others."

"Can you do this?" Phil hadn't ever worked with her, but they knew each other.

Brooke had no idea whether the doctor believed in God. But she had a feeling he might after this terrible nightmare played itself out. She smiled at him through fresh tears. "I'll be okay. God's carrying me."

Even before he led her to the next room Brooke had figured out the obvious. Since Heidi Jo was already gone, the young girl with the broken arm, the one whose injuries didn't seem life-threatening, had to be Amy Elizabeth. Which meant that the girls on life support were Clarissa and Chloe. Erin's two precious, outgoing teenagers. Knowing which girls were suffering and which had passed on somehow made the tragedy infinitely worse.

She stopped before he led her into the next room. *I need You again, Lord ... I can't do this. I'm so weak, Father.* She pressed her shoulder into the wall.

"We can wait." Dr. Clancy put his hand on her other shoulder. "Really, Brooke."

"No." She shook her head, and again she felt the still small voice of the Lord speaking to her, rescuing her. *I am with you always ... your refuge and strength.* The words were from Psalms 46, a Scripture Brooke had kept on her desk since Hayley's accident. She breathed in and again she felt the strength of God. The surreal otherworldly ability to take another breath and another one after that. "I'm all right. Go first please."

Dr. Clancy led her into an emergency room and Brooke rubbed sanitizing foam over her hands and fingers. As soon as she faced the hospital bed, immediately Brooke knew that this was Clarissa, Erin and Sam's talkative oldest daughter. Brooke could see something else, too. Just with a glance at the machines keeping the girl alive. She turned to Phil. "Brain damage?"

"Severe. Spinal injuries as well." He shook his head, as if this truth was something he could only now reveal. "It doesn't look good for either of the older girls."

Brooke nodded. Her sister would be devastated, which made her think of something she didn't have emotional room to consider. Were Erin and Sam still in surgery? And if so, how were they doing? And what about Peter? Whatever the emergency there had to be someone who could take over.

The tragedies kept piling up. Brooke breathed in. *Gracious God, carry me. Please ...* She closed her eyes for a long moment and thought about Hayley, about how she overcame the odds after her accident. When she opened them she went to the side of Clarissa's bed. "We believe in miracles, baby." She gently touched Clarissa's blonde hair. Her body was as lifeless as Heidi Jo's. Again the tears overcame her. With her voice breaking, she spoke again. "God is carrying you. Just hang on, okay?" She couldn't get as close to Clarissa as she had with Heidi Jo. Machines were attached to both her arms, her neck and her face. Brooke tried to think what Erin would do for the girl, and all she could think was to touch her hair again and tell her the only other thing that mattered. "We all love you, sweetheart."

She stepped away and looked again at Phil. "This is Clarissa."

Phil had a file and as he'd done with Heidi Jo he wrote down the name as Brooke spelled it. Finally the doctor took her to see Chloe. Of all Erin's girls, Chloe was probably Brooke's favorite. She wasn't as talkative as Clarissa, but she was a sunbeam and she laughed easily. Brooke always pictured her growing up to be a teacher or a counselor. She had that way about her.

Again she prayed as she approached the bed. This time she didn't wait to tell Phil. She looked back at him. "This is Chloe." She spelled the girl's name and then came up alongside her. The injuries to Chloe seemed very similar to those of her sister's. Which made sense. They were probably sitting together. "Same?"

"Yes." Again Phil looked like he was taking this as poorly as any of Brooke's siblings. "Severe brain damage. She's hanging on by a thread. I'm sorry. I don't know what else to say." He hesitated. "Do you know the name of the fourth girl, the one with the broken arm?"

By way of deduction, Brooke nodded. "Amy Elizabeth." She looked back at him. "Can I see her?"

"In a little while. She's got a team working on her."

Brooke nodded. The enormity of the situation was too much to grasp. She moved to Chloe's bedside. "Miracles happen, Chloe, baby." She touched the girl's blonde hair, amazed even in this broken state how much she looked like her older sister. "Jesus is with you, sweetheart. We're all here and we love you."

The tears came fast and steady, more tears than Brooke had ever cried in all her life. "Please ... I need to get back to my family."

Phil led the way, and Brooke was grateful. God had gotten her through the most difficult twenty minutes since Hayley's drowning, but without someone to follow, she wasn't sure she could make her way back to the others. When she got there, she found her family much the way she left them. But now she was the only one with the next bit of news. Which kids were still living, and which one was not. They turned to her and only then did she see Peter. He came to her and held her up, came to her just in time. It was her turn to break down, but before she did she uttered just two words.

"Heidi Jo."

Fourteen

THE THREE SISTERS SAT HUDDLED TOGETHER ON A SINGLE SOFA in the corner of the waiting room at St. Anne's. Ashley was grateful for Brooke. Her older sister had been in several times to check on the girls and Erin and Sam, but there was no news at this point. Besides, she was a pediatrician, not a surgeon. She wanted to respect the team working on Erin and her family, so for the most part Brooke stayed in the waiting room with the others. Same as their dad.

Ashley wasn't sure what time it was, or how many dreadful hours had passed since they walked through the emergency room doors and heard the news. She didn't think it was midnight yet, but it could've been. It was like they'd slipped into a zone of disbelief and heartache where time and life outside the Intensive Care waiting room had ceased to exist. None of them had pulled out their cell phones or contacted anyone outside of family.

Not when the shock still consumed them, and not when the news changed every hour. Ashley sat between Kari and Brooke, the three of them holding hands and going back and forth between rehashing the details of the surprise and their last conversations with Erin and then slipping into desperate, prayerful silence.

A silence like the one surrounding them now.

Eventually they would have to make phone calls, of course. Tomorrow morning they would call Pastor Mark Atteberry at Clear Creek Community so that a prayer chain could be started. Sam's work needed to be contacted, and they needed to tell the staff at the church Erin and her family attended.

But for now no one else needed to know.

They couldn't stand the thought of anyone outside the family joining them in the waiting room when things were so critical. When there was no way of telling which of Erin's family might even survive the night. Ashley closed her eyes. Where two or more were gathered, God was with them. That's what the Bible said. Certainly the prayers of the Baxter family were enough until they could see past this terrible night.

Dear God, I've never felt like this ... never felt so helpless. So many people we love on the other side of the waiting room door, Lord. Please ... help me not to live in the why of it all. Help me trust You. Help me breathe through the next hour.

Ashley kept praying, kept uttering phrases and after a minute or so comfort surrounded her, a comfort and love that was tangible. Not just the feeling of her sisters on either side. But a deep belief that whatever happened next, wherever things settled when this tragedy finished playing out, they would survive. She felt fresh tears, felt them slide through her closed eyelids and stream down her cheeks. The pain was greater than anything she'd ever felt, but she had these two certainties more than even an hour ago.

God loved them. And they would survive.

She might not know how they would get through the next hour, but the Lord knew and He was here. *I feel Your presence, Lord ... Please, stay. Don't leave us.*

My daughter, I will never leave you or forsake you. I have loved you with an everlasting love.

Ashley felt the voice of the Spirit whispering to her soul, felt herself nodding along, believing His assurance, needing it like she needed air. She blinked her eyes open and realized that her sisters were struggling again. Grief came in waves, and right now Brooke and Kari seemed to be fighting one of the worst of them. Brooke leaned her head against the wall, eyes vacant. On Ashley's other side, Kari leaned over her knees, her head in her hand. Her shoulders trembled and her breaths came in quick spurts between quiet sobs. Their dad sat with Luke and Dayne in three chairs nearby, their eyes dry, anxiety written into their strained expressions. Landon and Ryan had taken Katy, Cole, Maddie, and Jessie back to the house. Katy wanted to help Elaine and Reagan with the kids, making up beds on couches and placing sleeping bags throughout the house. Ashley was grateful for their help. Someone needed to stay back, but it couldn't be her. Not yet. Right now she needed to be here with her sisters and brothers and father.

Landon and Ryan had returned to the hospital only ten minutes ago, and now they stood shoulder to shoulder, facing the only window in the waiting room, talking in hushed whispers as they stared into the night. The situation was very, very serious. Ashley realized that, even though she couldn't get her mind around everything Brooke had told them. Serious brain damage sounded terrible, of course. But they could recover, right? Ashley wanted to think so, but she hadn't been able to bring herself to actually ask. Even with Brooke sitting right beside her.

The news at this point was that Sam and Erin had come out of surgery, both were in critical condition and both with spinal and brain trauma. They'd been moved to rooms in the ICU at about the same time as Clarissa and Chloe — who were still both on life support. Amy Elizabeth was worse off than they originally thought. She suffered enough internal injuries that she had also undergone surgery, but the operation had been successful and her condition was marked as serious. She was sedated in a room two floors down. Her doctor believed she would come through this without permanent damage — to her body at least. Doctors had placed her in a medically induced coma to keep her still, and to allow for healing of her internal injuries. They'd likely keep her in the coma for a week or so before bringing her back around and eventually releasing her to go home.

Wherever home would be when a week had passed.

Ashley was about to get up and go to the guys near the window, ask Landon if he and Ryan had found out any new information on their way back into the waiting room. But before she could get up a new doctor walked in and shut the door behind him. The man looked stricken.

Ashley watched her father nod in his direction. "You're the attending?" He looked relieved by the possibility.

"I am. Hello, John." The doctor walked up and put his hand on their father's shoulder. "I'm sorry."

"Me, too." Their father hung his head for a moment and then looked up. "More news." It was a statement. As if the decades John had spent working as a doctor told him it wasn't a matter of whether there'd be more bad news, but when. The accident had been that horrific.

The man sighed. "Yes. More news." Whatever it was, the man looked like he'd rather do anything than share it.

Ashley held tighter to the hands of her sisters, and she felt all of them stiffen as they anticipated what was coming. With so many deeply critical injuries, with so much injury to the brains of the people they loved, the news was bound to get worse. Ashley wished she could run from the room and live forever in a place where the doctor's words would never be said. Where the accident had never happened. But all she could do was lean hard into the comfort of Jesus and her sisters and hear the news like the rest of them.

The doctor looked around the room. "I'm Doctor Chris Hazel. I've been overseeing the care of your family since they were transferred to my unit." He pursed his lips, but he didn't look down. Didn't break eye contact. "We've lost Clarissa. She has no brain activity whatsoever."

Ashley felt like someone had lifted her up and slammed her against the wall. Clarissa? The talkative sweet blue-eyed, blonde teenager with all her life ahead of her? How could she be dead?

Erin would be devastated by this, changed forever. Two of her girls were gone? It was a blow greater than any Ashley could imagine. She released the hands of her sisters and linked arms with them instead. With this sort of darkness, she needed to know her sisters were alive beside her. Needed to feel the warmth of them and the familiarity of their voices. Kari groaned on her right. "No … no, God … please … no. Clarissa … sweet girl … we love you, Clarissa."

Brooke didn't say anything, but her crying grew louder. Ashley clung to them, praying silently. The doctor was going on, saying something to Luke, something about him being a lawyer.

"Someone needs to assume power of attorney for the girls." He hesitated, his face marked with painful shadows. "Indiana law allows for a relative to retain temporary guardianship and power of attorney in a situation like this, where the parents are incapacitated." He paused. "Decisions need to be made."

"Decisions?" Dayne's voice was broken, but he seemed to be the one in this moment most able to speak. "Can you be more specific?"

Ashley wondered, too. What decisions were needed now if Clarissa was already gone? She tried to listen, tried to focus on the doctor's next words, but instead she could only see Clarissa, the way she had looked at Bailey Flanigan's wedding. She had worn a yellow spring dress, and all night she and Chloe and their little sisters had danced and laughed and sang on the dance floor. One particular snapshot surfaced and Ashley clung to it, held on to it like a life preserver in the stormiest sea. The picture she had snapped of the girls with Clarissa in the middle. All of them had made silly faces for the photo, but Clarissa hadn't had time. Instead the camera had caught her midlaugh. Innocent and happy and certain as time that life as she knew it would continue like that for always.

That was the way she would remember Clarissa. Midlaugh.

She tried again to focus on the doctor's words. The word organ donor snapped her from the swirl of memories back to the moment. The doctor folded his arms, his words soft but serious. "There are girls across the state Clarissa's age waiting desperately for organs. A fourteen-year-old ballet dancer in Gary, Indiana, who needs a heart in the next two weeks or she won't make it, a soccer player in Indianapolis who needs a lung, and a young artist across the state who needs a new kidney."

Ashley's tears came in torrents as she pictured the situation, the girls across Indiana who needed transplants to survive. She watched her father, watched him silently weep even as he nodded and listened to his doctor friend. Only Brooke, on Ashley's left, wasn't openly crying. Almost as if the idea of organ donation had breathed a surreal new hope into her.

Dayne dragged his fist discretely across one cheek, and then the other. "Since Luke is an attorney, he could sign a document giving us the ability to make these decisions? Is that what you're saying?"

"I'd probably suggest John signing the document." The doctor looked from Dayne to their father and then to Luke. "I bring up Luke because he can help make some of this clearer to the rest of you as the next few days play out."

The next few days? Ashley couldn't imagine how they would stand it. The doctor might as well have said he expected the news to only get worse. She was grateful for her sisters, for their unity and the support they provided for each other. *You're with us, God ... You're with us ... please be with us.*

Ashley watched her dad nod. "I'll sign it."

"Timing is important." The doctor's eyes looked damp, too. He hesitated. "If you, as a family, could make a decision on this. The sooner the better. Once the heart stops beating, organs die." The doctor looked pained as he continued. "We're keeping Clarissa's heart going with a machine. Until you decide."

Dayne clenched his jaw, struggling to continue in his momentary role as the family's spokesman. "The others? How are they doing?"

"Sam's worse. He has an infection." The doctor hesitated, his tone marked with what sounded like defeat. "We're doing everything we can. For him and Erin and Chloe." He looked around the room. "I'll give you a few minutes. Then ... if you could let me know about Clarissa." He paused, as if weighing whether to share this next bit of information. "Erin and Sam are organ donors. Their driver's licenses indicate as much." He looked at their dad. "If that helps."

"Yes." Dayne put his arm around their father's shoulders. "Thank you."

The doctor started to leave, but then he stopped and looked at their dad again. "I couldn't be more sorry, John. Would you like me to call someone? Your pastor?"

As if God was holding him up, their dad seemed to find a new strength. He shook his head. "No, Chris. Not yet." His eyes held the slightest flicker of hope. "We have our God ... and we have each other. For now that's enough."

Dr. Hazel watched him for a few seconds, clearly wanting to make sure they were really well enough for him to leave. "All right then ... I'll be back in a bit."

When he was gone, they all seemed to look to their dad. This would be the hardest conversation they'd ever had, but until now Ashley couldn't believe the idea had even occurred to most of them. The possibility that they would have to make a decision like this in regards to their precious Clarissa.

Their dad seemed even stronger than he had seconds ago. He ignored the tears on his weathered face and breathed deep. "I don't think there's a question here." He looked at Ashley and then Kari. "It's almost impossible to imagine any of this. But if Erin and

Sam are in favor of organ donation, they would want the same for their girls."

Ashley nodded, and around the room Landon and Ryan, Luke and Dayne did the same.

"It's what Erin would want," Brooke's voice was soft but strong. "It gives purpose to something absolutely senseless." A slight anger colored her tone. Proof that the shock — though still thick throughout the room — was beginning to wear off. At least for Brooke.

"Hold on." Kari released her hold on Ashley's arm and stood, her legs clearly shaking. She walked a few steps away from the others, and then toward them again, like she was trying to form her thoughts into words. Finally she stopped and looked from Brooke to her dad. "If she still has a heartbeat, shouldn't we wait? In case she's not really ... not gone yet?"

Ashley felt for her sister, for the hope that rang in the words the doctor had said. That they were keeping Clarissa's heart beating. Ashley waited to see who would respond, and she was grateful her dad took the lead. There had been many times over the years when Brooke was at odds with the rest of them. This didn't need to be one of those times.

Their father stood and went to Kari, taking her into his arms and hugging her for a long time. When he took a step back, he left his arm around her. "Clarissa is gone, sweetheart." He seemed steadier than before, as if maybe his role as a doctor allowed him — like Brooke — to see the good in their very great loss. "No brain activity means a person is dead." He soothed his hand along Kari's arm and looked at Ashley and then the guys. "They're using a machine to keep her heart beating for the sake of her organs."

"Then I say we agree to this." Dayne sat back, resignation in his voice. "It's the right thing."

"Yes," their dad nodded. "It is."

Kari leaned against their father and turned her face into his shoulder. Her body shook, wracked by sobs. "I hate this." Her pained muffled words seemed to echo through the room, representing what they were all feeling. "Why is God letting this happen?"

Ashley wondered which of them would try to offer up an answer to that. Whether her father would find some bit of godly wisdom or if Luke would remember a Bible verse that applied to the situation. God had not abandoned them — otherwise they wouldn't still be upright. But when no one said anything, Ashley was grateful. Situations like this needed time and prayer and struggle before anyone could begin to answer Kari's question.

The truth was, they might never understand why.

Their dad led Kari back to her seat and again she linked arms with Ashley. At the same time, Dr. Hazel returned to the room. He came to them and waited for a few seconds. When he spoke, again he directed his question to their father. "Has your family reached a decision?"

Their dad was still standing near the sofa where Kari had just sat down. He folded his arms and nodded slowly. "Please use her organs. We think it's what Erin and Sam would want."

A hint of relief added life to the doctor's eyes. "I can't imagine how difficult this is." He paused, looking around the room again, his tone deeply sincere. "But it's a beautiful decision."

A beautiful decision? An irrational part of Ashley suddenly wanted to fight the possibility, wanted to believe like Kari that if they could keep Clarissa's heart beating, maybe they could keep her alive until she was healed. But that was an impossibility. She was already gone, like her dad said. And so it was a beautiful decision. The hardest one ever in all of life, but somewhere across the state, at least one teenage girl and her family were about to get the greatest news ever.

The news that their daughter had been given life.

Fifteen

ERIN COULDN'T MOVE. SHE KNEW THAT MUCH. THE WORLD around her wasn't dark and it wasn't light, but rather it was some sort of foggy blur of whites and colors and sounds, none of which she could completely make out.

Something was happening, because she had the sense that she needed to run, needed to find Sam and the girls. No, that wasn't it. She tried to concentrate. Something wasn't happening ... something had already happened. Something big and terrible and painful and final.

They were in traffic, stuck behind a line of cars bottlenecked around the construction on Highway 37. And they were almost at their exit, almost to Ashley's house where they were about to have a party. Erin forced her thoughts to make sense. Why were they going to Ashley's house? The party was a surprise ... yes, that was it. And then it came to her in a rush.

Her father's surprise seventieth birthday party, that's where they were headed. They were stuck in traffic, held up by construction, waiting to get off the highway so they could get to Ashley's house before their father got there. So they could be in on the surprise. But instead they'd been hit from behind by something. A train, maybe. It felt that way. And only now was anything making even a little sense.

She looked around, but the blurred images wouldn't form real shapes. *Sam!* She cried out his name. At least she thought she had. *Sam, where are you?* Her words slurred inside her mind, crashing off one side of her brain and into the other. Was anyone hearing her? *Someone ... help me! Where are my girls?*

An ache started in her arms and legs and moved to her heart where it grew. The hurting consumed her and became a brokenness that knew no limits, a bottomless ocean of pain and heartbreak. *Clarissa ... Chloe? Where are you, girls? Where are your sisters?*

Tiredness washed over her. She'd used all her energy calling for her family, but no one was answering. *Dear God, where are they? Where is my husband? How come I can't see anything?*

The truth took root somewhere inside her and slowly worked its way to her mind, to whatever hazy, half-awake place she was trapped in. She was injured. That had to be it, because she was alive. At least she felt alive. Still, something was wrong, because she couldn't move. As if every cell in her body had suffered some sort of traumatic event. The pain wasn't a usual kind, the sort that came from injury. It ran deeper than that. The pain of some very great loss. But what? Erin tried to concentrate, tried again to move, but her arms and legs wouldn't work. *What's happening to me?*

She wanted to scream, wanted someone to shake her and wake her up so she could see and so she could have answers. But she couldn't make her mouth move now, and she couldn't find anyone to tell, couldn't hear voices or any sounds that made sense other than a distant whirring. Like the sound of air rushing in and out, in and out.

Erin felt panic begin somewhere in her mind and course through the rest of her body like lightning, mixing with the pain and uncertainty. Where were Sam and their girls? *God ... please tell me. What's happened to them?* There were no answers, no reassuring voices. Instead the images before her began to take shape. Gradually like the arrival of the sun on a summer morning, lines began to form and the haziness cleared a little, then a little more.

A field came into view. The clearer it became, the more beautiful it grew. And as the images took shape, her pain and fear and panic lessened. The field was wide and long and lush with vibrant green grass. And at the center stood a picnic table. What was this? Where was she? Erin thought about straining, forcing herself to see more clearly but she somehow knew better than to try.

Let go, Erin . . . let go and watch. I am with you . . . drawing you to Myself.

The words weren't spoken, they simply were. As if they'd been stated at the center of her soul at the beginning of time in a place where only truth existed. *Let go . . .* she needed to let go. She felt herself relax, and as she did the images before her grew clearer. Without moving, she was closer to the picnic table and there were people sitting at it. People coming more into view even as the color of the sky took her breath.

It's the most beautiful thing I've ever seen, she wanted to say. But again she didn't have the ability to speak or open her mouth. The beauty took all her energy, all her pain and fear. The faces were coming into focus. A woman and children. Lots of children . . . or maybe just three children. Yes, that was it. Three children surrounded the woman at the picnic table. They were looking at her, talking to her.

Who is it, Lord . . . where am I?

But before the question could resonate through her mind, Erin could suddenly see everything. Every last detail and in that moment she felt a sense of elation and joy greater than anything she'd ever known.

The woman was her mother. She looked young and whole and beautiful, the way she'd looked many years before she'd gotten sick. She was watching Erin, her face filled with an expression of peace and love that seemed to say everything was okay. It was all going to be okay.

Mom . . . I've missed you. Erin wasn't sure if she spoke the words, and she didn't understand why her mother was in this place. At the same time, she remembered the children, and she looked at them. And again the images were lifelike, no longer cloudy. There was a little girl with brown hair and Ashley's face. Her mother had her arm around the child.

"This is your niece, Sarah. She's with me ... she's very happy here."

Her niece Sarah? Erin blinked a few times, and in the center of her heart the panic started to return. If her mother was here ... and if Sarah was here ... She didn't want to look, didn't want to know who the other children were, but she had no choice. She shifted her gaze and one at a time the faces of the other girls came into view. The first was her precious Heidi Jo. The girl sat on the other side of Erin's mom, the sweetest expression on her face.

"We're catching up." Her mother smiled, her words as real as if she were standing next to Erin. Wherever Erin was. "Your girls are lovely, Erin. They're well and whole. I'm taking care of them."

Erin nodded, unable to speak. She turned slightly one last time and the other girl's face became clear, too. It was Clarissa, her oldest. Her long blonde hair hung over her shoulders, and she stood near Erin's mother's side.

The great colors and vast landscape became more and more clear, and with a force she hadn't known in all her life, Erin was drawn to join them. This place was filled with perfect love and joy and peace. None of her loved ones were crying. She started to take a step in their direction. *I want to be with them, Lord ... please, let me go to them.*

But at the same time panic hit her once more, with an intensity triple what it was before. What was she saying? She couldn't go to them, no matter how wonderful the idea seemed for a moment. Because there was Candy somewhere in Texas plotting and planning to take away her daughters, and suddenly Erin felt herself push away, putting distance between herself and the glorious field, the place where her mother and daughters and niece were so happy.

She couldn't go because Sam and Chloe and Amy Elizabeth weren't there. The rest of her family needed her, and so she had to wait, had to fight a battle she couldn't quite understand. If she went to them now, she couldn't return to the other side, the place where the pain waited for her. She understood that much.

Not yet, God ... I need to help my family. Please ... heal me ... help me, Lord.

Erin, you are My daughter ... I know the plans I have for you.

The plans. Yes, that was it. God still had plans for her and Sam and Chloe and Amy Elizabeth. That's why she couldn't go to the wonderful field just yet. Her determination brought with it a renewed sense of aching and hurting and devastation. She needed to find a way back to them, to the rest of her family. She had to protect them from Candy Burns. No one was going to take her girls away from her, or put them in danger. No one. The memory of the exquisite place from which her mother had called to her would have to hold her over for now. It would have to soothe the pain and sustain her until she had done everything in her power to help Chloe and Amy Elizabeth. Because she would not leave her girls alone.

She would fight for them until her final breath.

Sixteen

JOHN HADN'T SLEPT MORE THAN A COUPLE HOURS IN A CHAIR IN Erin's room since they arrived at St. Anne's two days ago. Elaine had been by that afternoon, and she'd brought him fresh blueberries and a bag of almonds. Food he couldn't always find in the hospital cafeteria.

By now the rest of the world knew about the accident. The news had been reported on the front page of yesterday's *Bloomington Herald Times*, and since the family had clearly been notified of the tragedy, the names of Erin and Sam and the girls were all written into the story. All of the city and state, all of the nation for that matter, had been given at least a small version of the tragedy. It was that terrible.

John was alone in the waiting room at this hour, sometime after seven o'clock. The others had gone back to Ashley's house where Reagan and Katy had made chili and homemade corn bread. All of them agreed it wasn't healthy to stay at the hospital this long without a break. John just couldn't convince himself to leave. Not while his daughter was still fighting for her life.

The nurses needed to work on her, change tubing and tend to her various medications and IV fluids. John used the occasion to come to the waiting room, the place that was beginning to feel like some strange kind of new home. He walked to the window and stared out at the lights of St. Anne's north wing. He knew the hospital well enough to know what he was looking at.

It was the labor and delivery ward. The place where all of his grandchildren except for Erin's girls and Tommy had been born.

A place where even this moment life was being celebrated. He stared at the bright windows and dark brick walls and it helped, just a little. Knowing that amidst the death and dying, life still reigned nearby. He leaned against the window frame and let his thoughts go where he least wanted them to, the place he'd been fighting not to fall into.

The place of doubt.

Fragments of truth were in him and around him, no question. There was the Bible Promise app on his phone and a list on his phone's notepad of memorized Scriptures. He and Elaine had read sections in Ephesians and Revelation and 2 Corinthians as a way of surviving the minute-by-minute pain. The excruciating pain. But through it all he hadn't found a way to kill the doubt.

It came in the form of subtle questions. Why his family? When they had only ever loved the Lord and served Him, and when the girls had all their lives ahead, why Erin and Sam? And why would God need to take them home to heaven so soon, and how were the rest of them ever supposed to feel normal again? God could've stopped the whole thing from happening. He could've prevented the accident.

John felt his body tremble, the aftereffects of adrenaline and heartache that hadn't left his system since he heard the first terrible news. He left the window and spotted yesterday's newspaper on a waiting room end table. Having it there was like having someone standing in the room shouting the truth at him. The accident had happened. He wasn't having a nightmare or suffering from some delusion. Erin and Sam and the girls had been rear-ended by an eighteen-wheeler on Highway 37.

He picked up the paper, rolled it so the story was on the inside, and dropped it into the nearest trash can. The details were vivid, the way they would remain as long as John's heart beat. He leaned against the nearest wall and stared at nothing. The man who hit them had been a fifty-three-year-old truck driver named

Marty Cohen. A professional trucker with decades of experience and a clean record. The guy must've had his seat belt off, because he was ejected from his truck on impact. Dead at the scene.

Police were doing what they could to investigate the accident, but in the end witnesses provided everything they needed to know. The guy had fallen asleep. Several motorists were quoted in the article saying the guy had his eyes closed right up until he plowed into the van. Too many hours on the road, too many demands on his work load. He had a truck full of potatoes that needed to reach Indianapolis that day. That's what the newspaper said.

A truck full of potatoes.

As if having potatoes by that night would've been worth the lives of his precious Erin and her family. John breathed deep, and tried with everything in him to release the doubts. He wasn't a doubting man, not ever. Not when Elizabeth got cancer, and not when she died of it after Ashley's wedding. He thought back further and found no time like this where doubts seemed rooted in his soul. He had doubted the miracle they needed for Hayley after her drowning accident, but he had never doubted God Himself. Not when Ashley got pregnant in Paris, and not when Luke left the family during his college years.

Not 9 – 11 and not Landon's lung disease.

Nothing had shaken him like this.

The church knew by now, along with the rest of the town, and Mark Atteberry's wife had organized a prayer chain and meals for everyone staying at Ashley's house. The first meals had begun arriving that morning. Pastor Mark asked the congregation to respect the Baxter family's privacy by staying away from the hospital, but many of them had sent cards and flowers to the house. The show of kindness and the promise of prayer comforted all of them.

He checked his watch. The nursing staff should be finished working with Erin now. He wouldn't know until she woke up whether she could hear him during this part of her recovery or not, whether she knew he was in the room. But he had to be there. In case his presence encouraged her or calmed her or helped her to heal.

In case she didn't …

The thought swung dangerously from the rafters of his mind like a dagger capable of dealing a fatal blow. He couldn't finish it, couldn't acknowledge it. *Let it hang there,* he told himself. Never mind the truth it held. John had to be with Erin because a daughter in trouble needed her daddy.

And there was no question Erin was in trouble. It was enough to acknowledge that much without having to finish the terrifying thought. Erin was still critical. Sam, too. But like yesterday, Sam was worse again, the infection blazing through his body refusing to retreat to the powerful antibiotics. John had been in to see Chloe and Amy Elizabeth, both of them too sedated to show any signs of life. And he'd spent time with Sam, of course.

But mainly he wanted to be with Erin.

He started toward the waiting room door, but as he did his young friend Chris Hazel entered the room. At the sight of John, Hazel stopped short and his face fell. John felt his heart skip a beat, and then another. Not again … another of them. He leaned back against the wall, not sure he could stand up through whatever news the doctor was bringing.

"You're alone?" Chris came toward him.

"The others are having dinner. They'll be back in an hour." John looked around for the nearest seat. Already he could feel the blood leaving his face. *Not another one, please, God …*

"Let's sit down." Chris motioned toward the nearest set of chairs, and they both took seats, adjusting themselves so they were facing each other. "The news isn't good."

"Never." John clenched his jaw, hating the cynicism creeping into his tone. "I'm sorry. I just … I don't understand this."

Chris sat close enough that he reached out and put his hand on John's shoulder. "I'm sorry. I can't imagine this."

John couldn't imagine it, either. Not a week ago and not in this moment. He waited, wishing he could stop time and protect himself from what was coming. His silence lasted seconds, but it felt like a week. When he couldn't stand it another moment he hung his head. As he looked up, he could feel tears gathering once more. "Tell me. Please, Chris."

"We've lost Chloe and Sam. Their brain activity stopped within a minute of each other." Chris looked pale, his eyes searching John's as if waiting for some terrible reaction, a reaction like the one John had suffered when he first heard about the accident.

But this time the news came on stocking feet, creeping softly into his heart and not quite hitting the nerves of reality. Instead the doctor's words seemed more factual, like a detail John would have to work through later. Even in the middle of sorting through his strange feelings, John knew what was happening. The shock was too great, too much for him to bear. His brain knew this, and so it had created a barrier between reality and the place John had slipped into.

He felt himself nod, but otherwise he seemed to be in some strange dream. Chris Hazel was saying something about organs again, but John couldn't make out all the words. As if someone else was controlling his body, he heard himself say, "Yes ... please use whatever organs you can." Chris slid a clipboard to him and John felt his hand signing at the bottom.

But through it all he was no longer sure if he was even awake.

"Would you like to see them? Chloe and Sam?" Chris exhaled hard, and the sound seemed to gather up from his shoes. "Also, I can call the rest of the family, if you want. I have Ashley and Landon's numbers."

His questions floated in the space between them and took

a few seconds to come together. John felt a heaviness come over him. The heaviness of a broken heart. Suddenly he understood. Chloe and Sam were dead, and his doctor friend was giving him the chance to see them one last time, whether the man should call the others. John looked into his friend's eyes and nodded. That was all he could bring himself to do.

"Okay, then." Chris stood slowly. "Come on back when you're ready, John. I'll take you to them. And I'll call Landon."

That worked. John couldn't imagine calling them and telling them about this latest blow. He watched his friend leave and then he dug his elbows into his knees. For a long time he leaned over his legs and let his head rest in his hand. Chloe and Sam. His precious Erin had just lost her last remaining teenage daughter and her husband. When she woke up — if she woke up — she would only have Amy Elizabeth.

The whole last few days seemed so awful they almost had to be a nightmare. But then, that was the shock again, doing its job, trying to protect him. *I want to ask You why, Lord ... why You would allow this.* He waited for an answer, waited with only the beat of his heart as any sort of response. Doubt and anger tap-danced in his mind, rousing him to face the reality surrounding him. *You could've woken up that truck driver. You could've stopped this.* He exhaled, trying to rid his body of the strange and unusual feeling consuming him. He never doubted God. Never.

Help me, Father ... I'm sorry. I just don't understand. Please ... give me strength to take the next step.

Seconds passed and then gradually, like air filling a balloon, he felt the Lord breathe life into him, felt himself possess the strength to stand and do the one thing he absolutely had to do next.

Go see Chloe and Sam.

WITH EVERY BREATH, JOHN WISHED HE would wake up. That none of the things happening around him were really happening. But he was wide awake and they were playing out as surely as the clock ticking on the wall. Dr. Hazel had assured him the others were on their way back down. Many of them, anyway.

And he had other news, too. Erin didn't look well. Her vital signs were weakening, and her fever was up. Infection was a strong possibility, her body too badly damaged to fight the ravaging destruction throughout it. "I want you to be ready, John. That's all."

Be ready? How in the world could anyone be ready for forty-eight hours like they'd all just gone through? Either way, he nodded. Took the news like another sucker punch to the gut in a fight he had lost in a knockout three rounds ago. He went to Sam's room first, to the right side of his bed where there were fewer machines. On the other side his heart was still beating. Same as they'd done with Clarissa. His organs needed to be protected if they'd be worth passing on to someone else.

He stared at his son-in-law, and a collage of memories flashed in his mind. Sam Hogan coming to him when Erin was just out of college. *I'd like to marry your daughter, sir. I promise to take care of her as long as I live.* And then they were sitting around the Baxter family dining room table — back when the house still belonged to John and Elizabeth — and they were back from their honeymoon to Lake Michigan and ready to open wedding presents and Sam was smiling and saying, *Everything feels so new and shiny, just like our lives together.* And they were coming to him and Elizabeth — Sam and Erin, both — and they were asking for advice, how marriage could withstand infertility. And Sam's voice rang through the memory. *I love Erin with or without children, but the pressure is killing us.* With that the flashback changed and Sam and Erin were walking up to him with not one but four adopted daughters. And Sam was beaming and saying, *If I live to be a hundred years old, I'll never understand why God chose to bless us so completely.*

Ambitious, determined, loyal Sam Hogan.

John put his hand on Sam's head and felt him, the reality of him. *Lord, now the girls have their daddy again. Let them be together in heaven. Let Elizabeth be with them so that all my loved ones on that side are together with You. Please...*

It was a picture he hadn't allowed in his mind until only just now. Somehow the horror of the last few days had been so firmly entrenched in the here and now, he had forgotten about the there and then. The fact that as Erin's family — one at a time — left this world, they were instantly in the other.

A different sort of emotion filled his heart and soul and created tears where before the anger and doubt were consuming him. The feeling was peace. Because if Sam was in heaven with Chloe and Clarissa and Heidi Jo, and if the four of them were there with Elizabeth and little Sarah and if they were keeping company with their Savior, then how could he be angry?

He stepped back and the last memory, the one that would stay with him long after this painful day was over, was the image of Sam standing at the front of Clear Creek Church promising to love Erin as long as he lived.

"Well done, Sam, my son. Well done." A sad smile lifted John's lips as he saw his son-in-law the way he had looked that day. "You did what you promised."

With that he left the room and went next door to the bed where Chloe lay. This was harder, but still John forced himself to hold on to the truth. She wasn't here, wasn't in a bed attached to tubes and machines, her brain destroyed. She was alive and vibrant, running with two of her sisters and getting to know Elizabeth like never before. She was with her daddy. John walked to her bedside and put his hand on her shoulder. "Chloe ... I loved you so much." He whispered the words. They were for him, not for her, but he had to say them. "I hate that I didn't get to tell you good-bye, sweetheart."

She still felt warm and alive, the work of the machine keeping her heart going. He withdrew his hand and studied her, the beautiful child who had been old enough to know the horrors of her previous life with her birth mother, Candy Burns. Poor Chloe had seen drug deals go down and she'd witnessed her mother get beaten time and again. As she got older the beatings became hers and Clarissa's, devastating conditions that continued until finally the state intervened.

Yet through it all she never seemed anything other than a happy, well-adjusted teenager. Quieter than Clarissa, but marked by an occasional sense of spunk and humor that John imagined would've become defining characteristics as she grew older. But they would never know now. He tried to think of a memory of Chloe he could take with him, one that stood apart from the others and instantly one surfaced.

Last Fourth of July, weeks before Sam got word about the job opening in Austin, the whole group was gathered at Lake Monroe for their annual picnic and fishing derby. John had finished with more fish than usual, even though his team didn't win. Everyone dispersed from the lakeside and headed back to the picnic tables, back to apply mosquito spray and slip into sweatshirts and position their chairs so they could see the fireworks over the lake. In that moment of transition, Chloe had walked up to him.

"Papa, can you come here? I wanna show you something." She was tanned from a day on the beach, and her blue eyes sparkled in the reflection of the setting sun. She held out her hand and bounced a little. "Please? It's the coolest thing."

John went to her and she held on to his arm as they walked. "I think it's a bald eagle! It's the prettiest bird I've ever seen. And it has this huge nest." It was more talking than Chloe usually did in an entire afternoon — at least from John's experience. But that moment she was as chatty as her older sister. Together they walked along the shore fifty yards or so until they reached a point where they could see a nest in a distant tree. "There it is!" Her voice filled with excitement. "What do you think? Is it a bald eagle?"

John shielded his eyes and stared at the tree. As he did, as they both watched, a huge bird suddenly flew from the nest and took flight. "Well, look at that." John had laughed, surprised. "You're right, Chloe girl. It is a bald eagle."

"I knew it." She stood beside him, the two of them watching as the eagle effortlessly gained height and circled slowly over the water. "It's the most beautiful thing ever." Chloe turned and hugged him around his waist. Then she looked right at him. "You're the best grandpa in the world." She grinned. "I thought you should know."

With that she ran off to join up with her sisters. And John was left standing there knowing one thing with all his heart. He would never forget that moment, or the shared glimpse of a bald eagle he'd experienced with Erin's second-oldest daughter. Her sweet expression, her kind eyes, the way she told him he was the best grandpa. All of it combined to form a single image of the girl. The one he would take with him when he left her bedside.

And every day after that.

He turned away, grateful for the gift of remembering, and he left the room to find Erin. When the others arrived, that's where he wanted to be. Erin needed him the most, because she was still living. Which was why he had no time to waste, no moments to spend in the waiting room grieving the loss of Chloe and Sam.

Not when Erin was still alive.

John had just found a chair and positioned himself at the side of his daughter's bed when one of the nurses entered the room. "I need to give you this. It's been in one of the storage rooms." She held a tattered oversized brown purse, stuffed with what looked like torn papers and trash. In her other hand was a cell phone—again battered, but still in one piece. She handed the items to John. "We have a few boxes of other things that were scattered over the road during the accident. The suitcases in the back of the van ... there was nothing really left of those."

These were details John hated. The picture of their destroyed van decimated in the middle of the highway, their suitcases and clothing and iPods and magazines and purses—scattered on the roadway for all the staring motorists to see. He cringed as he took the purse and phone. They were Erin's, he could tell immediately. The same ones she'd had last March at Bailey's wedding. "We'll ... get the boxes in the morning. If that's okay."

"Of course." The woman looked beyond sad. "This is my first shift since the accident. The entire staff ... Dr. Baxter, we're so sorry."

"Thank you." He lifted kind eyes to the woman. "God is with us." The words came naturally. Like breathing. Because no matter how bad the doubts had been, they'd been replaced with this last blow of bad news. Doubt and anger wouldn't help anything. Only God and heaven could do that. The woman left, and John glanced inside Erin's purse. The papers were dirty and in some cases torn. They'd been shoved inside in a hurry. But it was possible that within the phone and purse they might find numbers and information that would help them know what to do next. John hugged the purse slowly to his chest.

As if by doing so he could feel Erin in his arms again.

His youngest daughter. He looked at her face, the way her brown hair even matted in the hospital bed, still framed her face much as it had Elizabeth's when she was younger. Once again he was reminded that of all their girls, Erin had always looked the most like their mother. It was the reason he couldn't bear to lose her. Her love for her family, her way of mothering, her mannerisms — all so much like Elizabeth's. Erin had always been the last bit of reminder of Elizabeth John had left. He couldn't do anything to help her now. So he did what he could. He sat at the side of her bed, clinging to her purse and her phone.

And praying for a miracle.

Seventeen

It was nearly ten o'clock, two days after the accident, and Luke Baxter felt sick to his stomach. He sat at a table in the waiting room, anchored by Ashley and their dad. Never mind that his father's birthday was tomorrow. None of them wanted to think about that now. The others were clustered in groups of two or three, taking turns comforting each other. It seemed like there was always someone crying or falling apart, and someone else strong enough to keep the others standing. And then the roles would reverse.

But tonight was the first time they'd thought at all about what would happen next. It was like as the tragedy unraveled time had stood still. None of them thought about e-mail or bills or work or getting online for any reason or even contacting Sam's employer back in Texas. It was all they could do to survive one hour to the next as the news grew worse.

Luke figured the turning point came because of Erin's purse and cell phone. Somehow his sister's phone still worked, and since she was in a coma, still fighting for every minute of life, their dad had gone through her text messages. He'd found several from a woman who seemed to be the girls' social worker.

"I feel like there's trouble back in Texas," his dad had told him an hour ago as he handed Luke the phone and Erin's purse. "Erin said something about the girls' biological mother wanting visitations. I think we should look into it."

Luke had done as his dad asked and what he'd found left him even more devastated. A battle had begun to brew between Erin and Sam and the girls' birth mother. Luke had sat alone going through the messages and clearly, by the tone of Erin's texts, she was worried. One text in particular deeply concerned Luke. It was sent the morning Sam and Erin set off for their trip, the last text Erin had sent Naomi Boggs. Luke pulled it up and read it again.

Look, something urgent has come up. I can prove to you that Candy only wants money out of this. I'll call you when we get back to Texas. This can wait until then.

The response had come sometime Monday morning. *Yes, it can wait. I'll tell Candy and her mother you're out of town for a week. When you get back, give me a call and we'll discuss your proof.*

Of course now there was no way for Luke to know what Erin had meant. He looked across the table. Ashley and their dad were waiting for his assessment. Was there trouble waiting for Erin back in Texas or not?

Ashley was the only one who had seen Luke get the purse. She must've recognized the bag — the way girls did with things like that. Because she crossed the waiting room immediately and asked whether the purse was indeed Erin's, and what else they'd found. Since then she'd waited patiently, sitting across from Luke for the entire hour. And now, while the others still talked with each other, caught up in conversations about past moments and the losses stacking up around them, Ashley wanted answers. Same as their father.

She leaned on her elbows, studying him. "What did you find?"

"It doesn't look good." Luke hated saying the words. After all that had happened over the last few days, they could use a little good news. But this wasn't that moment. "There's a trail of text messages here from a social worker, Naomi Boggs. She doesn't seem to be the original social worker who took care of the girls' adoption, but she's handling the case now."

"I'm confused." John crossed his arms and leaned back in his chair. He looked weary and broken. "Why is there a current case? The girls were adopted nearly a decade ago."

"Erin sort of explains it in here." Luke lifted his sister's phone and then set it back on the table. "It sounds like she and Sam made a deal with the girls' grandmother at the time of the adoption." He rehashed some of what they already knew, how Candy Burns had accidentally killed a drug runner in a deal gone bad, and how she'd served nine years in prison for the crime.

"I remember something about Erin agreeing to an open adoption so the grandmother could see the girls." Ashley looked worried, her brow knit together. "Erin thought an open adoption with Candy's mother was a bad idea at the time. But it was the only way she and Sam could get the girls."

"Apparently, the grandmother didn't care to see the girls. She visited them only a couple times since the adoption." He looked from Ashley to his dad. "But now Candy Burns is out of prison and she wants regular visits. Because the adoption is open and listed that way in the state of Texas, there could be some real problems ahead."

His father's expression seemed to change from confusion to a painful knowing.

"I don't get it." Ashley sighed. "I mean, what right does some drug-addicted prisoner have seeing these girls agai — " She stopped, clearly catching herself. There were no longer girls who needed to worry about their birth mother. "I hate this." She muttered under her breath and massaged her temples with her thumb and forefinger. "What I mean is, why should Candy see Amy ever again after what she did?"

Suddenly Luke felt his head spinning as a new reality hit him. Like Ashley, he had been worried about Candy trying to visit Amy — especially with Erin so injured. But the reality was worse. Much worse. He sucked in a shaky breath. "Think about this." He leaned closer, keeping his voice down. He didn't want the others hearing his concerns. Not when he was only beginning to understand them. "If Erin doesn't make it ... then who gets custody of Amy?"

For a long moment none of them said anything. They were too caught up in the suddenly very real possibility that Candy Burns might have a claim on Amy Elizabeth. Luke glanced through the text messages again. "A few days before they left, Erin said this to the social worker." He found the exact text he was looking for. "She said, 'Please, help me with this. Whatever it takes I can't stand the thought of Candy getting her hands on my girls. She never cared about them and you yourself said you're worried she doesn't care now. Taking parenting classes in prison doesn't change the fact that she offered to sell them before she killed someone. Can't the courts see that?'"

Ashley clenched her jaw. Anger met with a passion that had always marked her personality. She tapped her fingers on the table. "If Erin didn't want that woman to have visits with her girls, then ..." Her voice broke, and tears filled her eyes. "We absolutely cannot let her regain custody of Amy." Her voice fell to a pained whisper. "Absolutely not."

"I agree." Their dad had his hands clenched, like he would fight the woman herself if she dared come find Erin's little girl. "Of course, we're a little premature."

"We are." Luke was quick to say so. "Erin's still with us. God could still heal her." He had talked to Erin's doctor earlier tonight when the others were in with her, and the prognosis was grim. But he didn't want to say so. He also didn't want to share the fact that no matter how strongly Ashley or his dad or any of them felt, there might not be anything they could do. The open adoption status left the custody change a very real possibility.

"She won't have a case, right?" His dad sounded like he'd found a reason to live again. "I'm with Ashley. We can't let anyone take Amy."

Luke reminded himself to think like an attorney for a moment, and a plan began to take shape in his mind. He looked from Ashley to their father. "Okay. Here's what we'll do."

THE MOMENT GOVERNMENT OFFICES IN TEXAS were open, the morning of his father's seventieth birthday, Luke sat at the old Baxter table and placed the call. He got ahold of Naomi Boggs with only a few transfers. "Hello?" She sounded young, not old enough to be jaded by the system.

Luke prayed for the right words. If Naomi was young, that could be good for them. She might be more willing to fight for Amy. "Hello, ma'am, this is Luke Baxter. I'm Erin Hogan's brother."

"Oh." Naomi sounded confused. "Okay. Nice to meet you, Mr. Baxter."

"Thank you." His brain hurt. He stared out the window at his mother's roses in the backyard. "Mrs. Boggs I'm afraid I have very bad news." He barely paused. "My sister Erin and her family were in a terrible car accident over the weekend."

Naomi's gasp came across the phone line. "No! Is everyone okay?"

"They're not." This was the first time Luke had to tell someone outside the family. It was one of the hardest things he'd ever done. He breathed out, leaning his elbows on the wooden table. "They were stopped on the highway in traffic when they were rear-ended by an eighteen-wheeler. The guy was asleep at the wheel." His voice shook, and everything in his chest hurt. "Heidi Jo died at the scene."

"No!" Her breathing became jagged. "That's terrible." She might've been crying. Luke wasn't sure.

"There's more." He felt like hands were choking him, like the power of saying the words was enough to make them true again. "Clarissa and Chloe and their father, Sam, have also passed on at the hospital. They've been at St. Anne's here in Bloomington, Indiana."

"That can't be." Naomi's shock was evident, as if maybe Luke had called the wrong person or maybe he was referring to a different family. "It was ... a family vacation. I can't believe this."

"Yes." Luke remembered to exhale. "They were driving up for my dad's surprise birthday party."

"Dear God, why them ..." the woman's whispered words were barely audible. But the fact that she'd said them told Luke one very important thing. She must believe in God. And if that were true, he could only hope she would have their family's best interest at heart. "What about Erin and Amy?"

"Amy is in a medically induced coma after having surgery. But she's expected to recover." He hesitated. "Erin's very critical." This, too, was difficult to admit to a stranger. Luke still believed for a miracle, but the reality remained. "It doesn't look good."

"This is awful. I can't believe it." She sounded stunned. "Let me sit down. Hold on."

He waited while a bit of noise came across the line and the phone seemed to jostle in the woman's hands. After a few seconds she came back on the line. "So you're saying ... there's a possibility Amy could be an orphan in the next few days?"

Realistically it was a possibility in the next few hours. But Luke couldn't bring himself to say so. "Yes, ma'am. That's ... why I'm calling."

"Dear God ... help us." She breathed out, long and slow, like she'd been holding her breath since he gave her the news. "This is very serious, Mr. Baxter."

"Luke. Call me Luke."

"Okay. And I'm Naomi." Her tone suggested she was

distracted, as if maybe she'd pulled out a pad of paper and was taking notes. "Has anyone in the family signed power of attorney for the girls? They'll all—" She hesitated, as if—like Ashley yesterday—she didn't easily make the adjustment to the Hogans having not four girls, but one. Just one. "I'm sorry. Power of attorney for Amy Elizabeth."

"Yes. That took place a few days ago." He had gone down to the courthouse near the university and taken care of it after talking with the doctor about the idea of organ donation.

"The thing is, Candy has done a great job making the courts think she's rehabilitated." The woman paused. "I haven't figured out her motives, but she's absolutely determined to have visitation rights."

Luke let the possibility stay with him for a few heartbeats. "What do you think? I mean, my sister believes the woman is still a danger."

"I agree. But there's no way to prove it." She sounded defeated. "Because of the open adoption, I'm worried." Her shock was morphing into a deep sort of sorrow, at least if her tone was any indication. "The way the last social worker wrote this one up, Candy *and* her mother have more rights than if they'd done a closed adoption."

The possibility was beyond comprehension. If Erin died, when Amy woke up and when she learned that her family was gone, she might be ripped from the Baxters and sent to live with Candy Burns. Incomprehensible. "Mrs. . . . uh, Naomi. I'm calling because our family is not willing to give up custody of Amy to her birth mother. If . . . if our sister doesn't make it."

"I understand." Naomi was clearly on his side, but the resignation in her tone scared him. "Let's take this one step at a time. I'll make a few calls, and then we'll talk."

"What happens next?"

Naomi sighed. "Unfortunately, I have to tell Candy and her

mother. Again, with the open adoption we have to be forthright in the situation. Two of Candy's biological daughters are no longer with us. She needs to know."

Luke's mind raced ahead, trying to imagine how the felon and her mother would react to the news. If there wasn't any Erin or Sam to swindle money from, then maybe Candy would lose interest. In other words, no one to pay her to get lost. Still, he felt beyond uneasy about the situation. His lawyer sense told him that the woman was up to no good, and once she heard about the accident she'd find a way to use it against them.

Not until he hung up did he figure it out.

Immediately he dialed the number in Erin's phone for Sam's employer. Once he reached Sam's boss, Luke began the conversation by breaking the awful news to the man. After a few minutes of the man expressing his great sorrow and shock, Luke got to the point. "We need to know if Sam had a life insurance policy."

"Yes." The man didn't hesitate, didn't ask Luke to prove he was even actually related to Sam Hogan. Probably too much in shock over the news. "Everyone in the company is entitled to one of our life insurance packages. I can check for you and call you back."

Luke wanted to keep the details legal, even if the boss didn't ask for identification. "Look, I'm going to fax over my license to practice law and a copy of my identification along with copies of Sam's and Erin's ID's. That way you can know this is aboveboard, and you can feel right giving me the information."

The man was still so sorry about what had happened. He apologized for not requesting the verification at first and the call ended. While he waited, Luke closed his eyes. *Dear God, please heal Erin ... please breathe life into her. If we lose her, we might lose Amy. And that can't happen ... God don't leave us now. Please, Father.*

My son, be still and know that I am God. In all things, I am God ...

The response was the last thing Luke wanted flitting through his mind. Of course God was in control. But at a time like this he wanted promises from the Lord that everything would work out, and Erin would get better so she could raise Amy, and so that Candy would be shut down and the adoption would become closed. The way it should've been at the beginning.

Instead the Lord seemed to whisper to him again, this time to be still. *How can I be still? I need to act ... I need to fly to Texas if that's what it takes. This matters to Erin ... we have to keep that child from being taken away from us.*

This time there was only the sound of his racing heart. Eleven minutes passed and Luke was about to call Sam's boss again. He had a hunch here, a hunch that the life insurance policy wasn't one of those throwaway deals worth only enough money for a funeral.

The phone rang before he could call back. Luke answered it immediately. "Did you find out?"

"I did." Sam's boss still sounded broken over the news, but there was a little pride in his tone. Like he was glad he could get the information, glad to help. "It was a term policy."

Luke tried to be patient. If Candy knew about the life insurance — if she even suspected there might be an inheritance involved — she could be on her way to Indiana right now ready to assume her role as the only functioning parent in the situation. He closed his eyes. "Worth how much? Does it say how much it's worth?"

"Yes." There was a pause on the other line. "It's worth a quarter of a million dollars."

For a few seconds Luke couldn't say anything. Then he opened his eyes, thanked the man, and promised to call with funeral plans, whenever the family made them, which would have to be soon. But as he hung up all he could think was that once Candy found out Amy Elizabeth had an inheritance, she'd do everything in her power to gain custody of her and keep her forever from the Baxter family.

She'd have 250,000 reasons why.

Eighteen

ASHLEY WAS ANGRY WITH HERSELF.

They were back at the hospital waiting room, everyone but the kids, and like the others Ashley was taking a turn sitting by Erin's bed. Two floors down, Amy Elizabeth was expected to remain in her medically induced coma for at least another couple days. But she was doing better, her organs showing signs of healing. The news wasn't as good for Erin. Their sister was slightly worse that Tuesday morning, three days after the accident. Nothing about her prognosis looked hopeful.

Ashley had spent the last half hour at Erin's bedside assuring her comatose sister that the family was praying, and for that matter, prayer chains were underway around the clock at both Clear Creek Community and their church back in Austin.

"You look a little better," she told her sister and at the same time she regretted telling her a lie. The whole time she stood at Erin's bedside, holding her hand and doing her best to avoid the needles and tubes that seemed to be hooked to every part of her.

Ashley tried again. "We want you to wake up, Erin. We need you."

That last part was the truth, at least, but none of what she was saying was even close to what she planned to say. Their dad walked in and explained that Brooke was next. They were each trying to keep their visits brief so their Dad could spend most of the time with her. After he had a few hours they could go another round, and if they chose they could sit with her in groups of two.

But Ashley needed more time alone with her. So she could say things she didn't want to leave unspoken. She sat in the corner chair of the waiting room, her head back against the wall, eyes closed. She had blown it. She couldn't find the courage to talk to Erin even today—when her next few hours weren't promised.

Ashley remembered her conversation with Landon last night. They were climbing into bed and Ashley didn't crawl under the covers. Instead she sat cross-legged on the bed facing her husband. "I was never the sister I should've been to Erin." She rested her forearms on her knees and watched for his reaction.

He was lying down already and now he rolled onto his side and stared at her, his eyes kind and deep. "Don't be so hard on yourself. You loved her. You talked her into coming to the party."

Ashley looked down and guilty tears splashed onto her crossed legs. When she could find her voice she looked up at him. "Exactly."

"Ash..." he looked instantly worried, almost angry. "This isn't your fault. You can't think that."

"Of course I can." Her words were tight, and her lip quivered. She had to fight from letting the sobs take over. "I invited her." A shiver started at the base of her neck. "If I hadn't asked her ... they'd still be in Texas."

"Baby, no." Landon had sat up and stood on his knees holding his arms out to her. "Come here ... you can't think like that."

The weight of guilt from years of not really liking Erin, and then more years of not noticing her enough, along with the invitation to the party made it hard for Ashley to struggle to her knees. But she did, and she allowed him to pull her close. She rested her head on his chest and heard the strength of his heartbeat, felt the fervor of his indignation. "You will never, ever tell yourself this was your fault." He took hold of her shoulders and searched her eyes. "You can't do that, Ash. It'll destroy you."

She wanted a reason to feel differently, but she couldn't think of one. "How else can I see it?"

"You were just the one throwing the party." It was like Landon truly couldn't believe this was an issue for her. "She would've come no matter who invited her. That'd be like saying all of this is your dad's fault for having a birthday at the end of June."

"There's more." Ashley had wiped her eyes and they sat back down, facing each other on the bed again. "I always looked down on Erin, I think. I thought she was too needy and too dependent on our mom." Ashley felt sick just saying the words. "I always sort of dismissed her. Like, 'Oh, don't worry about her. That's just Erin.' That sort of thing."

"Baby . . ." Landon put his hand on her knee. "If you were ever like that it was years ago. You and Erin are fine now."

"Sure, we're fine." Ashley had heard the frustration in her tone. "But I never told her I was sorry. Things gradually got better, but that doesn't mean I ever apologized."

Landon had been quiet then, as if he finally understood a little of what Ashley was feeling. "You can tell her at the hospital."

Ashley had agreed. She had planned to go into Erin's room alone and hold her sister's hand and tell her all the reasons she was sorry. But then her chance to be with Erin came this morning and Ashley couldn't bring herself to say the words. She was too afraid. If this was the last time she ever spoke to her sister, she didn't want her last memory to be of a confession, of a dark admission without any real resolution. If she couldn't look in Erin's eyes and tell her how she felt, if she couldn't see the forgiveness reflecting back from her sister's heart, then she had no idea how she'd bring herself to say it.

Ashley felt a chill run down her arms. It was nearly ninety degrees outside on this second day of July, but here in the waiting room at St. Anne's it felt like winter. Or maybe that was just Ashley's heart making the rest of her cold. Because what sort of sister was she if she couldn't bring herself to say sorry? So what if she didn't have Erin's reaction? Somewhere in the depths of her being — no matter how bad things were — Erin might possibly be able to hear her, to understand her. And that should have been enough. To wait for Erin to wake up was to risk missing the chance to apologize altogether.

A memory worked its way to daylight.

Erin had been sitting with their mom on the front porch of the Baxter house, the one she and Landon lived in now. Ashley came home from her first week at Sunset Hills Adult Care Home and found them on the front porch, deep in some conversation. Ashley was headed right back out, so she parked near the front steps and when she saw her mom and sister, she stopped. "Isn't that nice? Another mother-daughter moment." She smiled, but she must've looked beyond rude. She didn't wait for a response as she hurried inside for an apple and a bottle of water.

On her way back out to her car, Erin called after her. "You can join us."

"That's okay." Ashley waved her off. "Wouldn't want to intrude."

Ashley shuddered with disgust at the memory of her voice, the tone she had used that afternoon. This many years away from that rebellious time, Ashley knew what the problem was. She was jealous of Erin, of course. Erin had done everything right. She earned the best grades and the craziest thing she ever did was ditch school once to get her hair done for prom. Erin enjoyed knitting and watching old movies with their parents and attending Bible Study Club at Clear Creek High. In their growing-up years, she was everything Ashley had never been.

But that wasn't all Ashley had been jealous of when it came to Erin. Most of all she envied the way Erin got along with their mother. The two were so close. Back when she was younger, Ashley sometimes felt like there was nothing she could do to make her mom love her the way she loved Erin. The wisdom of the years told a different story, of course. Erin had been close to their mother because she was introverted and liked being at home on a Friday night, and because Ashley, Brooke, and Kari all had a social life.

Over time, an understanding crept into Ashley's relationship with her youngest sister. Ashley came back to her faith and eventually married Landon, and in the process she became kinder and more compassionate. Erin just naturally forgave her, and when the family was together for barbecues or picnics or Sunday dinners, Erin never acted like she had anything against Ashley.

But even still Ashley took her for granted. In her worst moments she thought Erin boring and old-fashioned, and in her best she overlooked her sister. And now Erin was losing the fight for her life. Which meant, if Ashley was ever going to tell Erin she was sorry, it would have to happen here.

She was still wrestling with the guilt of her surface talk in Erin's hospital room earlier when Luke entered the room and approached her. He lowered his voice. "We need a meeting. Can you call Kari and see where she is? I'd like everyone here."

Ashley felt herself grow dizzy, felt the light-headed feeling she was becoming familiar with. "Did something else happen?"

"I spoke with the social worker." Luke looked like he could've been talking to a jury. The mix of somber confidence and determination spoke volumes. "I'll go back to the house and round up the others. The Flanigans brought dinner for tonight, so we need to meet before then. How about the waiting room in an hour?"

"Kids, too?"

"Not this time." Luke's intensity didn't lessen. "I have to make a few phone calls."

"Okay." Ashley thought about the kids as her brother walked away.

Elaine and Reagan and Katy had done an amazing job with

the children — feeding and clothing and cleaning them, and keeping them entertained with movies and coloring books and games. They'd even gone to the park a few times. There were thirteen of them including the older ones, who were also helping out. After the first day, Cole, Maddie, and Jessie had opted to stay back at Ashley and Landon's house.

"It's too sad, Mom," Cole had told her. "We're all praying for Aunt Erin and everyone, but we can't help by sitting in a waiting room."

A few of Cole's friends' families had also brought meals and had promised to pray, as well. Ashley was grateful for the support and for the freedom to stay with Landon at the hospital all day and come home to find all the kids loved and cared for. Not that there weren't times of tears even back at the house. Reagan had pulled her aside last night when everyone returned from the hospital.

"It's so sad, watching the older kids talking about the cousins they've lost. They pulled out scrapbooks and went through old pictures on the computer. None of us can believe this."

That was for sure. Ashley shivered now, her hands freezing. She took her cell phone outside so the sunshine might warm her body and melt the ice that seemed to be running through her fingers. As she walked down the hall she caught a glimpse of Brooke talking with Erin's attending physician.

Brooke had become the family's liaison, especially where Amy was concerned. They'd all taken turns visiting their little niece, and they were grateful for her medically induced coma. The trauma she would wake up to would be unbearable, even if she were perfectly healthy. Brooke had reported earlier that morning that Amy's internal injuries were healing, but they still wanted her to stay perfectly still. When they passed these early critical days, they would gradually bring her out of the coma.

Once she was outside, Ashley stopped and let the sun bake

her shoulders for several seconds. Then she walked to a spot against the warm brick wall. Luke was going back to the house, so she called Kari and found her at lunch talking with some friends from church who had heard about the accident. She promised to meet in the waiting room at St. Anne's in an hour. Ashley stayed outside after the call was over until her body and fingers were finally warm.

When she went back inside, she walked straight to Erin's room and stopped at the open door. A curtain was pulled across the front of the room for privacy so that only the lower part of Erin's hospital bed was showing. But from where she stood Ashley could hear their dad's voice, soft and hopeful as he talked to Erin. Ashley crept into the room and again took the chair at the foot of the bed, against the wall. Even then her dad didn't seem to notice her.

"Remember that Valentine's Day when everyone had somewhere to go, someone to be with? And you and your mom and I celebrated by ourselves? You made me that beautiful scarf, remember?" He was holding Erin's hand, leaning over the bed and speaking closer to her face than if he were sitting down. "We went out for Chinese food that night and we watched *Sleepless in Seattle*." His tone was rich with nostalgia. "You told us you knew God had a special man for you somewhere. But in the meantime you didn't care if other people thought it was silly to spend Valentine's Day with your parents." He sounded stronger than he had a few days ago. His emotions under control. But at this point his voice grew shaky. "You said there wasn't anyone you loved more, so why not?" He hesitated. "You were eighteen that year."

Ashley's sick stomach felt worse as she watched. Her youngest sister had been a model daughter, caring for their parents and loving them even when it wasn't the most popular choice with kids her age. Every wrong feeling she'd ever felt about Erin had been her own fault. Ashley could see that now more than ever before.

Their dad looked over his shoulder and straightened. "Hi, Ash." His smile didn't reach his eyes. "How long have you been here?"

"Not long." She breathed in sharp through her nose and folded her hands in her lap. "I can leave. If you want this moment."

"No, it's fine." He came to her and she stood so the two of them could hug. "I like having you here."

"Hmm. Me, too." She stepped back, regret casting shadows over her heart. "That was beautiful. That story about Erin and Valentine's Day."

His eyes looked like they might stay sad forever, but still the hint of a smile remained. "She's always been so thoughtful."

Guilt added in with Ashley's regret. She folded her arms and moved to the foot of Erin's bed. For nearly a minute she just stood there, watching her sister's chest rise and fall and thinking about the past, the times she could've been more loving or kind. More inclusive of her youngest sister. Finally she turned to her dad. "I'm sorry."

"For what?" He came to her and put his arm around her shoulders. "This isn't your fault, Ash." He glanced at her. "Landon told me to watch you ... he said you had some crazy notion that this was your doing for inviting her to the party."

"No." She gave a quick shake of her head. "I mean, yes, I sometimes think that. But that's not why I'm sorry." Her father was solid and strong beside her, something Ashley desperately needed. She leaned into his shoulder. "I'm sorry for not being more like Erin."

Her dad was quiet, his hold on her as close as before. Almost as if he was letting her words simmer in his heart before he might respond. After a while he took a slow breath. "I never expected you kids to be the same."

"I know." Ashley's tears returned. They fell down her face and dropped onto the floor, and she did nothing to stop them. "But

I was a brat, Dad. We both know it. I broke everyone's hearts by running off to Paris, and when I came home I wasn't very loving." She sniffed and looked at her sister. "Especially to Erin." She swallowed a few times, working to keep her composure. "I think ... I was jealous of her. The relationship she had with you and Mom."

"That was a hard time for you." Her dad kissed her cheek and then watched Erin again. "But God had you in His hands all the time. Look where you are today."

"Thank you." Ashley stepped away and took a single tissue from the box on the back counter. She blew her nose and then returned to her dad. "I guess I'm feeling a lot of regret. Like I could've been a better sister to Erin."

Her dad put his arm around her again, and with his other hand he took hold of Erin's foot through the sheets. "You've been great for a long time, Ash. And you can be the sister she needs, now."

"Now?" Ashley looked at Erin's still figure, and a sense of defeat filled her. "What can I do now?"

Her dad smiled at her, and this time a little of the sadness in his eyes lifted. "God will show you."

Ashley nodded and with her free hand she took gentle hold of Erin's other foot. "I love her ... I wish ..." A sob caught in her throat and she stared at the floor. She released her hold on Erin and pinched the bridge of her nose. "Dad, I don't know if I can do this."

"We can't do this." He tightened his hold on her shoulders. "Only God working through us, that's the only way any of us are still walking this road. He's with us, sweetheart."

Ashley used her forearm to wipe her wet cheeks.

Another minute or so passed, and her dad looked at her. "What do you wish?"

Ashley sniffed and felt her face contort under a sadness greater than all of Indiana. "I wish ... I was a better sister."

Her dad faced her and then he wrapped his arms around her. "Shhh, Ash ... it's okay." He soothed her dark hair and held her the way he had when she'd come home from Paris. "Erin loves you. Never worry about that."

"I ... know she does." She didn't want to trouble her sister, or make her concerned. In case she could hear them. So she kept her voice to a whisper, and cried into her father's chest. "I just want another ... chance to ... love her."

"Then maybe God will give you that. Keep praying."

For the rest of the hour they stayed with Erin, Ashley eventually returning to the same chair and her dad moving back to Erin's bedside where he continued to recall old stories and happy times. Anything that might connect with Erin and stimulate a change for the better. But before they left her room, Dr. Hazel found them. He entered the room and shut the door behind him.

"Would you like us to leave?" Her dad understood doctor protocol, how as long as the care his family was receiving was top notch, he was better not to interfere. He joined Ashley, standing against the wall near her chair.

"No. Please stay." His tone was beyond somber. Ashley watched him take a few minutes to check Erin's numbers, her chart, her physical responses. He jotted down something in her file, and he released a sad sigh as he faced them. "You already know what I'm going to say, John." He looked at his friend. "Don't you?"

"Yes." Her dad put his hand on Ashley's shoulder. "I'm praying for a miracle. That the evidence of my eyes might be wrong."

What evidence? Ashley wanted to scream. *Why hadn't he told her when they were talking earlier?* Her mind spun and her heart pounded. All the sounds tried to blur together. *Dear God, help me focus. Don't let her be worse, please.* She forced herself to listen.

Whatever the doctor said next, Ashley only caught bits and pieces. Erin wasn't responding, her numbers were failing, her brain activity was minimal. Wait! Again she wanted to shout at the man, at her dad, even. They couldn't give up on Erin. She was still fighting, still making progress — even if only because she was still breathing. But as she fought the idea in her mind, the doctor's final words screamed through her heart and soul, as clear as any words ever spoken. They needed to tell the others, he told them. Because the truth was this: Erin was failing.

"She's fading fast." He sounded like he might cry. "I'd say it'll be sometime tonight."

Everything about the past hour swirled together and Ashley could only think of one very terrible sad truth. If Dr. Hazel was right, then her father was wrong. She would not have time to make things right with Erin, to be the sister she'd always meant to be. Unless God gave them a miracle, she'd run out of time. And there was nothing she could do to make up for it.

Not if they only had a few hours left.

Nineteen

LANDON FINISHED THE CLEANUP WITH RYAN, AND THE TWO OF them hurried back to the hospital. Luke had said there was no real news with Erin or Amy Elizabeth, but that he needed a meeting with them all. Whatever had happened, that sounded important. Landon prayed as he drove that Ashley would handle the news well, that he could be there to hold her up and help her through.

The way he'd done at difficult times since he first fell in love with her.

Even with their efforts to hurry, Landon and Ryan were the last to the meeting. They found the others holding down two tables in the waiting room, which was thankfully otherwise empty. Brooke and Peter sat across from Kari. Ryan took the empty chair next to her. Landon did the same, sitting next to Ashley, with Luke and Reagan at the far end. Dayne and Katy sat next to their dad, and Luke was about to take charge of the meeting when John Baxter held up his hand. His face looked gravely sad.

Only then did Landon notice the sorrow on Ashley's face, too. He had the sudden certainty that something else had happened. John looked down for a long while and when he lifted his eyes, there were tears on his cheeks. "Erin only has a few hours." They might've been the most difficult words John had ever uttered. "They told Ashley and me a few minutes ago in her hospital room."

Kari hung her head and Brooke glanced at the waiting room door, as if she might run back to Erin's room herself and see if there wasn't something else that could be done. But in the end she relaxed and rested her head on Peter's shoulder. Luke held tight to Reagan and Dayne did the same with Katy. They'd had enough bad news that week that they weren't shocked. Just deeply sad.

The thing they had prayed and hoped wouldn't finish off this horrible week was about to happen. Barring a miracle, they would have to say good-bye to their sister.

They absorbed the news and John prayed for them, prayed that even in this moment God would take this cup and deliver Erin from her debilitating injuries. "Give us new strength, Father. We don't understand." His voice was a mix of sorrow and defeat. "We might never understand. But we lean into You this hour. In Jesus' name, amen."

A few more minutes passed, and then Luke broke the silence. "We really need to talk. Especially now."

Landon felt Ashley tense up. She pressed her shoulder into his and looked at Luke, the way all of them did.

Luke had a notepad full of what looked like bullet points. His pen was poised on the first one. "I've talked with the social worker. She's new to the case and she's with us. She's very concerned about Amy's birth mother." He looked from one side of the two tables to the other. "Of course now, we're talking about more than visitation. We're talking custody."

The word hit Landon hard enough to take his breath. He tightened his hold on Ashley and caught the desperation on the faces around him. The situation was so much worse than he'd expected coming into this meeting. If Erin died — and it looked that way — then Amy could end up being raised by her birth mother.

Brooke frowned. "Are you saying ... this woman could get full custody of Amy?"

"Absolutely." Luke moved his pen to the next bullet point. "Which leads us to this. Sam and Erin both had life insurance policies. Looks like they total about three hundred thousand dollars."

Again the blow hit Landon full force, the way he could clearly see it was hitting the others at the table. John was the first to recover. He coughed a few times, his throat tight from what was obviously a terrible revelation. "I'm assuming Amy would be the sole heir."

"Exactly." Luke sat back in his chair and dropped the pen on the notepad. "This is very, very bad. The social worker — a woman named Naomi Boggs — will tell Candy and her mother the news about the accident today. It won't take long for them to figure out that if Erin dies, Amy will get the estate. Not that they'll know the amount right off. But the life insurance ... that's enough for Candy to hire an attorney and fight hard for custody. It's more money than she could possibly imagine."

"There has to be some kind of protection built into the policy," again Brooke looked upset.

Landon studied her, the oldest Baxter daughter. Brooke was a fighter — much like Ashley — but Ashley fought with passion. Brooke fought with brains — as if she could outthink a problem like this. But Luke's tone and expression told them this would be harder than they thought.

"A level of protection, yes." Luke frowned. "But it assumes a level of trust with the parent or guardian raising Amy. It allows for ordinary and customary expenses in raising the child, and then a mandatory twenty percent that must be saved for Amy's college costs."

"What?" Ryan raised his voice. "Twenty percent of three hundred thousand wouldn't get her through a four-year degree."

"Exactly." Luke worked the muscles in his jaw. "Again, the policy assumes a level of trust. Meaning if Sam had died and Erin was in charge of the money, she wouldn't abuse it and Amy would have enough to pay for a college education and a house one day."

Landon watched Luke, waiting. Clearly there was more coming.

Luke picked up his pen again and tapped the third bullet point on his list. "That brings us to the main reason we're meeting today." He paused, looking intently at each of his siblings. "I told Naomi we were going to fight this. I have temporary power of attorney where Amy is concerned. She's a minor and that gives us permission to authorize treatment or any decisions a parent might make on her behalf."

"Does that mean we have custody?" Dayne released his hold on Katy and leaned his forearms on the table. "Maybe we'll have the edge over the birth mother."

"It's a step in the right direction, for sure. But it doesn't guarantee anything. The fact is, Candy Burns — Amy's birth mother — has legal right to her. The open adoption allows for it, as long as the court has no proof that Amy would be in danger going to live with her."

"That's ridiculous." Brooke slapped her hand softly on the table. "How dangerous does it have to be? Any time a child goes through something this traumatic, this life altering, of course the last thing she should have to worry about is whether she'd be sent to live with a felon she doesn't even know."

"I'm working on that. Erin texted Naomi, alluding to the fact that she had proof Candy wasn't fit. She didn't elaborate, so I'm trying to imagine how she might've gotten that information. And where I can find it." Luke looked from Brooke to their dad. "Here's the main thing. We need a plan. One of us has to be willing to take custody of Amy if . . ."

He didn't have to finish his sentence.

The reality spread through Landon's heart like warm rain, like everything inside him was crying for Erin's loss, for Amy's loss. The child was nine. How would she ever be okay if she woke up and found that everyone else in her family had been killed?

But then another thought came with the rain. How much worse would the situation be for Amy if she had to live with her birth mother?

Several of Ashley's siblings and their spouses began talking quietly, and Luke quietly interrupted them. "You don't need to decide now. Pray about it, sleep on it. Let's make a decision tomorrow morning. In the meantime, pray for me. That I might figure out this evidence Erin was texting Naomi Boggs about."

In the time it took for Luke to say those last words, Landon made a decision. He looked at Ashley, softly crying beside him, and he knew the answer. Brooke and Peter worked full-time, and Kari and Ryan didn't have room in Ryan's custom log cabin, unless they added on or moved. Luke and Reagan had their hands full, and Dayne and Katy lived too far away to give Amy the extended family she would need.

Which meant he and Ashley needed to take their niece. The thought created a perfect fit in Landon's heart. He and Ashley had been through a great deal together. But God had given Landon a fairly clean bill of health last time he was in, and Amy would fit right in with Devin and Janessa.

They all agreed to talk about the matter in the morning. Before they could get up from the table, John reminded them about Erin. "I'll be in her room the rest of the day." His eyes filled with tears. "Any of you who want to come in and talk to her, feel free. I already asked the nursing staff. They don't mind how many we have, as long as we're quiet."

The sobering reality settled in around them, displacing the fighter mode they were ready to assume. First they had to surround Erin, pray for a miracle and believe God would bring good out of whatever the rest of the day held. They would stay with Erin until she improved or went to heaven.

And later tonight Landon would talk to Ashley about Amy Elizabeth.

ASHLEY WAS EXHAUSTED, BUT SHE HAD an idea. A way she could be the sister to Erin she'd always meant to be. As tired as she was, she needed to talk with Landon before they turned in for the night.

Erin had held on through the day, and even then Ashley hadn't found the right time to say what she wanted to say. When they weren't taking turns visiting the still-comatose Amy Elizabeth, the family filled Erin's room. Then just before midnight the attending physician told them she looked stable enough to survive another day. His words sent them shuffling out to the parking lot and back to the old Baxter house. Ashley and Landon's house. Even their dad was staying with them. He and Elaine were using the spare bedroom on the main floor.

In the morning, she told herself. She had to find a moment alone with Erin in the morning and tell her exactly what was on her heart. The fact that she still had another chance was a gift from God alone. They walked through the front door at just before one in the morning, and like other days when they'd come home from the hospital this late, the lights were off, the kids asleep. Landon had held her hand as they drove and now as they walked inside. But they'd ridden home in mostly silence. It was enough to have him near. And besides, she needed time to formulate her thoughts.

"Let's go kiss the kids," Ashley whispered near Landon's ear.

He caught her gently, working his fingers through her hair and taking hold of the back of her head. His kiss took her by surprise, but it felt wonderful. A reminder that they were still alive. That life still had a chance even with so much death. He smiled at her, his eyes still marked by the constant sorrow they were all feeling. "Follow me."

She did, and they walked to Cole's room first. Devin and Janessa were in sleeping bags on Cole's floor, freeing up their rooms for several cousins. Ashley and Landon took turns stooping over their sleeping children and kissing their foreheads. She breathed in deep, savoring the combined smell of dirty shoes and clean sheets, and the innocence in each of their faces.

Cole was really struggling. He had texted her several times each day since the accident, telling her he was praying for her and asking her if she was okay. He was a good boy, a young man, really. His blond hair was darker now, nowhere near as light as Devin's still was. Devin and Janessa seemed concerned, but it was still a great week for them — same as it was for the other younger Baxter cousins. It was a time to play and laugh and be together. Like summer camp, only better.

A sort of cousin camp.

Landon put his arm around her and prayed in a quiet whisper, that the kids would sleep safely and that their hearts would be protected from bitterness or doubt in the wake of what had happened this week. It was a prayer they'd all uttered on behalf of their kids. Over and over again.

They poured glasses of water in the kitchen and took quiet steps back to their bedroom. Ashley shut the door behind them and flipped on the ceiling fan and the light. The room was stuffy, but since temperatures had dropped since sundown, she opened the window and let the cool breeze in.

A small sofa sat against one wall of their bedroom, and now Ashley took Landon's hand. "Can we talk for a minute?"

"Sure." He looked like he had something on his mind, too. "I was going to say the same thing."

Again Ashley felt her exhaustion. She would need a second wind to get through the next half hour. Before they could take another step, Ashley turned to him. "Thank you. For staying with me all day."

"Of course." Landon eased his arms around her and held her body against his. "My heart's breaking, too. I needed you as much as you needed me."

"I always need you."

"Mmm." Landon nuzzled her neck and left a light trail of kisses along her jawline and finally on her lips. He kissed her fully, and the moment turned more passionate.

Ashley loved how his kiss made her feel, like there was still hope that some day they could all be happy again. She smiled at him, even if she didn't feel her eyes quite come to life. In a move that made the world fade away, she touched the tip of her nose to his, their bodies connected in the embrace. "Yes." She kissed him once more. "I definitely need you."

They swayed that way for a minute or so, finding energy in the realness of each other, the warmth of the way their bodies fit together. "Okay, then." Ashley took a quick breath and a step back. "That's what I needed."

Landon's smile barely lifted his lips. "Me, too." He nodded to the sofa. "Can we sit?"

"Definitely." Ashley had thought all day about how she would begin this conversation. Now she couldn't remember a single option. "Okay, so I want to talk about the future." They faced each other. "All our lives, Landon ... all of it. I've never made life easy for you."

A softness appeared in Landon's eyes. "I never wanted anyone else."

"But it wasn't easy." She folded her hands, her knuckles white from the pressure. "You took on Cole as your own son when you married me and you never ..." Her voice cracked, and she stopped. She didn't want to cry again. So many tears over the last few days. "You never made me feel like a pariah for coming back from Paris pregnant. You just ... you just loved Cole like he was your own. Even when I wasn't ready for love. Even then you loved him. And you loved me."

"He was the most adorable little boy." Landon tilted his head, the light in his eyes a reflection of his soul. "If you never would've wanted me, I would've always loved him."

"See?" She tossed her hands and let them fall in her lap. "I was awful back then. I'll thank God every day as long as I live that He got my attention and snapped me out of my selfishness. To think I might've lost you …" She shook her head and the first tears hit her cheeks in earnest. "My whole painting thing and the purchase of this house, the way you did that for me." She shook her head a few quick times. "Really, Landon. It's never been easy."

He took both her hands in his. "Is this going somewhere?" His eyes danced the way they used to. Before the accident.

And suddenly in that moment it occurred to Ashley that the rest of time would be defined as life before the accident and life after it. Such a sad reality. She blinked a few times and remembered what was happening. Maybe she was too tired to have this conversation now. Maybe it should wait till morning.

She tried to focus. "No. I mean, yes. It's going somewhere." She tucked a few strands of her hair behind her ear. "What I'm trying to say is … I have an idea about Amy." She hesitated, holding her breath, waiting for his reaction.

He only nodded thoughtfully. "I think we should adopt her."

She had to find the right words, had to state this in a way that didn't sound crazy. Because she needed his support. That much was certain. "See, it doesn't really make sense for the others to — " She felt her eyes fly open. For a long time she only watched him, searched his eyes trying to understand if she'd really heard what she thought she just heard. Her voice was a tortured whisper when she finally spoke. "What did you say?"

He ran his thumbs along her hands and his eyes told her what his words had already said. "I think we should adopt her. I've been thinking it all day." He leaned forward and kissed her slowly. When he opened his eyes, he looked for her reaction. "If none of the others feel strongly about it. I mean, we'll have to wait and — "

"Landon!" She was in his arms like that, pulling him to his feet and holding on to him as if they'd been apart for a month.

"Are you serious?" Her tears were happy for the first time in what felt like forever.

"I am." His tone softened, and there wasn't a hint of anything but sincerity. "I'm ready to raise her as my own daughter." He kissed Ashley once more, and she felt herself getting lost in his arms, the closeness of him. "You were wrong what you said earlier. About it never being easy to love you." He brushed his face against hers and kissed her ear, her cheek, her lips. "It's been an adventure, Ash. It always will be." He leaned back and took hold of her shoulders. "If God takes Erin home, if He leaves Amy alone, then you and I will raise her and love her and be here for her — same as if she were our own little girl."

Ashley studied him, tears streaming down her face. "I . . . don't know what to say."

"Say you love me." Landon looked lost in her eyes, the same way she felt about his. Again he brushed his cheek against hers and kissed her.

When they came up for air, Ashley put her hands on either side of his face. "I love you, Landon Blake. Even before I was willing to admit it to myself, I loved you." She kissed him again. "I've always loved you. All my life."

It was true. But here she was pretty sure she'd never loved him more. She thought about the times when the hospital waiting room vigils were for him, and all she could think, all she could manage to utter in the recesses of her soul was a cry of gratitude to God. And at the same time a plea. Because in His very great mercy — though life was His to give and take — the Lord had given Landon his health back, and helped him find a way to fight his lung disease.

He had given her Landon.

Standing there in his arms, she felt convinced that God would grant them long life together — something she prayed for every night. For now and for the years ahead. She clung to him, her body needing his. *Let us live, Lord ... please. Protect us and bless us with long life, that we might grow old together. So that we can impact Cole and Devin and Janessa.*

And maybe even Amy Elizabeth.

Let heaven wait awhile longer, Father, so that we can be a light for the Baxter family, a light for our nieces and nephews and one day for our own grandkids.

Landon nuzzled his face against hers. "What are you thinking?" He tightened the hold he had on her, swaying with her, needing the life here in this moment as badly as she did.

"You. Me." She smiled at him, even while new tears blurred her eyes. "That God would let us live a long, long time. And even then," her lips touched his, "it wouldn't be long enough."

"No. It would never be enough." He crossed the room, flipped off the light switch and returned to her. Then he swept her into his arms and carried her gently to their bed. And for the next hour — despite their exhaustion — with everything in them they remembered what it was to truly love, even in a week seeped in death. Through passion and tears and the need they had for each other, they did the one thing they could do in light of the loss they'd suffered that week.

They celebrated life.

Twenty

JOHN HATED THE SAMENESS OF THEIR ROUTINE, THE WAY THEY woke up each morning and spent precious little time with the living, only to head off to the hospital and wait for death. That's what it felt like by the time Wednesday rolled around. A waiting game for death.

That morning was a little different. After having Cheerios with Devin and Tommy and Malin, John shared a cup of coffee on the front porch with Elaine, and he prepared to do something else he'd been dreading.

Make the call to Clear Creek Church and schedule the funeral.

The morgue had been holding the bodies of Sam, Clarissa, Chloe, and Heidi Jo, pending notification about arrangements for a memorial. But there was so much more to arrange than that. Kari and Reagan had promised to pull together a memorial, but they all wanted to wait and see what happened with Erin today.

If ... if she didn't make it, then everyone agreed they'd rather bury them together. The whole family except Amy Elizabeth. If Kari and Reagan planned the service, then John could take care of today's business. Before he called the church, he called the caretaker at the local cemetery, the place where Elizabeth and Ashley's little Sarah were buried. John had bought several plots when he purchased Elizabeth's.

At the time the guy had promised not to sell the plots adjacent to theirs, in case the day came when he needed more in the years to come. This was that day.

Elaine finished her coffee and gave him a half smile. "I think I'll go in with the kids."

He understood. Clearly John might want to be alone in a moment like this, when he would have to talk about his first wife and her cemetery plot and the reality of the funerals yet ahead. He squeezed her hand as she left and then turned his attention to the job ahead.

In the end, the task was simpler than he had thought. People who worked at cemeteries and churches and funeral homes knew how to handle the process of death. John was grateful. The caretaker at the cemetery sold John an additional ten plots — bringing the total to fifteen.

"Again, I've got another dozen plots you could pick up if you need to."

The man didn't mean to sound crass, but John closed his eyes at the thought. "I hope … it's a long time before you hear from me."

"Yes. That's what I mean … just want you to know you've got room."

"Thank you." John brushed off the sick feeling as he ended the call. So that was that. They could all be buried near Elizabeth. Far too many of his family members, memorialized in the same small section of grass just outside Bloomington. He breathed in deep, filled his lungs with the fresh summer air and faint smell of Elizabeth's roses.

He wondered about the reunion she must be having even at this moment. She loved her kids and grandkids so much. When little Sarah died of anencephaly the whole family found comfort in the fact that the baby would have her loving grandmother to hold her in heaven. He smiled despite his teary eyes. Now it would be a party up there.

His energy waned as he placed the call to the church and Mark Atteberry took his call. "We're praying, John. Around the clock. Literally."

"We can feel it." John narrowed his eyes, staring past the back porch to the rose garden. Elizabeth had loved those flowers. *I hope she has a rose garden up there, Lord. Please ... let her have a rose garden.* He blinked and tried to focus on what Mark was saying. "The prayer chain. Yes, thank you for that." He explained that they needed a service. Maybe as early as Saturday — especially since Dayne and Katy might need to leave on Sunday. Dayne had a movie he was involved in that started principle photography in Santa Monica that Monday.

"The thing is, I'm not sure about Erin." John hated saying it. He felt like he was betraying her somehow, the way he'd felt when he gave up believing in a miracle for Brooke's daughter, Hayley. But the reality remained. "They tell us she doesn't have long."

"Let's do this. We'll get things going. Let's assume it's Saturday. You keep in touch and let us know if things change."

John thanked him and with that he headed back into the house.

It was time to go to the hospital.

JOHN ARRIVED BEFORE THE OTHERS, AND he sat alone in the waiting room except for a woman sitting by herself a few seats down. She was reading a Bible. When John walked in she looked up and smiled and nodded, and he did the same.

Something about her looked familiar, but John couldn't quite remember where he'd seen her before. The woman was tall and slender, blue eyes and blonde hair and probably about his age. After a few minutes she closed her Bible. "Are you John Baxter?"

"I am." He narrowed his eyes. "I feel like I should know you."

"I'm Elizabeth Larsen. My daughter went to school with your son Luke."

Now he remembered her. They'd served on a few parent committees together. The woman was kind and helpful, a great asset to any project from what he recalled.

A shadow fell over her eyes. "I heard about your accident. My daughter works here as a nurse, so I thought ... I figured I'd come sit in the waiting room and pray." She looked at her watch. "I'm leaving in a few minutes. I've been here since seven this morning. Praying for your family."

Again John felt the tears in his eyes. How amazing that a woman who hadn't spoken with them in years would feel compelled to come here and pray. He waited until he could find his voice. "Thank you, Elizabeth. We certainly feel your prayers. They mean more than you know."

They talked for a few minutes about the condition of Erin and her family, and then, as she said, her daughter got off work and the two of them left. But even after they were gone, the sweet presence of the woman and her very deep faith remained. Proof that even in the darkest times, God cared about them.

And in this moment He must've wanted John to know.

The others arrived, and they met at the same two tables, and again John was grateful for the privacy of this waiting room. There were others associated with the ICU — all of them small and intended to give families moments like this. But still, there were times when other people had been in there with them. People like Elizabeth Larsen. As touching as John's moment with her had been, he was glad they were alone now.

Yesterday Luke had done his job, explaining the legal mess they might face if they lost Erin. Today, in light of the assignment Luke had given them, they needed to talk about who would take Amy. John had already told Luke that this meeting was one he would lead.

"I want to tell you all how much I love you." John folded his hands and looked at his kids, oldest to youngest, at the love and depth in their eyes, at the way they cared so deeply. "You've always been there for me and, before she died, for your mother. You've always been there for each other."

Around the table he saw movement, and when he realized

what was happening he felt the first catch in his voice. First Ashley and Kari and then gradually each of them joined hands, creating an undivided circle as they came together for what would inevitably be one of their most serious family moments ever.

"I'm proud of you." John tried to stay strong, but when tears filled his voice he didn't fight them. "We raised you to remember that you are Baxters, and that in this community that means something. But you ... each of you ... far exceeded that meaning. I want you to know that. I couldn't be more proud."

Several of them were crying softly now, the reality of what had happened over the last few days finally hitting some of them, the ones who didn't cry as easily like Landon and Ryan and Brooke and Peter. John ignored his tears, and he felt a new sort of strength fill his being. God was carrying him. The truth was freeing. He felt the weight of his next words before he even spoke them. "I'm assuming you've prayed about little Amy, about which of you might be able to take her."

He pulled his Bible from his bag and set it on the table. With ease and familiarity he opened it to Lamentations. "Before any of you respond, I want to read this. You all know it, but I read it again this morning and it reminded me that death will never win. Not in the end." He flipped to Lamentations 3:22–23. "Because of the LORD's great love we are not consumed, for his compassions never fail. They are new every morning; great is your faithfulness."

The Scripture settled in around the hearts and hands gathered at the table. He felt the words hit their mark for each of them, reminding them of the truth. Death would never have the last word.

"Listen." His tone was intense and kind, and he could feel that his eyes were, too. "There isn't one of you here who wouldn't do this. Each of you, all of you would say yes. But there's a right answer here at this table. If you've prayed about it, let's get that answer out so we can move forward."

Landon drew a sharp breath. "Ashley and I are ready to take her. We feel we could adopt her and raise her as our own."

Kari covered her face with her hands, her tears instant. At first John wondered if maybe his second oldest daughter might have come to the same conclusion. But Ryan cleared up the situation. "We didn't feel we could do it. But we were willing. We prayed someone would respond quickly when we got together this morning. That would be our answer."

Luke and Reagan nodded, their relief evident. "Same here."

Around the table the response was the same, and not until they'd all added their comments did John realize something. His tears had stopped. Their family had come together at yet another tremendously difficult moment, and John had proof once more that everything was going to be okay. They would hold each other up and help each other out and when one of them was without a home, someone would offer theirs. The way Ashley and Landon had stepped up this morning. They would live again and they would love again and they would keep their faith.

Because they were the Baxter family.

And because God's mercies really were new every morning.

ERIN WAS WORSE, AND THE MOMENT the meeting was finished John returned to Erin's bedside. The others were there, too. They'd been told that Amy wouldn't come out of her coma until the next day, so for now all their attention was on Erin. Their precious Erin.

John took the spot at the top of her bed, his hand on her pillow, stroking her hair the way he had done when she was a baby. Erin was their last little girl, and she'd always been young. Young in actions and young at heart, and young in her willingness to spend time with her parents. When she was five or six, she would come sit on the floor in front of wherever John was sitting.

"French braid my hair, Daddy. Please?" She'd hand him a hair tie and turn so her long blonde hair hung straight down her back.

It started off as something silly, but John became good at it. He mastered the ability to take three sections of Erin's hair from the top of her head and add to each section while braiding the pieces together. He remembered the last time she had him braid her hair.

She was twelve years old and she skipped in and sat on the floor in front of him. "I'm playing a prairie girl in a skit tomorrow, Daddy." She grinned over her shoulder at him. "Could you French braid my hair today? One last time?"

By then it had been a couple years since he'd done that, so he knew she was right. This would be the last time, and it was. John wondered what he would give now to have the chance for one more day back then, back when she was whole and alive and could run into the house with childlike abandon wanting nothing more than for her father to braid her hair.

Her blood pressure was lower now, her brain activity almost nonexistent. Dr. Hazel was right. She should have left them yesterday. Somehow he believed she was holding on for some specific reason. He figured it had something to do with Amy Elizabeth.

Another conversation came to mind, one he had with Erin just a week ago over Skype. They were talking and Amy Elizabeth had run up and climbed into her mother's lap. "Braid my hair, please, Mommy."

Erin had simply looked into the screen and laughed. "Feels like yesterday, doesn't it?"

John had laughed, too, because at the time there was no reason to be sad. They all felt like they had forever ahead of them. Erin began braiding Amy's hair and even told her daughter that her papa was a better braider than her. "He used to braid my hair when I was your age."

"Really?" Amy was squirmy. She giggled at the thought of her papa braiding her hair, and the moment Erin finished the girl was off and running.

John ran his hand over Erin's still head again. How could she be leaving him? His baby girl ... none of it was supposed to end this way. He pictured her with her girls at their last Fourth of July picnic, the happy way she looked and the friendship she had found with her sisters and brothers. For so many years Erin hadn't felt like she fit in. But she did now.

She did.

One at a time the others came in. They told Erin they loved her and that they'd see her when it was their turn to come home. It wasn't that it was too late to pray for a miracle, but they wanted their last words to be meaningful. Not ignorant of God's plan at work before them. If He was taking their sister home, they wanted to say good-bye.

Ashley was the last in the room. By then, Erin's breathing was raspier, more shallow. A transplant team had already been called in to harvest Erin's organs. A woman with two young children an hour away was slated to get her heart. It was the sort of detail John only knew because he had worked at the hospital for so many years.

"Hi." Ashley came up alongside her dad. "How is she?"

"She's leaving us." John leaned in and kissed Erin's cheek. "It's okay, baby. I know you need to leave. It's okay."

"I'm glad she's still here." Ashley was crying, but her voice was strong. "I have ... some things I need to tell her."

John nodded and took a half step back. "Is it okay if I stay?"

Ashley smiled through her tears. "Definitely." She moved in close and took hold of her sister's hand. "Erin ... I have some things I should've told you last time I was in here. But ... I couldn't find the words."

John watched, waiting. He hadn't known this was coming.

Ashley sniffed and used her shoulder to wipe her tears. "The thing is, Erin, I wasn't always the best sister. And I've thought about that a lot lately."

This wasn't what John was expecting at all. He crossed the room, found a tissue, and slipped it into Ashley's free hand. She thanked him with her eyes and dried her cheeks and nose. "I know we're good now, me and you. Our last talk was ... it was beautiful. I couldn't wait to see you. Really." She waited, searching her sister's face as if maybe somehow she would open her eyes and respond. One more time.

Ashley leaned a little closer. "The problem is ... I never said sorry. The way I acted back when ... when I came home from Paris? That was my fault. I was jealous, Erin. I wanted what you and Mom shared, and I was so far from it." She dabbed her tears again. "I didn't know what to do, so I was mean. Very mean." She scrunched her face, and fought a series of sobs. "I wish ... I wish we could go back. You and me. Just have one more time together when we were that young. So I could tell you how much I love you." She held the tissue to her eyes for a few seconds.

John came up beside her and put his hand on her shoulder. He hadn't known Ashley was wrestling with this, but he was more proud of her than ever before. *Help her find the words, Father ... And if this is Erin's time, help us give her what she needs to let go.*

Ashley lowered the tissue. "I do love you, Erin. And ... I've asked God to give me one more chance to prove it." A few quiet sobs escaped while Ashley fought for control. "And so He has given me a way. It's Amy Elizabeth." Gradually the tears slowed and Ashley seemed to find another level of strength. "I want you to know, that I will not let her go back to that woman. Candy Burns will not have a single visit with your sweet Amy. Because ..." She caught her breath a little more. "Landon and I are going to take care of her. Amy will be just fine, Erin. I promise you."

John squeezed Ashley's shoulder. This was exactly what Erin should know at this hour, that her little girl was going to be okay.

"We found your text … about the evidence you have on Candy. And we're going to find that, too. Luke's working on it." She leaned closer and released Erin's hand. She ran her hand along Erin's hair, her cheek. "We'll take care of her and love her like you have. Until we all come home to meet you."

"We'll all be together again, Erin." John was at Ashley's side again. He held his youngest daughter's hand and felt the lifelessness of it. "I love you, honey."

"I love you, Erin. I should've said it more." Ashley bent close and kissed her sister's cheek. "When I see you next time … we'll have a lot to catch up on."

Something was happening with the monitors. Erin was on life support, but the machines were set up to let her heart and lungs work on their own. It was one way to evaluate her actual condition. Now, almost as if she had been waiting to know Amy would be okay, a look of otherworldly peace seemed to fill Erin's expression.

John straightened and looked from Erin's face to the monitors and back again. "She's going." He looked back at one of the nurses who had just entered the room. "Please … get the others."

"Yes, Dr. Baxter." The woman hurried off.

Ashley sucked in a slow breath. "Dad … what's happening?"

"Her heart's giving up." He brought Erin's hand to his lips and kissed it. "It's your time, baby girl. It's okay. Go be with your mom. She's waiting for you. Look for Sam, baby. Look for your girls. They're there. Waiting for you."

Ashley looked like she wasn't sure if she should run from the room or stay. "Dad," she leaned into him. "I don't know if I can do this."

"You can." He was calm, his cheeks dry. "Picture your mother, Ashley. Picture Sam and Clarissa and Chloe and Heidi Jo. All of them looking for Erin and excited." He felt the joy in his voice, the real joy. "She's coming home. Nothing could be greater than that."

Every Bible verse about life and death came together in John's mind. *To be absent with the body is to be present with the Lord ... those who love the Lord will never taste death ... death is swallowed up in victory ... Jesus answered, I tell you the truth: Today you will be with Me in paradise ... Whoever believes in Him will not perish but have eternal life ... If anyone keeps My word, he will never see death ... Whoever lives and believes in Me will never die.*

Do you believe this?

John could almost hear the Lord asking him the same question he asked his disciples more than two thousand years ago. *Yes, Lord ... yes, I believe.*

The others were piling into the room now, and like John most of them were dry-eyed. The apostle Paul said it best. *For me, to live is Christ and to die is gain.* How could they do anything but celebrate this moment? All of them would face it one day ... in a fraction of an instant, in the midst of a lifetime it would be their turn.

But not everyone got to go home like this.

John reached out his hand and took hold of Ashley's on one side and Kari's on the other. In no time the group had formed a circle around Erin's bed. John remembered the Bible verse from earlier and suddenly he knew what they needed to do. With a steady voice, steadier than he would've imagined for this moment, he slowly began to sing.

"Great is Thy faithfulness, oh God my Father. There is no shadow of turning with Thee."

Kari and Ryan and Dayne and Katy added their voices. "Thou changest not, Thy compassions they fail not. As Thou has been, Thou forever will be."

One by one every voice added in as the song grew and built. John didn't need to watch the monitors any longer. He could see on her face that she was leaving. He wished with all his heart he could be in that place where she was going — even for a few minutes. To see the look on Elizabeth's face and to experience the eternal reunion that would be happening any moment now.

"Great is Thy faithfulness. Great is Thy faithfulness … morning by morning new mercies I see." The chorus built until all the Baxter family was singing together, their voices united as one. John saw in the corner of his eye nurses and a few doctors joining them near the door, giving them this moment but wanting to share it, too. Several of them were crying.

But not the Baxters. Not this time. The circle seemed to grow stronger, their voices sweeter. As if they wouldn't consider sending their sister and daughter home to heaven without letting her know exactly how much she was loved. How certain they were of her place in heaven.

Gradually, the sound of the machines slowed until they stopped. They watched Erin's body relax a little, watched her spirit take flight. And even then they kept singing.

"Pardon for sin, and a peace that endureth. Thine own dear presence to cheer and to guide." Their voices weren't overly loud, but they were as sweet as any angel chorus. John knew he would remember the sound as long as he lived. "Strength for today and bright hope for tomorrow, blessings all mine and ten thousand beside."

John couldn't have planned this moment better if he'd scripted it. Ashley wasn't crying anymore. Her eyes were trained on Erin's face, the same way they all seemed mesmerized by her. They didn't need words beyond the song because John could see they were all thinking the same thing.

As the song wound down, as Dr. Hazel moved in and confirmed that Erin's body had given up, John was struck by the very great truth in the moment. God's faithfulness was unequaled, His mercies new every single morning. For this was no longer a tragic moment, sad and devastating. It was his family holding each other up, believing God's promise that those who loved Him never tasted death. Never. It wasn't so much that Erin was leaving them. It was like he had told Ashley.

She was coming home.

THE SINGING WAS ERIN'S FAVORITE PART. The special hymn from so many Sunday services, sung by the voices she loved most. The voices of her family. And before that there had been her father, reminding her of so many beautiful moments, and Ashley.

Dear sweet Ashley.

Erin tried to tell her everything was okay. She already knew Ashley was sorry for the things she'd said way back then, the way she'd acted. There was no need for Ashley to feel bad or conflicted. The past was behind them.

But every time Erin tried to open her mouth nothing came out. She pushed and strained, and finally she ran out of effort and did the only thing she could do. She enjoyed the words being spoken to her, the message in the words — not just from Ashley and her dad, but from all of them

Her entire family.

But then gradually she began to feel herself slipping. Not slipping away, just slipping from the place she was to another place, slowly ... like the opening of a flower in spring, the stunning place she'd seen before appeared before her eyes again. The beautiful field, even brighter than before. The greens and blues and purples and yellows more vibrant than anything she'd ever seen.

Even in Ashley's paintings.

And there in the midst of the field was the table again and one at a time faces that she dearly loved came into view. Her mother, healthy and smiling, and beside her more of her family. A sense of elation filled Erin and worked its way through her heart and mind and soul. There was Sam and Clarissa and Chloe and Heidi

Jo. So many of them, and they were calling to her, welcoming her and she knew this would be the most unbelievable time of her life.

But ... but where was Amy Elizabeth?

"I'll go find her," she yelled to the others. They mustn't have heard her because they were still smiling and talking with each other and having what looked like the best time ever.

"I can't come now!" Erin couldn't hear her own words, either, but she tried to find her way back to the other side. Turning and searching for the place with less colors. The place where Amy Elizabeth was. "Amy ... where are you?"

The colors disappeared again and there was the blur of grays and blacks and whites and she could hear Ashley once more. Erin tried to focus, tried to hear what her sister was saying. Something else, not the part about being sorry. *Dear Lord, You're here with me. I can feel Your Spirit ... help me hear my sister. I can't understand ...*

Daughter, be still ... I am with you.

And with that Ashley's voice was suddenly clear, the message unmistakable. Ashley was going to take care of Amy. She wasn't going to let anything happen to her. The news relaxed her and gave her the permission she needed, permission to find her mom and Sam and the other girls. Ashley would take care of everything. She would keep her safe from Candy Burns. She and their dad were telling her it was okay, she could go to the place of the blues and greens and purples, the place where God's love felt like the brightest color, the one overlaying all the others.

Amy Elizabeth would be okay.

The peace inside her became a song and everyone she loved was singing it. The beautiful words from her favorite hymn filled her and surrounded her. *Great is Thy faithfulness, Oh God my Father ... there is no shadow of turning with Thee ...*

It was true. He was calling to her even now, at this very

moment, and this time she could see it all, colors and sounds and smells more alive than anything in any place Erin had ever been. "Mommy!" It was Heidi Jo, and Erin began to run across the grass. And the field felt like silk beneath her feet. They were coming to her now, all of them. Erin couldn't hear her siblings' voices anymore, couldn't hear her father. But that was okay. They would all be together soon. She knew that without asking.

For now she was consumed by the reality of this new and wonderful place and the people she was with. Sam and the girls, and her mother. Erin smiled as she flew into their arms, as Sam swung her around and her mother pulled her close and the girls and her little niece took turns hugging her. This place was wonderful, and she could sense the Lord with them. Not like before, but in a much more real way. And no one was in a hurry. Suddenly the reunion was all she could think about, all she could imagine. She could hardly wait to sit at the picnic table with them.

She and her mom had so much to talk about.

Twenty-One

EVER SINCE THE ACCIDENT, DAYNE FELT LIKE HE WAS DRAGGING the broken pieces of his heart around on a rope behind him. Like he never had time to stop and pray and put things back together again. The drama had played out that quickly. Yes, he was grateful he'd been there with the others, and there were moments they'd shared this past week that would stand forever as some of his most beautiful. He was sure about that.

But still he and Katy needed a break from the sadness, even just to pray and find the strength to help the others. And so that Friday morning, he and Katy left the kids with his dad and Elaine. The time away had been his father's idea. "I need to be with my grandkids," his dad told him. "You and Katy go live. We all need to embrace life. That's what Erin would've wanted."

Dayne made a plan that he and Katy would use Kari and Ryan's boat at the Lake Monroe Marina, and they'd take two of their favorite people with them: Bailey and Brandon Paul. Dayne and Katy had mentored the young couple before their March wedding. Katy had known Bailey for eight years. Since Bailey was fifteen.

The two had honeymooned in the South Pacific on Turtle Island in Fiji, and now they lived on the lake in the house Dayne once bought for Katy. It would be great to catch up with them, hear how married life was going and how the two were doing with their plan to expand Christian Kids Theater.

A few phone calls later and Dayne had set the plan in motion. Both Bailey and Brandon were available. Dayne and Katy would swing by in their rental car to pick them up at the lake house, and they'd spend a good part of the day on the water. The others were still waking up and making coffee, talking about taking walks or going to the park. Dayne thanked his sister and brother-in-law and they promised to be back for dinner.

"Good." Their dad smiled. "We have enough casseroles for the whole neighborhood."

They weren't back to laughing. Not yet. But the celebration of Erin's home-going had been so beautiful that this much was true: The depressing sense of tragedy had passed. There were still tears, of course. Even that late morning as Dayne and Katy left. But the Baxter family was surviving.

When he was behind the wheel, the window rolled down, a warm summer breeze in his face, Dayne exhaled in a way that made him wonder if he hadn't been holding his breath all week. "I need this."

Katy put her hand on his knee and stayed quiet. Every statement didn't need a response. It was one of the things he loved about her.

"I mean ... everyone's been talking about when Erin was three and when she was eight and how sweet she was in high school." He held tight to the wheel. "But none of that applies to me. I didn't know her until she was married with kids."

"Honey ... you should've told me." She drew closer, watching his face even while he watched the road. "I didn't know you were feeling that way."

"It added up." He glanced at her, his eyes soft. "I wasn't mad. Just that it made me realize again how much I missed."

"Hmm." Katy seemed to mull that over for a long moment. "I bet you learned more about your family than you knew before."

"Volumes." Dayne let the reality hit. "Definitely. I know all of them better. For sure."

Again Katy was quiet. She settled back into her seat and put her window down as well. "A day at the lake will be good. For both of us."

He realized then that Katy hadn't really had a break from the kids and the cooking and caring for the group since the accident. She'd only spent part of the time at the hospital, and despite her hours of serving, she hadn't complained.

"Katy ... I'm sorry."

"What?" Her smile was as genuine as the smell of jasmine in the air. "Why are you sorry, Dayne Matthews?"

"I haven't thanked you. For all the hours you stayed at the house helping Elaine and Reagan." He reached out and touched her blonde hair, ran his fingers through it. "I miss you."

She turned her head and this time her eyes smiled at him. Even for just a few seconds. "I miss you, too."

"It's almost more than I can grasp, all the loss in the last few days."

"Which was why yesterday was so wonderful." Katy's voice sounded dreamy. "I never looked forward to heaven more than watching Erin go. Like one minute she was here and earthbound and trapped by machines and wires, and the next ..."

"The next she was in paradise." Dayne felt the deepest sadness mix with the greatest possible joy. "With her husband and girls." He paused, staring at the road ahead. "And with our mother."

"Since then I've been too hopeful to feel trapped in pain."

"I like that." Dayne felt his tension let up. "Too hopeful to feel trapped in pain. Very nice, Katy."

"Thanks." She laughed, and then she seemed to catch herself. As if she didn't want to violate the unwritten rule about how long after a tragedy people needed to wait before they could laugh.

"Don't stop yourself." Dayne slipped his fingers between hers and cherished the feel of her skin. "We're alive. We're supposed to laugh." He glanced at her. "Think about those little girls. Of course it's okay to laugh, Katy."

A quiet fell over the car and Dayne thought about his youngest sister. The loss of Erin and Sam and three of their girls hit him differently than the others. At least his siblings had grown up with Erin. They had a lifetime of memories with her. Dayne's memories with Erin and her family were limited. He would feel the difference tomorrow, no doubt. The funeral was set for noon at Clear Creek Church, one service for all five of them. Dayne was grateful he and Katy were here, grateful they could all be together.

But today he needed to pray, needed time on the lake so he could face tomorrow.

Bailey and Brandon were waiting outside, checking on the blueberries that grew in a small garden on the side of the house. They had a plastic container full of the berries and a beach bag as they approached Dayne and Katy's rented car.

Dayne slipped it into park and he and Katy hurried out to meet the younger couple. They exchanged hugs and a subdued greeting. Before they climbed back in the car, Bailey put her arm around Brandon's waist, her eyes beyond sad. "How are you, really?"

"Really?" He looked at Katy for a long beat and then back at Bailey. "I'm worn out. Since Saturday the days have been the very worst, and then yesterday ... I don't know — that was maybe one of the best."

Katy took hold of his hand and explained how they had watched Erin go to heaven — right before their eyes.

Not until two hours later when they were on the other side of the lake and Dayne cut the engine did the conversation turn to Bailey and Brandon. "So ... how's married life?" Dayne joined the others at the back of the boat. They were in a cove with almost no boat traffic, so the air around them was still. The warm sun and gentle swells of the lake beneath them felt good on Dayne's soul.

"Amazing." Brandon was quick to answer.

"Waking up with your best friend ... being together like this," the sparkle in Bailey's eyes was brighter than the sun on the lake. "It's the most wonderful time ever. I never dreamed it would be like this."

The couple shared how they were growing their theater business, still keeping CKT, but adding a more professional round of shows and auditions. "It'll be open to people of any age, but we'll incorporate a Bible study with the rehearsal process." Brandon's expression told them how happy he was about this. "I never want to live in LA again."

Dayne chuckled. "It's not for everyone." He was proud of his friend. Brandon left at the height of his public popularity. He was still one of the favorite actors in the nation, maybe even in the world. But he had grown tired of the constant paparazzi and insanity.

"It's like I dreamed it would be." Brandon leaned back and turned his face to the sun. He had his arm around Bailey's bare shoulders. "We get to live our lives. We wake up and read the Bible together. We go to the store and to church and to the theater." His smile looked marked by peace. Something that had often been missing before. "It's like I was born for this."

"And we love working together." Bailey turned to him, and for a moment they were lost in their own world. She looked back at Dayne and then Katy. "We have so many dreams for CKT and the theater. Like maybe one day people will think of Bloomington as a place where they'd come to see live shows."

"We've made an offer on some storefront space on either side of the building we already own." Brandon laughed. "We're not taking over downtown just yet, but we have a vision for it."

They explained how part of their ideas for renovations included free office space for people in mission work. "Theater meets mission." Bailey laughed lightly. "We can fill the downtown with people who want the world to know about Jesus, and still make it the most artsy place this side of New York City." She grinned at her husband. "With a coffee shop and boutiques and little restaurants. That's the dream, anyway."

Somewhere through the course of the day, Dayne realized something that made his heart feel light, made him feel like he would find his way back to daylight at the end of this week. He hadn't thought about death for more than an hour. He took the wheel of the boat again and drove them along the edge of the lake to a private beach a ways down. Dayne and Brandon worked to dock the boat, and the four of them sat in beach chairs, their towels spread out on the sand.

There the conversation continued and eventually it returned to the accident.

"The news reached every part of the country." Brandon's voice fell a notch. "I can't imagine what it's been like for your family. We're just so sorry."

Katy looked out at the lake. "At first it was like ... this can't be happening. I mean, we're all gathered at Ashley's house waiting to give John Baxter this surprise party and there're these sirens. Like everywhere and all around us. Just sirens and more sirens."

Bailey hung her head for a moment, and reached for Brandon's hand. "How terrible."

Dayne nodded. "Everyone who arrived at the house was talking about it. Kari and Ryan, Luke and Reagan, Brooke ... we all heard them, and a few of us saw ambulances. We had no idea what was happening. The last thing that occurred to most of us was that Erin might be involved."

"The driver didn't make it, right? That's what I read."

"He didn't." Dayne put his elbow on the arm of the chair and felt Katy's skin brush against his. "He fell asleep, but his seat belt was off. Almost like he must've been thinking about pulling over and getting some sleep. Like his body somehow thought he was already parked and he could climb out of his seat and into his bunk. That's all we can figure."

"His family must be devastated." Bailey shook her head. "The reports say it was one of the worst accidents in Indiana history."

"I think about all that, and then I picture Erin last night." Katy lifted her face to the bright blue sky. "She's not worried or hurting or frightened. She's alive, more than ever before. Same as the rest of her family. All except Amy."

They were quiet for a moment, letting the gravity of the situation, the hope of it, settle between them. After a while, Bailey told them how her family was doing, the boys with their sports, and Connor with his singing. He was on a scholarship to Liberty University and enjoying being home for the summer. His plans to audition for *American Idol* were on hold for another year, since his college singing and touring commitments wouldn't allow him time at this point.

"What about Cody Coleman?" Katy asked the question.

"He's great." Bailey smiled and leaned in a little closer to Brandon. "In fact, he and Andi got engaged on Saturday." Bailey didn't seem to connect the fact that the engagement had happened on the same day as the accident. "The wedding will be around Christmas sometime. Andi said they're working on a date."

Dayne was glad for the young guy. Cody had gone off to war and lost the lower part of his left leg. Before that, like Katy, Cody had lived with the Flanigan family. In the early days, Bailey and Cody had shared feelings for each other, but God had moved them past that time. Cody lived in Southern California now, coaching high school football. Andi was Bailey's former college roommate. Even though that time in Bailey's life was long past, Cody was enough a part of Bailey's history, that Dayne wasn't surprised to hear Katy ask about him.

"Andi must be thrilled." Katy's voice held a joy that had been missing since Saturday. "She's been through so much. I'm thrilled for them."

They kept talking about Bailey's friends, about the past and the faithfulness of God, but Dayne felt himself tuning out, distracted by certainty that even on days marked by the deepest sorrow, life and love still reigned. On the day of the accident, while death had its way out on Highway 37, people were celebrating summer and boating on Lake Monroe, welcoming babies and falling in love.

Cody and Andi had even gotten engaged.

It was further proof that the song they'd sung around Erin's hospital bed was rich with truth. God was faithful, His mercies ever new. And no matter how dark the night, this much would always be true.

Morning would come.

CANDY BURNS HAD TRIED EVERYTHING TO remove the Facebook post, but she was out of options. Nothing worked. She had left the private message on Erin Hogan's page and now there was no way to get rid of it. She sat at her mother's computer and silently cursed herself for being so careless. That night she'd gone out with some of her old friends and gotten drunk. Not a little wasted, but drunk. Smashed drunk. She barely remembered writing the post, and now as she read it for the twentieth time she cursed herself again.

The post might be the very thing that would do her in this time. She might as well have walked herself into the child protective services office and signed away her rights to ever coming out ahead where Amy was concerned.

She leaned back hard in the plastic computer chair. The accident was a new twist. The death of two of her girls. Candy tried to feel sad about their loss, but it was difficult. They were in heaven — that's the way Erin and Sam had raised them to believe, no doubt. And now Candy had less kids to worry about.

Less kids and more money.

It was her mother who first thought about the possibility of an inheritance. That was after they got word that Erin was dead, too. Candy and her mother had been sitting at her mother's small kitchen table, looking out the window of her third-floor apartment when her mother's expression changed. "They had to have insurance."

"What?" Candy didn't get it at first. A lot of good insurance would do the family, now that most of them were dead. "For Amy's hospital bills?"

"No." Her mother snapped at her. The woman had been more testy than usual lately. "Life insurance. A couple like the Hogans? Probably had a boatload of insurance."

Candy might not have been the sharpest knife in the drawer but it took no time to reach the conclusion her mother was hinting at. "So you're saying..."

"I'm saying you just hit the lottery." Her mother laughed, but not in a mean sort of way. Usually her mother was a pretty stable person. It didn't make her bad, just because she was happy for Candy over this new development. "Wherever Amy goes, the money will go. We could live very, very comfortably."

Candy didn't correct her mother about her use of the word *we*. Besides, the woman couldn't stay in one place longer than a few months. She got cabin fever too easily. Already she'd hinted a few times that her style had been cramped by Candy — who had no job, no car, and nowhere to live except with her mother. Candy's release from prison made it less possible for Lu to think about getting work on another cruise line — something she wanted to do before the summer was up.

At first when she realized there was probably money involved, she actually talked her mom into driving to Indiana so they could show up at the hospital and sit with Amy. So it would be clear that she was theirs and not anyone else's. She and her mom packed a couple bags, tossed them in the back of her old Buick and headed out of town.

They got about ten miles down the interstate when the Buick threw a rod. Her mother had to call a friend with a tow truck and they spent the rest of the day at the shop, while her mom complained about how much Candy was costing her.

It didn't matter. She'd pay her mother back.

With very little imagination, Candy could see this working just fine. She and Amy could live in the house here, rent free, and have all the money just to live on. A new car, new clothes. The jewelry she had never been able to buy for herself. She could probably find a nice man with that kind of money.

Not that she knew exactly what kind of money they were talking about. But life insurance was usually a whole lot. Enough to live on for years and years, at least that's what her mother had guessed. So maybe a hundred thousand or two hundred thousand. Something like that.

The thought made Candy giddy with anticipation. She could hire a sitter for Amy, so she could go out with her friends at night. Every night if she wanted. Sure she and Amy would have some time together. She wouldn't want the girl to run away or anything. But she could hardly wait to have a little cash in her pocket. She could take her girlfriends somewhere nice for a change. The kinds of places where the rich men hung out.

Yes, everything was about to change for Candy, and according to Naomi Boggs — the social worker — there was going to be a hearing in a week or so. More of a technicality from what Candy understood. Because of the open adoption agreement, with the adoptive parents dead, Amy officially belonged to Candy's mother. But since Candy was out of prison and since she'd taken those tedious parenting classes, and of course since she was Amy's actual mother, the judge would probably give her custody.

Candy and her mother had decided the hearing was more of a formality. Erin had a bunch of sisters and brothers — at least that's what Candy's mother had said. She couldn't imagine anyone wanting Amy. Maybe visits once in a while so they wouldn't feel guilty about moving on. But Amy wasn't a blood relative. She was adopted from a felon, after all.

What use would Erin's family have with her?

That's what Candy had figured until just this very moment. Now, as she sat in the Friday evening dark staring at her stupid private Facebook message to Erin, Candy was haunted by a possibility. If she wanted Amy for the insurance money, maybe someone in Erin's family would feel the same way. And if they felt the same way, they would fight Candy for custody of the girl. And if they fought for custody, the private Facebook message could ruin Candy's chances forever.

That was definitely a possibility.

Which would be the greatest tragedy of all, because the kid was probably worth a fortune. But only to the person who raised her.

"How could you be such an idiot," she whispered out loud at her reflection in the computer screen. A string of expletives rolled off her tongue. She'd sent the message early Friday morning. Just after she'd stumbled in the door from her wild Thursday night. There was a chance no one from Erin's family had seen it, but then the social worker had called. Candy tried to ask sly kinds of questions to see if Naomi Boggs knew whether Erin or Sam had seen the message.

She used her most sad voice. "So ... when did the family leave for Indiana?"

There was a long pause. "When did they leave?" Naomi seemed puzzled. "Two of your daughters were killed in a car accident. And you ask when did they leave?"

"Look." Candy had to think fast. "I don't appreciate your tone,

Mrs. Boggs. I'm trying to ... to picture my girls in their final days. I just wondered if they drove straight through or what?"

The woman seemed super irritated. "As far as I know they left Friday morning."

"Do you know what time?" Candy regretted the question immediately.

"Again ... I'm not sure I understand your interest, Mrs. Burns." The social worker came across awfully high and mighty. "I thought you might have questions about Amy, since she's still alive."

"Give me time." Her voice was a little too angry, so she toned it down. "I'm only trying to understand the whole thing. Like ... did Erin or Sam say anything about me? Like after they started for Indiana?"

"Mrs. Burns, I'm sorry. I need to get back to work." The woman sounded downright angry now. "If you have questions about your surviving daughter, feel free to call me. Until then, and unless you're willing to be more transparent with the purpose of your questions, I have other duties to tend to."

Now, as Candy replayed that conversation in her mind and a second one she had with Naomi Boggs late yesterday, she had a horrible feeling the social worker knew about the private Facebook message. Why else would she be so short on the phone? Candy blinked, her mind a foggy mess. Of course, if Naomi knew about the message, why hadn't she said anything?

It was possible Erin and Sam hadn't seen it before they left Friday morning, and if they had ... it was just as possible that they hadn't shared the news with Naomi. They would've been busy driving and talking and looking forward to the family visit in Indiana. Yes, that was it. Candy smiled to herself and pushed back from the computer. No one would ever see what she'd written that drunken Friday morning. They would have the hearing and she would win back Amy, and the insurance money would be hers. She had nothing to worry about.

Who checked their private Facebook messages the morning before a trip?

Twenty-Two

ASHLEY SPENT ALL OF FRIDAY AT AMY'S BEDSIDE.

She and Landon were both there when her doctor eased her out of the induced coma before sunrise, and when Landon returned home to the other kids and the rest of the family before noon, Ashley stayed. She'd been mostly sleeping, but a few times she opened her eyes and spotted Ashley and Landon. Amy would look around the room, as if she was looking for her parents or her sisters, and then she'd close her eyes again.

"She's going to be very tired for the first day or two." Brooke had been in constant contact, doing what she could to help Ashley understand the process. "What do the doctors say about her injuries?"

"They're healing. Her arm's in a cast, of course. And she's still very bruised. But they say she can go home Saturday evening." Ashley paused, feeling the weight of the sadness to come. How would she tell Erin's youngest daughter that everyone else in her family was gone? "I guess overall everything's healing the way it should on the inside." Everything but her heart, Ashley wanted to add. The part that might never heal.

"Are you coming home tonight?" Brooke was already back at the Baxter house with the others. "She'll be okay, Ash. She won't know you're there."

"I'll know." Ashley sat in the chair closest to Amy's bed. She reached out and took the child's small hand. "I promised Erin I'd take care of her."

Brooke didn't push the issue. None of the others did, either. And so now that it was Friday night, Ashley grabbed a quick salad at the hospital cafeteria and thanked the nurses for putting a cot in Amy's room. She would sleep when it got late enough. For now she intended to sit next to the little girl and hold her hand. *Please, God ... soften the blow. Protect her heart from the enormity of what she'll be waking up to. Father ... she needs You so badly.*

Do not fear, daughter. I will carry you and her ... now and always.

Ashley felt the whisper of God to the center of her anxious being. Even yesterday while they were singing Erin toward heaven, Ashley couldn't stop thinking about little Amy. If the child would belong to her and Landon, then her emotional and physical well-being would be their responsibility.

Amy's room was the first place Ashley went after they said their good-byes to Erin. Even before the doctor started bringing her out of the coma. Landon left to sleep at home for a few hours, and before he did he cautioned her. "You can't take away the pain, Ash."

"I know." She had studied the little girl, imagining her unsuspecting heart. "I just don't want her to be alone." Her eyes found Landon's. "Erin would want me to stay."

Now it was a full twenty-four hours later, and the funeral was tomorrow. Ashley planned to leave the hospital around eight in the morning, get dressed at the house, and attend the service with the rest of the family, from the church service to the cemetery. The moment they were done, she planned to be back here. Especially if tomorrow night Amy might get to go home.

The child was still on an IV and other monitors, but she was stable. Whatever that meant in light of the losses she faced. Ashley watched her roll onto her side. She grimaced, her brow forming a V over her sweet face. Her nurse had told Ashley the child would be in quite a bit of pain for a while, the result of major bruising and strained muscles throughout her body.

Ashley still had a tender hold of the girl's hand when her eyes began to flutter. Then, for the first time since the accident, her eyes opened all the way. She closed them again and after several minutes, she blinked them open again. Instead of looking away or searching for someone else, in the dim light of the hospital room she squinted at Ashley. And for the first time since the accident she opened her mouth and tried to speak. It took work, and her pain was evident in her expression, but finally she eked out, "Hi, Aunt Ashley."

This wasn't the time to cry, but Ashley had to blink away her tears so she could see the girl clearly. "Hi, sweetie. How do you feel?"

"Sick." She frowned again and shifted herself one way and then another. "Everything hurts." She let her eyes make a careful search of the room. "Where am I?"

"In the hospital. The doctors are taking care of you."

"Why?"

The child's single word undid Ashley. She held her breath, silently begging God for the words. The medical team working Amy's case had advised that when she woke up, they should tell her the truth. "Tell her gradually," the doctor had said. "Don't worry. You'll know what to say and when."

"Aunt Ashley," her words were croaky and barely more than a strained whisper. "Why am I in the hospital?"

Ashley felt panic rise within her until it was up to her neck, threatening to consume her. *Help me, God ... I'm not sure I can do this.*

I am with you, Daughter ... I am always with you.

The truth settled her heart. Ashley leaned closer, and with her free hand she brushed the blonde hair off Amy's forehead. "You were in an accident, baby. Your whole family."

Amy blinked, her eyes beyond blue even here in the shadows. "Was my family hurt, too?"

"Yes." This time Ashley could feel the Lord's hands on her shoulders, feel Him beside her, His spirit bringing calm to the moment. Ashley tried to divert the conversation. "You were sleeping for a long time."

She blinked again, confusion still coloring her expression. "I'm still tired." She squinted again, as if maybe her head hurt or she was trying to see clearly. "I had a dream."

"You did?" Ashley's heartbeat quickened. "Tell me about it."

"It was pretty." The girl smiled, a shy, slight, little smile that was gone as soon as it came. But still it gave Ashley hope. "We were having a picnic in a field." Her words were slow, her tone still groggy and hoarse. "Everyone was there. Mommy and Daddy ... Clarissa and Chloe ... me and Heidi Jo." Her eyes lit up a little. "There was someone else. I think she was our grandma. That's what she told me. And there was another little girl named Sarah." She thought for a second. "Remember that pretty painting, Aunt Ashley?" She stopped, tired from the story. "The one in the playroom?"

If Ashley hadn't been sitting down, she probably would've fainted. Amy was describing a scene she'd painted years ago, one that hung in their playroom to this day. The painting was of her mother in heaven with baby Sarah, the two of them in a beautiful field of flowers. She struggled to find her voice. "Yes. I remember."

"It was like that." Amy yawned and her eyelids looked heavy again. "It was so beautiful, Aunt Ashley. I didn't want to leave. But Grandma said we'd all be back there one day."

And like that the girl yawned again and closed her eyes. She was asleep before Ashley had the chance to exhale. Was it possible? That somehow Amy had been given a glimpse of her family in heaven? That her mother had spoken to the child and that little Sarah had been there, too? Had God allowed this as a way of lessening the blow for Amy? If not for her faith, Ashley wouldn't have believed the child's account of her dream. She would've thought the girl was confusing the painting with some strange vision and an overactive imagination.

After all, Amy was little more than a baby when her grandmother died. As far as Ashley knew, she'd never asked about the painting in the playroom. Even if she knew a little of what her grandmother looked like, that wouldn't explain the child having a conversation with her. In a beautiful grassy field, surrounded by the rest of her family?

Ashley noticed the chills on her arms, the ones still making their way down to her feet. She remembered a passage from 1 Corinthians, chapter 13 . . . something she'd read in preparation for tomorrow's memorial service. It was the section of Scripture most known for its description of love. But tucked in the midst of that was a verse that said, *Now I know in part; then I shall know fully, even as I am fully known.*

Now we only know in part, right, Lord? That's what You're showing me. Because there was no real explanation for the dream Amy had shared with her. Whether it was an actual visit or a vision or simply a dream given to her from God alone. And no way of knowing whether she'd remember it again in the morning. For now if nothing else it gave Ashley the chance to see something she desperately believed to be true.

The picture of Erin and her family, and her mother and Sarah, all of them together and in a most wonderful place called heaven. If God would give Amy a picture like that, then Ashley had nothing to worry about.

God would carry them through whatever heartache lay ahead.

THE QUESTION DIDN'T COME WHEN AMY stepped from her hospital bed into the wheelchair and was pushed down the hall with Ashley and Landon and Cole. It didn't come as they went through the glass double doors or as the nurse who walked them out made sure they were okay, and as she headed back inside with the wheelchair. In the tense quiet, Ashley and Cole stood on either side of Amy, their arms around her frail shoulders, as they waited while Landon went to get their Toyota 4-Runner.

"It's hot out here." Amy looked up at her. Katy and Dayne had bought Amy a few new outfits on Friday after their day at the lake. She wore one of them now, a pretty pink and white shirt, pink leggings and white Converse tennis shoes. She seemed strong, able to handle the work of standing as they waited for Landon to pull up. "It's still summer, right, Aunt Ashley?"

"Yes, sweetheart. Summer's just getting started."

Cole swapped a nervous look with Ashley. At fifteen he was already taking on the role of older brother to his new little sister. But even with the concern in his eyes, neither he nor Ashley pushed the conversation. They were following doctor's orders, letting Amy ask the questions, but at some point soon the truth had to come out. She understood his concern. The question about her family had to come up soon. Cole pulled out his phone and stooped down next to Amy. "Have I showed you Devin's frogs? He's caught about twenty this week."

"Really?" She looked interested, but not overly so. She looked at the pictures and smiled, but then she quickly turned her look to Ashley, and her smile was gone. "Are we leaving the hospital?"

"Yes." Ashley put her arm around Amy's shoulders. "We're going back to my house. The Baxter house." Ashley felt her heart begin to race. "Remember that?"

"Yes." She looked over her shoulder, straining to see someone, anyone. "What about my mommy and daddy? Are they coming?"

Ashley felt herself falling, felt gravity double its hold on her.

"Well ... honey ..." She turned and faced Amy, just as she heard Landon pull up behind her. She had told him about the previous night, about Amy's dream and how strangely real and comforting it had been. Now she hoped Landon could help her remind Amy of the details.

"Want me to get Dad?" Cole asked his question in a whisper. The fear in his voice reminded her of her own.

"Yes." Ashley nodded, and she watched Cole hurry over and open the passenger door. She focused all her attention on the blonde girl, her arm in a sling, the cast from her shoulder to her fingertips. It looked half as big as her. "Amy." She closed the distance between herself and the girl and hugged her. As she did, Landon and Cole returned and took up their positions on either side of her. Amy didn't return the hug, but she didn't fight it, either.

Finally Ashley took a half step back. "Honey, we need to tell you something. Can we do that when we get to the house?"

"I can't leave." She took a shaky step to one side and then the other, glancing over her shoulder to the left and right. Then she looked from Ashley to Landon, from Landon to Cole, and then back to Ashley. "We can't leave them here. Where are they?" Her face looked pale, her eyes wider than before. "My mommy and daddy? And my sissies? Are they in the hospital?"

Ashley's thoughts froze in place, and her tears were instant. She pictured this conversation happening at home in a quiet bedroom. But Amy thought they were leaving her family behind — and so she needed to know now. Landon seemed to notice Ashley's struggle. He started to stoop down to Amy's level, but Ashley put her hand on his shoulder and shook her head. This was something she needed to do. The promise to Erin had been hers, and she felt personally responsible for telling Amy Elizabeth the truth.

She filled her lungs and begged God to give her the words. Because for the rest of her time, regardless of what wonderful or tragic things might happen in Amy's life, she would remember the next few minutes always. Ashley knelt down on the ground in front of Amy. She felt Cole and Landon put their hands on her shoulders, and their presence helped.

"You're crying." Amy brushed lightly at the tears on Ashley's cheeks. "Are you sad?"

"I am." Ashley sniffed. *Please, Lord ... help me handle this. I need You.* She breathed in again, deeper this time. As she exhaled she saw the image of her painting, the one with her mom in heaven. Heaven the way she pictured it. And a sense of peace filled her soul. "Sweetheart, remember your dream?"

This time she only nodded, her eyes never leaving Ashley's.

"What do you remember about it?" Ashley put her hands on Amy's slim shoulders, praying her touch would give the girl strength. She would be tired of standing soon.

"My dream?" Amy gulped a mouthful of air, her fear tangible. "I was in a really pretty place with green grass and flowers. And my mommy and daddy were there. And Clarissa and Chloe and Heidi Jo. And my grandma and a little girl named Sarah."

Ashley was stunned at Amy's recall. Was it a dream, then? Or something else? Something they wouldn't understand until they were all in heaven. "Remember what you told me ... how you didn't want to leave?"

"Because it was so nice." She gulped again. "Everyone was happy." Again she looked over her shoulder, straining a little as if her parents might come into view at any moment.

Ashley felt Landon squeeze her shoulder. She understood. There was no way to delay the news another moment. "Amy ..."

"Yes." She locked eyes with Ashley again. "So do you know where they are? My family?"

"I do." Tears overflowed from Ashley's heart, but she blinked them back. "Your family is in that beautiful place. Where you saw them in your dream."

"But that ... that was a dream." Amy's little body began to tremble.

"No, sweetie. It was real." Ashley brushed her knuckles against Amy's velvet-smooth cheek. "Your mommy and daddy and your sisters are in heaven with your grandma and your cousin Sarah."

Amy looked down at her new tennis shoes. She twisted one foot, her body still shaking.

"Amy, sweetie ... do you understand?"

She looked up, and though the fear remained, her eyes were dry. "How did they get there? To that pretty place?"

Ashley wanted to take the girl in her arms and never bring this up again. But this was only the beginning. "You and your family were coming to the party, do you remember that?"

She nodded. "For Papa's birthday."

"Exactly." Ashley's heart raced. *Please help me, Father.* For all the things Ashley had been through, this had to be one of the most difficult. "On your way here, your family was in an accident. Your mommy and daddy and your sisters went to heaven, Amy. That's why God let you see it in your dream."

"Why didn't I get to go?"

"Well ..." Ashley felt Cole crying quietly beside her. "The only reason any of us is here is because God still has plans for us. We still have more work to do."

"Oh."

Amy's precious question was still ringing in Ashley's head. It wasn't the question she'd expected. She thought Amy would ask why God had taken her family away from her. But she'd been given a glimpse of heaven. Of course she didn't want to know why they had gone. She wanted to know why God had left her behind. Ashley could barely draw a breath for the ache in her heart. "Do you understand, honey?"

Amy nodded. Again her eyes were dry, but the fear had dissipated some from her expression. She looked over her shoulder back at the hospital once more, and Ashley could see her search-ing, hoping. Wanting so badly to see her mom or dad ... one of her sisters ... come running into view. But the lobby was empty.

She turned once more and looked at Ashley, her sweet eyes full of concern. "Who's gonna take care of me?"

"I am." Ashley's answer was immediate. "We are. Uncle Landon and me, and Cole and Devin and Janessa. You're going to stay with us."

Amy lifted her eyes to Cole, and then to Landon and back to Ashley. She nodded once more. "Okay." She looked like she might faint, like shock had completely taken over, and caused a shut-down in her heart and soul.

"Come here." Ashley gently pulled Amy into her arms. And as she did, she could see herself standing over Erin's bed again, talking to her for the last time, telling her Amy would be safe. That nothing would ever happen to her. That final conversation.

Amy still didn't return her hug, but this time she fell against Ashley, as if she couldn't stand for another moment. Ashley tried to imagine the questions Amy must have. Questions about her home back in Texas and how they were going to get her things, and whether she was going to stay for now or forever, and a hun-dred others. But for now she didn't ask any of them.

"I'm ready to go." She stepped away from Ashley and hugged her broken arm to her chest. "My arm hurts."

Ashley stood and shared a look with Landon, a look that said they had a long way to go. Cole, too, had the look. And as they helped Amy into the car, as Ashley finally allowed the tears that had been building in her heart, it occurred to her that they wouldn't only need God's *help* to get through this season of pain with Amy.

They would need a miracle.

THEY DECIDED TO CELEBRATE THEIR FATHER'S birthday Sunday afternoon.

Since they'd all come with letters and plans to make this birthday unforgettable, Ashley and the others thought it only right that before Katy and Dayne flew home Monday morning, and before Luke and Reagan drove home to Indianapolis Sunday night, they take a few hours and do what they had set out to do from the beginning.

Let their father know how much they loved him.

Amy had gone to bed right when they got home last night and she was sleeping now. The way she had most of the day. Ashley helped her brush her teeth, and the whole time she said very little. She was up for breakfast this morning for a short while, and all the cousins talked to her, hugging her and telling her they were glad to see her.

Amy was pleasant and kind. But she was definitely in shock. Like she had found a way to convince herself she was merely having a visit at her aunt's house, and that somehow she'd find her way back home, back to her family when the trip was over. She still hadn't cried or gotten angry or asked another question. Ashley had set her up on the sofa where Jessie had been sleeping until a few nights ago. After Erin's death, after their around-the-clock vigil at the hospital was over, Kari and Brooke and their families and their dad and Elaine had returned to their homes.

But by Sunday at noon everyone was back at Ashley's.

Landon and Ryan were out back getting the barbecue ready. Ashley noticed something she hadn't heard in a week, a week that felt more like a year. The guys were laughing. Not loud raucous laughter that at times had marked so many of their family get-togethers. But a quiet easy laughter, the kind that took first steps toward living again. Laughter also marked the sound of the cousins playing Frisbee at the back of the property. The sky was blue and cloudless, cooler than last week.

Luke and Reagan were still at the house, since they lived an hour away. Luke found Ashley in the kitchen as she was chopping a fruit salad.

"I just talked to Naomi Boggs." His features were tight, the concern in his eyes at a new level. "Things aren't good, Ash."

"What'd she say?" Ashley set down the knife. Adrenaline flooded her veins.

"She talked to the judge. The hearing's set for a week from Wednesday."

Ashley steadied herself against the kitchen counter. "That's … ten days."

"Right, and we either have proof Candy isn't fit to be a mother, or she gets custody. It's an open-and-shut case."

"Proof?" Ashley's hands were shaking. "Erin's texts … she had proof, right?"

Luke released a heavy sigh. He stared at the floor for several seconds before looking up. "Since I can't ask her …" He hadn't cried much or often since the accident, but here his eyes welled up. More out of frustration than anything else, by the looks of it. "Since the first time I saw that text, I've been trying to figure out what proof she could've had."

"What have you done?" Ashley was still trying to get past the news. Amy could be taken from them as quickly as ten days from now? They couldn't let that happen. If Erin had proof that Candy had wrong intentions, they needed to find that proof. Immediately.

"I contacted Erin's neighbor. She was listed in Erin's phone as an emergency contact." By then the neighbors knew what had happened. Friends from Erin and Sam's church had contacted everyone acquainted with the family. "The neighbor knew where Erin and Sam kept an extra key." His frustration seemed to grow. "I had her go in and look around, scour the place for anything with Candy Burns's name on it." He shook his head. "Nothing."

"When does the moving company come?"

"Thursday, after our trip. So we can stay there."

"And I can put together a suitcase of clothes for Amy." Ashley couldn't grasp the sadness ahead. "I'm assuming the neighbors will keep an eye on the place until then?"

"Yes. Sam and Erin had an alarm, so their things should be safe."

The moving van was a great idea. Dayne had thought it up, and he and Katy had paid for it. A moving company would pack up the house much as if the family had only moved. The truck would bring everything from Erin's house here, to Bloomington, where it would be put in storage until the entire family could take a weekend and go through it. That was the only option that made sense — since they could hardly all take a trip to Texas.

Ashley felt herself rally, felt the fight rise inside her. She straightened and looked at her brother, really searched his eyes. "We have to fight this."

"That's what I came in here to tell you." His eyes were still filled with doubt. "It doesn't look good, Ash. But we have to try. I was thinking we'd fly in that Tuesday so we could be there for the hearing. We can at least present Erin's side."

"We're going to win." She walked to him and hugged him. "We've got the best lawyer in the country."

They talked for a few more minutes, and when Luke went outside with the others, and after Brooke and Kari and Reagan joined her in the kitchen to help put the rest of the dinner together, Ashley slipped away for a few minutes to do one very important task.

Book a flight to Austin.

Twenty-Three

JOHN HADN'T BEEN SURE ABOUT THIS PLAN WHEN HIS DAUGH-
ters brought it up Saturday after the funeral service. His birthday
seemed so insignificant in light of the week. Elaine was the one
who had pulled him aside and reminded him how important the
celebration might be. Not just for him but for the whole family.

So on Sunday just after noon — when they would usually
still be at church — he and Elaine pulled up at Ashley's house and
parked. For a long while John didn't move, didn't try to get out of
the car or hurry inside. "Was it really just a week ago?"

Elaine didn't say anything. She understood, he could see that
in her eyes.

"I mean, it feels like yesterday." He stared straight ahead at the
grassy land and shade trees that marked the side of the property.
"We were pulling up and I was sure the kids had planned some
kind of surprise, and the phone rang." John felt a fresh wall of
sadness surround him.

A phone call.

That was the way life changed for anyone who went through
something like this. One minute they were going about life concerned with getting someplace on time or making dinner or running errands or planning a party. Then just like that, in the middle
of an everyday-life kind of moment, the phone would ring. And
nothing about life would ever be the same again.

In their situation, the whole country knew about the tragedy,
and literally every citizen of Bloomington. The memorial service
yesterday was packed to overflowing, people lined up three-deep

along the back and sides of the church. It had been a simple memorial — no time to do anything else.

They talked about postponing the service until Amy was out of the hospital, but her doctor didn't see the need. Funerals and memorials were mainly for adults, people who understood the sometimes great length of time between here and heaven. Pastor Mark had arranged beautiful music, and since he knew the Baxter family better than anyone at the church, he gave the message.

Up front there had been large photos set up on easels — one of Erin and Sam, and one each of Clarissa, Chloe, and Heidi Jo. The pictures were surrounded by flowers of every shade and color, brilliant purples and whites and yellows and reds — further proof of life here, and life there. A reminder that Erin and her family had lived and they were living still.

The service hadn't taken long. They had agreed to keep the caskets out of the church. It was too many, too much. The loss far too great. Instead they asked the funeral home to work out the details with the cemetery. Once the service at Clear Creek was over, the family walked from the front pew to their waiting cars, while hundreds of people stood on either side, quietly watching them go.

"The cemetery was rough," John still sat in his car outside Ashley's house. He was grateful for Elaine's patience, the fact that she wasn't in a hurry to get inside. They all needed moments like this, when they could be quiet before God and realize the enormity of what had happened that week.

"Seeing the caskets ... that's what got me." Elaine's voice was tender and soft. She took John's hand and again she waited. Giving him this chance to remember.

"For me, too." Getting out of the car and seeing not one casket or two, but five. Caskets representing five lives that had mattered so dearly to him. His sweet granddaughters — all with so much life ahead — and his son-in-law who had been deeply determined to take care of his family. Even if it meant moving them away on more than one occasion so he could get work and support them.

And his precious youngest daughter. His sweet Erin.

Yes, they were in heaven and they were better off for it. He would believe that always. His days of questioning God for taking all five of them were over, although hours of struggle were bound to come along in the process of living without them. The times when looking at Amy Elizabeth would be enough to move him to tears. He didn't doubt that Erin and Sam and the girls were happier than ever.

He simply missed them.

"I feel like ... they should be inside waiting for us."

"Standing there with everyone else, the girls running around with their cousins." Elaine ran her thumb over his hand.

"Right." He smiled, even as a few tears hit his cheeks. "Clarissa talking a hundred miles an hour and Chloe with her sparkly eyes and Heidi Jo, holding hands with Amy. Erin and Sam, their arms around each other."

John sighed, wondering how he would get through the next few hours. The others wanted so badly to make him feel appreciated, to celebrate this milestone birthday. But right now John only wanted to find a quiet place and a scrapbook, or take up his position on the couch and roll home movie reels. Anything to spend a few more hours believing that Erin and her family were still with them, still alive. Their voices still ringing out somewhere under the same sky.

When Elizabeth died, someone told John that he would find a way to laugh and live again, and the days would bring him back to a routine that didn't involve crying every day. But even still, he would carry the loss with him forever, as if someone had ripped away a part of him. And he would go through life aching for it. The wisdom had proved true, even so much as to letting him find new life with Elaine.

But not a day went by when he didn't feel the loss of his Elizabeth. And it would be that way with Erin and her family. The reunion was coming, the one where they would all be together in heaven forever without heartache or tragedy or this very great pain he was feeling now. But here ... in the moments before his birthday barbecue ... heaven felt very far away, indeed.

He wiped his tears and smiled at Elaine. Again he didn't have to say anything. She understood that he was ready now, he could face his family and his birthday barbecue. He could go inside the house where he and Elizabeth had raised their family and he could enjoy an afternoon and evening with them.

Even when everywhere he looked he would remember Erin.

THE BARBECUE WAS GOING BETTER THAN John had expected. Rather than a constant effort to fight tears and feign happiness, the infusion of life from his family created a joy deep in John that stood in stark contrast to the loss they'd been dealt that week. Throughout the dinner, the kids proved they were already back to life as it had been. The prekindergarteners — Janessa, Sophie, and Annie — clamored for their mothers' attention wanting more juice or less fruit or help washing their hands. The three girls were inseparable, playing dolls in the living room and lost in their own world of make-believe and pretend. Their high-pitched little-girl giggles filled the air with a joy the family desperately needed.

The little ones — Johnny and Egan — were with their mothers, Reagan and Katy, and out back Devin, RJ, and Malin were hanging out with Amy. The four of them hovered around the pond looking for tadpoles or frogs or anything that slithered. Every spotting or near catch was celebrated with shouts of victory and a happiness unfettered by last Saturday's tragedy. Amy wasn't as enthusiastic as the others, but she was at least off the couch and outside. And her cousins were definitely going out of their way to

include her and keep her mind off the incalculable loss she'd suffered, the reality of which couldn't possibly be fully grasped yet.
Not by Amy or any of the younger kids. Her expression looked
like that of someone who wasn't quite fully awake. The look of
shock, for sure. On top of that, her arm still hurt quite a bit, and
she was achy everywhere.

John could only imagine what was going on in her heart.

The older kids — Cole and Jessie, Maddie and Hayley — had
finished eating and were shooting baskets out front. The sound
of the ball on the asphalt, the clang of the hoop — all signs that
life would go on.

John sat with Elaine on the back patio, surrounded by his kids
and their spouses and he couldn't help but smile as he watched
Devin, every bit the ringleader that Cole had been at that age.
"No wonder God tells us to be like little children." He smiled at
the others. "Amy is in shock. Her situation is very different, of
course. But the other kids could teach us something about living."
He looked back at the children near the pond. "They were sad and
they cried like all of us." John turned his attention to Devin and
RJ, Malin, and Amy. "But maybe they accept death a little easier.
They believe in heaven, and they believe in life here." He smiled,
feeling the sorrow written into his expression. "Faith like a child
… that's how I want to live."

"Me, too." Ashley was watching Amy. "Erin lived like that.
More than the rest of us, I think. With a simple childlike love for
God and life and family." Her eyes grew wet, despite the hint of a
smile on her face. "If she has a window right now, she'd be smiling
bigger than anyone in heaven. Just watching us all together for
Dad's birthday … watching the cousins play."

John loved that picture, and he held it close to his heart for
several minutes while the others talked about the logistics surrounding the accident, the void it had left, the struggles with the
social worker, and the pending trip Luke and Ashley were taking

to Texas. The idea of losing Amy to her birth mother was more than John could imagine, same as the others. So they didn't spend much time on that topic.

"I might write a letter to the wife of the truck driver." John looked from Kari and Ryan to Ashley and Landon and on to the others.

They each nodded, their eyes suddenly sadder than before. "Her loss comes with shame ... which must be so hard." Brooke bit her lip. "I hadn't thought about that."

"Me, either." Kari sighed. "So many people were affected." She set her plate down on the patio beside her and leaned over her knees. "If only he would've pulled over. Gotten sleep on the side of the road, even."

They were quiet for a while. "What would you tell her?" Dayne's expression was kind, thoughtful. He was clearly intrigued by the idea.

"I'd like to tell her we're praying for her ... and that we aren't angry with her husband. Just let her know that we believe God is sovereign even in very tough times like this. Maybe let her know a little about Erin and Sam and the girls, and how strong their faith was. How sure we are that they're in heaven."

Luke shifted in his chair. "What if her husband wasn't a Christian?"

"I thought about that." John settled back, glad they could talk through this. "Most people assume their loved ones go to heaven when they die. Whatever the eternal state for the trucker, his family needs to see Christ's love in action. This isn't about the woman's husband. A letter like this could make a difference for her and her family."

Another few seconds passed while the group considered this, and eventually Ashley smiled. "I think I'll add a letter to yours." Around the patio, the others agreed, nodding and catching John's vision.

"Maybe we should pray for them now." John hadn't planned on this, but it seemed the right thing to do. The others bowed their heads or linked hands and John simply began. Because praying was as simple as talking to God throughout the day, whenever the need arose. This was one of those times. "Father, we lift up the family of Marty Cohen. They're dealing with a very great loss, like we are, but they're also facing humiliation and shame. Please bring people alongside them and help them find You through this tragedy. Use our efforts to help their faith increase or to find faith in You for the first time."

John heard a few of them wiping tears. He continued, his voice marked by a peace that could've only come from God. "Be with us today, too, Lord. This evening we celebrate life. The sound of the children laughing around us and the love among us ... You give us these reminders to keep us from falling apart. But times will come for all of us when we don't feel like we can take another breath. Be our strength, Father. We need You every day, every hour." He stopped, his own emotions welling up again. "Please let our dear Erin and her family know how much we love them." He reached for Elaine's hand. "And let the reunion with Elizabeth and baby Sarah be the sweetest time ever. Thank You for conquering death, Lord. We love You. In Jesus' name, amen."

THE DINNER WAS FINISHED, THE DISHES were cleaned, and the cake was out on the counter waiting for them.

It was time to read the letters.

John had found out about them several days ago, but he hadn't said anything. He wasn't sure if they would have a moment like this before everyone fell back into their routines, and he didn't want to force it. But now they were all gathered in the living room of the old Baxter house, and each of his adult kids held a piece of paper in his or her hands. He sat in an overstuffed recliner, with

Elaine next to him in a hard-back chair from the dining room. The room was packed, most of the kids filling in spaces on the floor. Amy sat next to Ashley, clinging to her arm with her healthy one. Landon was on her other side.

Dayne spoke first. "Ashley wants us to go in age order." He smiled at her and then back at John. "I'm supposed to be good at reading in public." Soft chuckles came from around the room. Dayne's smile faded as he looked at John. "But I have a feeling this won't be easy." He pursed his lips and exhaled hard. "Okay. Here goes." He looked down at the paper and at John again. "Dear Dad, In some ways I really hate that you're seventy." Again a light ripple of laughter came from the room.

"Way to start off," Ryan teased, and John was grateful for his son-in-law's attempts at keeping the mood light. "He's still pretty young."

"True." Dayne smiled and sniffed at the same time. He found his place on the page. "I hate it because it reminds me how many years I lost." He looked slowly at the faces around the room. "Years when I would've given anything to be a Baxter."

He went on reading, telling John how grateful he was for the effort he had made in bringing him into the family, the times when they would meet at the park downtown and talk about logistics and practicality and how his siblings might react to a movie star being their brother.

"Through it all you treated me like a son. From the beginning." He hesitated, composing himself. "I realize now ... that even though the idea of being a Baxter was new to me, and the idea of being your son was as crazy as some movie plot ... it wasn't a new idea to you. Because you and Mom loved me from the day I was born. Even when you couldn't raise me, even though you couldn't find me."

Elaine handed John a tissue, and he used it to catch the first tears.

Dayne finished his letter by saying that though his adoptive parents were kind people, they were never a family. He looked at John for a long moment and then back at his letter. "I would easily trade all the awards and accolades and movie roles I've ever played for the chance to be raised in this family." He looked around again. "With all of you. Because being part of the Baxter family, learning about your faith and sharing in it now ..." He smiled at Katy, his eyes still watery as he finished the letter. "Finding Katy, having a family with her ... everything that's happened since I found out I was a Baxter has been the highlight of my life." He paused. "So, happy birthday, Dad. I only wish I'd been here to celebrate all the ones I missed."

John stood without hesitation and went to his oldest son. He wrapped him in his arms and held him the way he had longed to hold him through the first three decades of his life. "I love you, son. You belong here."

One by one, the others took to their feet and joined the huddle, clearly as moved as John was by Dayne's letter and his honest admission of how grateful he was to be a Baxter, and how much he regretted missing the chance for so many years. Eventually they all made their way back to their seats.

Brooke was up next. Her letter thanked John for never giving up on Hayley, and for teaching her how to believe in God again. "I'm not sure who I'd be today if it weren't for you. When I think of our family, I see you, Dad. At the center, praying for us, leading us. Happy birthday, even though I refuse to believe you're getting older. You'll always be my hero."

John had known that if the time allowed and they found this moment together, it would be emotional. He wiped his cheeks again, his heart full, and he crossed the room to hug Brooke. It was impossible to hear one of his kids share their deepest thoughts and love toward him without going to them afterward. Their words meant that much to him.

Kari recalled in her letter the way her dad had rushed her to Ryan's side when he was injured. "You always knew what I needed, Dad. Even before I knew myself." She thanked him for standing by her decision to love Tim, her first husband, even after his affair. "But then, I wouldn't have expected anything less. You have always told us that love is a decision, and you've lived that out with Mom and with each of us here. Thank you for still being that example, Dad. I love you."

John squeezed Elaine's hand before walking to Kari and pulling her close. "I love you, too."

Ashley cleared her throat and unfolded her letter. "Dear Dad, I told this to Landon the other day, and I can say the same thing to you. Through the years I was never easy to love. At least not in my younger days." She went on to thank her father for standing by her no matter how great her rebellion. "I came home from Paris with a jaded heart and a little boy." She stopped and smiled through her tears at Cole. His eyes held a depth beyond his years as they shared a look.

Ashley blinked, trying to see the paper in her hand. "I brought shame on the family and difficulty to all of you. But Dad," she looked up for a few seconds, "you stood by me even then. You and Mom treated Cole like he was your own son, and over time you loved me back to God. You really did. I'll always be so thankful for that. Otherwise I might never have let the walls of my heart down enough to love Landon Blake. Like Brooke, I can't imagine who I'd be without you. Your love made me who I am."

Ashley started to cry as she finished reading. Because of that, the hug between John and her lasted longer than the others. When she found control again, and as she sat down, Amy took hold of her arm again and Janessa scurried over and sat in Ashley's lap. "It's okay, Mommy. You don't have to cry."

Again the laughter was greatly needed, and the atmosphere

in the room lightened immediately. Ashley hugged her little girl, and put her other arm around Amy.

It was Erin's turn, and a few awkward seconds passed while Luke opened an envelope and pulled out his letter. "I titled it, 'The Prodigal,'" he smiled at John and then began reading. His letter recalled how growing up he had thought his parents were perfect. "And so I tried to be perfect, too. I thought that's what Baxters were supposed to do."

He went on to explain that when he fell, he fell hard because he didn't think there was any way back. "I was no longer perfect ... So, I guess I figured I wasn't part of the family." The others were quiet, listening. Except for Dayne, all of them had watched Luke make this journey. But hearing him talk about it was insightful for all of them. "I don't know if it was learning about Dayne or the talk you had with me that night, but I learned something through my fall. I learned I was never perfect before, and I would never be perfect at any time in the future."

He stopped and lifted grateful eyes to John before looking back at his letter once more. "Being a Baxter means we celebrate each other's victories, and we pick each other up when we fall down. It means never letting someone go. The way you never let me go, Dad. You and Mom gave us the greatest gift with this family. Now I want to take that legacy and make that same sort of wonderful life for mine."

John hugged his youngest son and thought about the time a decade ago when he would cry out hourly for his return, for his restoration and redemption. God was faithful above all things, even in this. The knowing after all these years that his refusal to give up on Luke was what eventually led him home again.

They were finished, but there was something none of them knew about. The reason John had learned about the letters before anyone mentioned them this afternoon. He sat slowly down and

Elaine handed him a tattered piece of paper. John took it carefully and looked at the others. "I was given Erin's purse after the accident. A few days ago I went through the mess inside and I found this." He held up the piece of paper. "The letter Erin had written for my birthday."

A slight gasp came from Kari and Ashley. Even the kids seemed to sit a little more still in light of the revelation. "I've already read it. Alone, where I could hold on to this ... last message from Erin to me. But I thought I should share it with all of you." He gave Ashley a sad smile. "The way she would've done a week ago if ... if things had gone differently."

John drew a full breath and began to read, "Dear Dad ... I can't believe I'm going to see you in just a few days. I like to think that'll be one of the best parts of your surprise." His voice caught, and he stopped. He looked at the faces of his grown kids, their tears and breaking hearts. He shifted his attention to Amy. She had her face tucked close to Ashley's arm, but even now she wasn't crying. As if it was too soon to have any idea what it meant that her family now lived in heaven, or the way her entire existence had changed so drastically in a single instant.

He somehow found the strength to continue. Erin had written about missing the family and sometimes feeling different than the others. "Growing up, I never quite fit in with my sisters. But you and Mom were always there for me, always encouraging me. And because of the way you loved me, Dad, eventually I stopped feeling sorry for myself."

John looked from Brooke to Kari and then Ashley before he found his place again. "When that happened, I found a friendship with my sisters that I wouldn't have had otherwise. It's why I hate living so far away." She finished her letter asking him to pray that somehow their family would find a way to make a permanent move back to Bloomington. He felt more tears in anticipation of the way Erin's letter ended. He steadied his hand so he could see the words. "For now, I'm just so glad to celebrate your birthday with you ... so glad we're coming home. I'll love you and admire you always, Erin."

As the others rose slowly to their feet and crossed the room toward him, as they stood once more in a group hug, their tears and hearts joined the way they would forever be joined, John was struck by the only thought that could possibly bring him comfort now. Erin was right about coming home ... that's exactly what God had planned for her and Sam and the girls. Right now they would be celebrating and remembering and enjoying each other's company. The reunion must've been beyond description because they were indeed home.

Just not the way the rest of them had expected.

For the rest of his life, John would hold close the memories of the past hour, the kind words from his kids and the ways they felt loved or helped or changed by having him as their father. His greatest accomplishments had been shared one at a time, and he would be grateful always for their desire to tell him. In a way it was a snapshot of his entire life, all seventy years.

Summed up in six beautifully written letters.

Twenty-Four

IN THE PREDAWN DARKNESS, ASHLEY CREPT THROUGH THE house and kissed each of her kids good-bye while they slept. First Cole then Devin, Janessa, and finally Amy. It was Tuesday, the day before the hearing in Texas, and Landon was about to drive her to the airport. She lingered near Amy's bed. *Dear Lord ... please let her open up to me. I haven't found a way to really reach her.* Ashley hesitated, but there was no audible answer. Just the truth her dad had always lived out.

Love was a decision.

She had promised Erin she would love Amy, and she was committed to keeping that promise. Whether that meant fighting it out in court tomorrow or patiently waiting for Amy to show some kind of emotion. Tears or anger, frustration or questions ... anything that would give Ashley a window to what the girl was feeling.

A sigh came from the deepest part of Ashley's soul as she hurried down and grabbed her bag. Ten minutes later they were on the way to Indianapolis, and Landon put his hand on her knee. "I'm proud of you ... fighting for Amy like this."

"I have to." Ashley felt cold, even though the temperatures hovered around seventy degrees. "I made a promise."

For a few minutes neither of them said anything. Landon was the first to break the silence. "Have you thought, Ash? What if we don't get to keep her?"

She wanted to come back with a quick answer, a certain belief that of course they would get to keep her. But Luke had called again last night and said the same thing. Now she stared at the dark empty highway in front of them. "It could happen. Luke says he's worried."

"Me, too." He slid his fingers between hers. "You care so much about this, but we have to go in with a realistic approach."

"You know what I'd rather do?" Ashley turned and looked at him, her voice tender. "I'd rather ask God for a miracle." She paused. "Erin said in her text that she had proof. We just have to figure out what it is."

Landon seemed about to say that they didn't have long to make that happen. But he stayed quiet. "I think you're right. We all need to pray for a miracle."

"I called everyone. They're all praying." She leaned her head back against the seat. The call with Luke last night had gone later than she intended. Now she was exhausted. "Everyone knows we need a miracle."

The one who understood the least, of course, was Amy. Ashley had taken her for a walk around the property yesterday and explained that she was going to Texas to talk to Candy Burns. "You know who she is, right?" Ashley's tone was gentle, the conversation unrushed.

"Yes. She gave birth to me and my sisters." She turned frightened eyes toward Ashley. "My mommy didn't want us to see her."

"I know, sweetie. That's why I'm going to Texas."

But there was no possible way to help the child understand how high the stakes were for tomorrow's hearing. She would've had to go to the hearing if she hadn't been injured. In no time they were at the airport. Landon took her suitcase from the car and set it on the curb, then he wrapped his arms around her and held her. "I wish I could be with you."

"Me, too." She kissed him, drawing strength from him. "The

kids need you." Ashley had asked the social worker if Landon could sign the paperwork later, provided they win custody. She had agreed, but again she had warned Ashley that the case didn't look good.

At least Landon would help the kids miss Ashley less, help keep things normal. Even Cole hated that she was going away. Since the accident his good-byes even when she went to the market were more drawn out. As if he was more aware that there were no guarantees beyond the moment.

Landon kissed her once more. "I'll pray constantly." He smiled, his eyes still concerned. "Keep me posted."

"I will." She took her suitcase and pulled it behind her as she headed for the door. She stopped just once to look back and wave. And once she was inside and had her boarding pass she met up with Luke at the gate.

He'd been practically going crazy trying to find the proof Erin had referred to. "I've talked to a number of people at her church, and even some of the neighbors near Candy Burns's mother's house. I've checked with the local police, in case Candy made some sort of threat and Erin documented it." He frowned. "I've spoken with Naomi Boggs ten times a day this past week and neither of us can come up with anything."

Then — and only then — did it hit Ashley how critical the situation was. Yes, Luke had been telling her things didn't look good. But suddenly the reality was at hand. They could lose tomorrow's hearing, and in a matter of days Amy would suffer one final blow. She would have to be sent by plane to live with a woman who once tried to sell her. A woman who, at least according to Erin's understanding, was far from rehabilitated.

"There has to be a way." Ashley was quiet the rest of the time at the gate. Seated beside her, Luke continued to check his phone, then Erin's phone, then his list of notes. As if he was searching everything he knew to be true about Erin's patterns and contacts and history to figure out what she must've meant when she told the social worker she had proof.

Proof that would make all the difference in Amy's future.

THE HEARING TOOK PLACE IN A nondescript paneled room, not much bigger than a classroom. The judge sat at the front behind a long built-in desk. Her hair was curled and she wore a floral dress. She looked more like someone on the potluck committee at church than a certified judge.

But whatever her background or political bent, she was about to make a decision that would change Amy's life. The room held just four rows of seats. Ashley sat next to Luke on one side of the front row. At the other end of the row, a public attorney sat with two files open on his lap. He looked focused.

Right in the middle sat Naomi Boggs. She, too, had a file open on her lap.

Ashley remembered to breathe. *Please, God … we need a miracle.* Decisions like this one happened every day in cities all over the country. How could they let the judge know that this wasn't any other case? She closed her eyes for a moment and then looked at her brother. He'd been texting up until a minute ago. "Anything?"

He shook his head. The frustration and concern in his eyes darkened his expression. "We'll have to use her text. That's all we've got."

Erin believed she had proof that Candy Burns intended to use the girls as a means of extortion — same as before. No, Ashley and Luke didn't have proof. But the fact that Erin believed she had seen such a thing, had to count for something.

At least that's what they were praying.

Luke had Erin's fully charged phone in his possession. He hoped to have the chance to let the judge hold the phone in her hands and read the text for herself. But even then Luke had been up front about the gravity of the situation. "It's really not proof at all," he told Ashley before the hearing. "Just keep praying."

Candy Burns took the stand. She was thin and weathered, but for the occasion she wore what must've been one of her best outfits. Polyester dark pants and a matching dark blazer, over a white blouse. Even with her worn-out look, she seemed at first glance absolutely fit to be a mother.

Ashley clenched her jaw as the woman took her seat on the witness stand. *Where are You, God? Please ... help us. We're going to lose if we don't have Your help.*

I will never leave you or forsake you, my daughter. Never.

The words echoed across her heart and brought a comfort she needed. But they weren't a guarantee. She narrowed her eyes, studying the Burns woman. Ashley wasn't a psychiatrist, but as an artist she had learned to read people, study them. Candy Burns was nervous, no doubt. And something about her eyes looked guilty. But again that wouldn't matter compared to the court's assessment that between parenting classes and drug rehabilitation the woman was safe to resume custody of her daughter.

Naomi had assured them that Candy had filed for full custody the day after she learned about the accident. "I think she smells an insurance policy." Naomi looked like she was angry with the system. "If Erin said she had proof Candy wanted money, I believe her. But we need something tangible."

Candy was stating her name for the court. Once that was done, the judge turned to Candy's attorney for an explanation of the case.

The man stood. He couldn't have been a day over twenty-five. "Your Honor, Ms. Burns's mother participated in an open adoption of her three daughters after she was sentenced to prison many years ago. As you know, open adoptions include terms agreed upon by both the birth mother — in this case the grandmother — and the adoptive parents." He walked over a copy of the open adoption contract and handed it to the judge. "I'd like you to read the clause in item number 14-A. It allows that if something happened to Erin and Sam Hogan — the adoptive parents — then Ms. Burns's mother would regain custody of the girls."

Ashley couldn't believe Erin and Sam would sign something like that. They must've been desperate for the girls, certain nothing would ever happen to them while the girls were still young. Besides, the adoption probably hinged on the clause. Her heartbeat struggled to find a rhythm anything close to regular.

Up front the lawyer paced back to his seat and sorted through another file for a moment. "Unfortunately, the Hogan family was in a terrible car accident ten days ago. The adoptive parents and three of their adopted daughters were killed. Only Candy Burns's daughter, Amy, survived."

Without any sense of ceremony, without the depth and seriousness befitting the stakes of this case, the man simply said, "Candy has been through parenting classes and she's rehabilitated from her drug use. She's out of prison now, and since the adoption agreement allows for it, she wants to step in instead of her mother and regain custody of the child." He hesitated and looked from the judge to Naomi Boggs and back again. "If there are no objections, your Honor, I believe the court has other matters more pressing than this one."

"Can I say something?" Candy's voice was a mix of shrill fear and anger.

The judge turned and stared at her. Then she looked back at the woman's attorney. "You can question your client, council, but your client cannot yell out."

"I'm sorry, your Honor." The man looked frustrated, like he hadn't intended for this to be such a big ordeal. "I'd like to question my client."

The judge waved her hand like she was shooing a fly. "Please."

Candy looked outraged at the man. She smoothed her shirt and straightened her back. As if she wondered how dare he consider ignoring her thoughts on the matter. Her attorney approached her. "You've been through parenting classes. Tell me why you want to be a mother now."

Candy cleared her throat. "I've always been a mother. I mean … I always wanted to be a mother." She lifted her chin and looked at Ashley. "I've had it rough, you know? Like it's never been easy, but now …." She looked at the judge, and pointed back at Ashley. "Now that family gave the okay to have my little girls' organs donated!" She glared at Luke. "Without my permission, by the way. And then two of my babies were buried in Indiana! When they should be here in Texas with me!"

The judge held up her hand. "The question was why," she lowered her brow and a V formed between her eyes. "Why do you want to be a mother now?"

"Because …" Candy blinked and her face went blank. As if she'd never actually thought about the reason. "Well … I mean, I'm the girl's real mother. I should have the benefit of raising her."

The benefit? Ashley felt the blood drain from her face. *Please, Lord, let the judge see through this woman.* The idea of loving Amy or missing her or wanting to raise her so far had not even come up.

"At any rate," her lawyer checked his watch. "My client's testimony isn't the issue. She's the biological mother and the adoption agreement allows for the child's grandmother to have full custody in the event of the death of the adoptive parents. The only reason we're here is to ask the court to allow the girl's biological mother to take the place of the grandmother." He did an exaggerated shrug. "We all have places to be, your Honor. If the court wouldn't mind making a decision."

Luke was on his feet. "Your Honor, I object."

Ashley could've jumped up and slapped the man. How dare the other lawyer minimize the importance of this case? And what did he know about Candy Burns's ability to be a parent? What about wanting the best situation for Amy? She pressed her fists into her knees and held her breath.

The judge pushed her glasses higher up the bridge of her nose and peered down at Luke. "Who are you?"

"Luke Baxter, your Honor. I'm an attorney from Indianapolis. I'm here with my sister, Ashley Baxter Blake." He sounded cool and calm, the picture of professionalism. "Ms. Blake and her husband have made a commitment to adopt the child in question, in keeping with the wishes of the adoptive parents."

"How are you connected to the adoptive parents?" The judge seemed irritated. No doubt she had a full docket of cases to get to.

"The adoptive mother — Erin Baxter Hogan — is also my sister."

Ashley could've hugged him for the way he kept his words in the present tense. Erin might be gone, but she would always be their sister. *Exhale*, she told herself ... *please, God ... we need help right now! Please ...*

Candy's attorney looked bored, like anything Luke might say was nothing more than a waste of time. Ashley still thought Candy looked nervous, like she was hiding something. But she looked even more outraged at the possibility of losing Amy.

She's probably nervous about the evidence Erin knew about, Ashley told herself. *Lord, if it's something we can find, please make it obvious. We're out of options ...*

The judge was still trying to put the pieces together. "So your sister Erin was killed in a car accident along with her husband and three of her four adopted girls. Is that right?"

"Yes, your Honor."

"I see." Her expression softened. "I'm very sorry for your loss."

Luke nodded once. "Thank you."

"And now ..." She peered at Ashley. "You and your husband want to raise this surviving little girl as your own?"

Ashley stood alongside her brother. "Yes, ma'am. Your Honor."

"And you think that's what your sister would've wanted?"

"We do." Luke took a step forward. "Ever since Ms. Burns was released from prison, our sister felt very strongly that her only interest in the girls was a financial one, the hope that she might gain financial means through her connection to her daughters."

"What?" Candy Burns shrieked out and rose to her feet, and then apparently thought better of the idea and sat back down. She looked outraged at the suggestion.

"I object." The young attorney's face grew instantly red. "Nothing has been introduced here to suggest Ms. Burns has anything but pure motives for wanting custody of her daughter."

"Actually," Luke took another step forward, still calm and professional. "I have Erin Hogan's cell phone, and I can show you a text where she says she has proof that Ms. Burns's motives are rooted in financial gain."

"A text?" The judge twisted her face in confusion. "Do you have actual proof, Mr. Baxter? The proof she was allegedly referring to?"

"No, your Honor." Luke was clearly doing his best to hide his disappointment, but Ashley knew him better. The subtle change in his posture gave him away. "Unfortunately my sister was killed before we could learn what the proof was."

Ashley kept her eyes on Candy Burns. And in that moment — as soon as Luke mentioned the proof on Erin's phone, her face went pale. She shifted her eyes and locked on to Ashley's, and there was no question the woman was guilty. Whatever Erin had been referring to, Candy was aware of it.

The judge was going on, explaining the difference between real evidence and hearsay as if Luke would need the definition. "For instance, if someone comes into my courtroom and blames someone for bashing them indirectly on Facebook, that's not evidence. It's gossip. But if that same person brings a tape recording or a video or even a letter from the person supposedly bashing them, well then, that could be considered evidence."

Something had happened. Ashley was still standing, but beside her she could feel Luke practically bursting with possibility, with some sudden revelation. As if in the last few seconds he had been given a breakthrough. Ashley returned slowly to her seat. *Father, whatever it is, let it be the answer. Please, help Luke … He needs You.*

Luke held up his hand. "Thank you, your Honor. I appreciate your clarification. If the court doesn't object, I'd like to ask for a ten-minute recess."

On the witness stand, Candy looked like she might shout out again. Clearly she wanted the proceeding over, probably so that whatever she was hiding couldn't somehow be discovered. She glared at her attorney, but the man shrugged slightly.

The judge hesitated. She sighed, like the whole matter was a bother to her, and she checked what looked like her docket. "Is this about the evidence, Mr. Baxter? Because we have a number of cases yet to hear today."

"Yes, your Honor. Absolutely." He managed to contain his grin, but Ashley loved the way his eyes shone. Whatever it was, he clearly believed he'd thought of the answer. "This is definitely about the evidence."

"Fine." She smacked her gavel on the desk. "This court will resume in ten minutes." With that, she stood and disappeared through a door behind her bench.

"Luke!" Ashley tugged on his jacket, bringing him back to the seat beside her. "What is it?"

"Facebook." He sat back in the seat and began scrolling though the options on Erin's phone. "I didn't think about it before, because clearly Candy Burns and Erin weren't friends."

Ashley's mind was spinning. "But … anyone can leave a private message. Is that what you're thinking?"

"Exactly." He glanced at the woman, stepping down from the stand and hurrying to her attorney at the front of the room. "Did you see how she reacted when the judge brought up Facebook?"

Luke was talking fast, his words running together in his excitement. "Something's up, and we're going to find it."

He worked his way through Erin's apps until he found Facebook. "Here we go." His fingers shook slightly, but he was able to open it. The screen filled with a login page, and Luke reacted like he'd been sucker punched. "No ... a password can't stand in our way."

She mustn't have ever used the app, otherwise it wouldn't require a password. Ashley felt her heart sink. "Use her e-mail address for the sign-in." Ashley checked the time on the wall. They'd already used three of their ten minutes. Naomi Boggs was talking with Candy and her attorney, all of them using hushed tones. Naomi had told Luke that she had to play a neutral role at the hearing, even though she agreed with Amy staying with Ashley and Landon instead of Candy. But it was hard to tell that here, by the way she was acting.

Ashley tried to think what her sister might've used as a password. "Try using just the sign-in, and then it'll ask you if you forgot your password."

"Good." Luke raced his fingers across the screen, and just like Ashley said, a message flashed asking if the password was forgotten. Luke clicked yes, and another message appeared. Your password has been e-mailed to you.

Once more Ashley checked the clock. They had four minutes left. "Check her e-mail."

"I'm trying." He was definitely tapping the buttons as quickly as he could, but when he finally found the mail app, it required a password, too.

Desperation crept into Ashley's heart and bones. "Please, God ... we need Your help," she whispered the prayer out loud.

"What about Spotlight?" Luke was shaking worse now, their time down to only a few minutes. "Her phone has it, I can tell. But I have a Droid, so I'm not sure how to use it on this phone."

"Here," Ashley had an iPhone, too. "Let me do it." She took Erin's phone and slid the screens to the right until the page was black with only one search line at the top. "What should I search?"

"Type the word, 'Passwords'. It's not a smart idea, but some people keep passwords stored in their phone. In a document or on a notepad."

Ashley couldn't believe this would work, but they had no choice. As quickly as she could make her fingers fly across the keyboard, she typed in 'Passwords' and then she hit the search button.

According to the clock they had less than two minutes. But in as much time as it took to exhale, a document title suddenly appeared. Ashley tapped it and it opened to reveal exactly what Luke had hoped for. An entire list of passwords.

"Facebook ... Facebook ... Facebook ..." They both kept their voices to a whisper, but even so Candy had shot them several angry and nervous looks over her shoulder during the break. Ashley scrolled down the list of passwords, and there ... there at the very bottom of the list was this entry: Facebook: SECCHA2911.

Ashley's heart pounded so hard, she wouldn't have been surprised to see it burst from her chest. She tried to still her fingers enough to open the Facebook app again and enter the information. First, Erin's e-mail address, and then the password. S-E-C-C-H-A-2-9-1-1.

And suddenly she was inside Erin's Facebook page. Ashley couldn't quite catch her breath, but she didn't care. They had thirty seconds at the most.

"Hurry." Luke gave a quick look at the bench and then back at Ashley and the phone in her hand. "The judge'll be out any second."

Again Ashley was familiar with the app because she had the same phone. In a matter of taps, she was looking at Erin's private messages and there at the top ...

There at the top was a message from Candy Burns.

"Dear God, You've done it," she whispered. "Luke, this must be it. The proof Erin was talking about." Ashley raced through the message, noting that the date was the day before the accident, and the time was early that morning. It was probably the last thing Erin had seen before she left the house.

Luke read the message out loud in a panicky whisper, his words fast and jerky again. "Dear Erin, as you know I'm out of prison and I'm a changed woman. I really do think I'd make a good mother now. But I'm also open to a deal." He stopped and stared at Ashley. As he finished, his tone was full of an excitement he could hardly contain. "My expenses are very high and I don't have a job." Luke swapped another look with her. Disgust flashed in his expression. "If the deal is right, I'm sure I could move on, start a new life, if you know what I mean. In the right situation, I could have other kids. I hate to mess up your happy family. Let me know your thoughts. Candy B."

Ashley shook her head, amazed. "She even signed her name? What sort of crazy person would put this kind of thing in writing?"

"I'm not sure," Luke stood, ready for the judge, and Ashley did the same. He leaned close, keeping the whispered tone as they finished the conversation. "The kind of crazy person who just lost custody of her little girl."

Elation swept through Ashley, but she wouldn't believe it, wouldn't stop praying until the judge returned and Candy Burns took the witness stand again and her brother held up the phone once more. "I have the proof, your Honor." He raised his brow. "May I approach the bench?"

The judge looked intrigued. "This isn't that text, is it?"

"No, your Honor."

"Okay, then ... you can approach."

Luke walked past the younger attorney, his expression humble and kind. His faith evident in his eyes. The judge seemed to like Luke, his candor and determination. The woman was clearly interested in whatever the evidence might be.

"You mentioned Facebook." He held up the phone, and the judge took it from him. "If your Honor would please read the private message written — in letter form — to my sister. The letter is from Candy Burns."

Ashley loved how Luke used the word "letter" to describe the private message. The judge had already said that a letter was evidence, whereas a Facebook post was usually nothing more than gossip.

Again Ashley couldn't draw a full breath while she waited to hear the judge's response. The evidence was there. Now it was a matter of the judge fully seeing what Candy Burns was referring to, what she meant by wanting to make a deal with Erin. Ashley looked at the witness stand. Candy Burns's confidence was shredded. She anchored her elbows on the stand and rubbed her face, her eyes. As if she couldn't bring herself to watch what was about to happen.

The judge knit her brow together and scowled at Candy. "Ms. Burns, are you familiar with a private message you wrote to Erin Hogan on Facebook?" She seemed to check the date. "It was on the last Friday in June?" She hesitated, angrier than before. "Please remember you are under oath, Ms. Burns."

Candy twisted her hands together and glanced from Naomi Boggs to her attorney and then to the judge again. She was so squirmy she looked like she was being attacked by fire ants behind the witness stand.

"Do you understand the question?" The tone of the judge's question proved she was beyond appalled.

"Yes. I understand." She pursed her lips, clearly angry with herself. But in the next few seconds, she seemed unwilling to commit perjury, either. "Fine." She spat the word in the direction of Ashley and Luke. "I wrote the letter." Her eyes found the judge again. "I didn't see anything wrong with it. I still don't." She cleared her throat and sat a little higher in her seat. "I was just out of prison and I was desperate to have a little money." She managed a laugh, but it was completely without any sort of humor. "I didn't really mean it. I was sort of testing Erin. If she really loved my girls I figured I could ask her to help me out." She hesitated. "Plus I went out drinking the night before and I got a little carried away. Which hurt my judgment."

With every word, every line Candy sunk herself deeper. The judge sat back in her high leather chair and let Candy ramble. At one point she looked at the court stenographer, as if to check that the woman was getting all of this. At the same time, Candy's lawyer lowered his head and rubbed the back of his neck.

Candy was winding down. " … Which was why I thought a Facebook message would work. I mean, it's private and all and I really didn't need a lot of money. I was willing to let Erin keep the girls if that's what she wanted."

"What about your mother, Ms. Burns? She's not here today, so can I assume she doesn't want custody of her granddaughter?"

"No. She doesn't want her." Candy seemed to relish the chance to make her mother look bad. "She wants to work on cruise ships. She said she'd only stay with me and Amy if there was a lot of life insurance money."

Ashley wondered if the judge might laugh out loud or call for Candy Burns's arrest. In the end she did the latter. "Ms. Burns, by acknowledging that you wrote this Facebook message, you just incriminated yourself on the witness stand. You understand that, right?"

Candy blinked. She seemed at a complete loss for words. "Yes?"

The judge looked from Candy to the bailiff near the door and back to Candy. "You are under arrest, Ms. Burns, for attempted extortion. The bailiff will read you your rights." She looked at the deputy again. "Please submit Ms. Burns to drug and alcohol tests and cuff her. I'll contact the DA to determine exact charges in the next day or so."

"Wait!" Candy shouted out. "Can I have a second chance, here? It's not like I knew this was coming!"

"Be quiet!" The judge snapped and held up her hand. "Don't make me add other charges!"

Candy shut her mouth. While the bailiff approached her with handcuffs, the judge turned to Luke. "Mr. Baxter, does someone in your family have temporary power of attorney over the minor child in question?"

"Yes, your Honor."

Ashley could barely stand it. She wanted to jump up and wrap her arms around Luke's neck and celebrate like they'd done when they were kids when their team won. Only this was so much bigger. She folded her hands, and kept quiet.

"Very well, I'd like a home study conducted on your sister," she checked her notes. "Ashley Baxter Blake, please stand."

Ashley practically leapt to her feet. "Your Honor."

"Are you and your husband willing to adopt Amy Elizabeth Hogan?"

"Yes, we are." Tears flooded Ashley's eyes. "It is our greatest desire, your Honor. We love her like she is our own child."

"Very well. Once the home study is complete, this court will void the previous adoption agreement, thereby allowing you and your husband to adopt her free and clear."

"Thank you." Ashley refused her tears. Instead she smiled at the judge. She wanted to tell the woman about her promise to Erin and about how well the girl was adjusting in her new home already. How far they had to go to tap into her emotions. But the judge had other matters so she kept her response short. "My husband and I truly appreciate this."

For the first time, the judge allowed the hint of a smile. She looked at Luke and gave a slight nod. "It's all about the evidence."

Luke and Ashley were dismissed, and when they were out in the hallway, Ashley did what she had wanted to do since the matter swung their way. She locked her arms around her brother's neck and held on to him with everything she had. "I can't believe it . . . Luke, thank you. Dear God, thank You! It's a miracle!"

He swung her around and then took a big step back. "We have to call the others. They're all praying, waiting for word."

Ashley tilted her head back and laughed. If she would've had a window, she could almost see her sister smiling from heaven. They had begged God for a miracle, and He had delivered. And in the process Ashley could finally for all time be the sister Erin deserved. This was the second chance she had wanted when it came to loving Erin. Because for all the ways she had failed to be a loving sister to Erin, this one time she had done it right.

She had kept her promise.

Twenty-Five

Ashley walked through the front door the day after the hearing at just before noon — both exhausted and elated. She had talked with Landon a number of times since the judge made her decision, and each time they were both emotional. Pausing on several occasions because they couldn't get over the goodness of God. His faithfulness.

"Landon?" She set her bag down and looked through the main floor. But it was empty. Then she remembered. He had said he was working out back, since he'd taken the past few days off to be with the kids while Ashley was in Texas. Cole and Devin were at a friend's house, and Kari had picked up Janessa to take her and Annie to the park.

Only Amy was home with Landon. She'd been invited to go with Kari, but she wanted to stay home. Ashley walked to the back kitchen window and stared out. Sure enough, there was Landon digging near the pond. The filter was broken, and he needed to dig up a pipe to fix it. And there, sitting on a bench near the gazebo, was Amy. Her shoulder-length blonde hair looked particularly pale in the bright sunlight. She sat back far enough on the bench that she could swing her legs. Ashley studied her. This was better than a week ago when she barely got off the couch. But even from this far away Ashley could tell she wasn't happy.

But this news was bound to help. Ashley savored the relief as it washed over her again. Amy was home for good. She felt the tension in her shoulders ease, felt her heartbeat settle into the rhythm it had before the accident. The thing was, they could understand if Amy had gone to heaven. Going to heaven was a goal, a gift ... a gain, according to the apostle Paul in Scripture. They would've grieved her loss and celebrated her home-going — all at the same time.

But going to live with Candy Burns?

That would've been something Ashley and Landon never could've understood. With that woman raising her, there was no telling what would've happened to her or who she might've become. But now ... now she was forever in the Baxter family. She would continue to learn what Erin and Sam had been teaching her. She would grow up loving Jesus and helping others and surrounded with family. Because of the miracle God worked in the courtroom yesterday, Amy was home.

Where she would be loved all the days of her life.

Ashley went outside and walked over to the bench where she was sitting. "Can I join you?"

"Sure." Amy slid over and made room for her. "How was your trip?"

"It was good." She took hold of Amy's hand. The girl was quick to cling to her fingers. "Do you know why I went there?"

Amy lifted her eyes to Ashley's. "You had a talk with my social worker?"

"Yes, that was part of it." Ashley watched Landon put down the shovel and join them.

He stooped down and gave Ashley a quick kiss. "I missed you."

"I missed you, too." She looked at Amy. "I was just telling her about my time in Texas."

Landon straightened and put his hand on Ashley's shoulder. The two of them had decided that Ashley should give the girl the news. "Then I think I'll let you two talk and I'll go back to digging." He winked at Amy and she responded with a grin.

This was new, and it touched Ashley's heart to the core. Her husband and her niece building a bond. It was a small step but it was definitely a step in the right direction. When Landon was back working on the pond, Ashley turned to Amy again. "You asked about the social worker. I talked to her about making you part of our family."

Amy looked up, her blue eyes full of the familiar fear. "What about my birth mother?"

"Well ... that's the good news." Ashley stroked Amy's hair. "Your Uncle Luke and I talked to a judge, and the judge said you don't ever have to go see your birth mother. Not ever. You can live here and you never have to go back to Texas again."

Ashley wasn't sure how she expected Amy to react. But the one thing she didn't expect was what was happening now. Huge, crocodile tears gathered in Amy's eyes and dripped onto her jean shorts. She hung her head and her shoulders began to shake. The motion must've hurt her broken arm because she hugged the cast to her chest.

"Honey, what is it?" Ashley put her arm around the child's shoulders. She hadn't cried since she came out of the coma, and many times Ashley had spoken to Amy alone, hoping she might open up about her feelings. But now? "You want to be here, right?"

She wiped her face and her nose on her arm and in a move that seemed to take all her effort, she stood and fell into Ashley's arms, collapsing against her, sobbing and crying as if her little heart wasn't only broken.

It was broken in a million pieces.

"I ... miss my ... mommy ... so much." Amy put her healthy right arm around Ashley's neck and held on tight. "I wanna be ... in heaven."

So that was it. This wasn't Amy rejecting the idea of living with them. It was the emotional breakthrough Ashley and Landon had been praying for. She ran her hand lightly along

Amy's back and let her cry. A few times Landon stopped shovel-
ing and looked over. But Ashley signaled to him that they were
okay. Amy needed this.

"It's okay, honey, I'm here. I understand."

"But . . . why didn't . . . God take me home . . . to heaven, too?"
Her sobs still came in a rapid series, the tears flooding her eyes
and running down her face, her nose still runny. "I miss them. I
want my sissies. And . . . and Heidi Jo is . . . my best friend."

"I know, baby." Ashley held her with both hands, rocking her
and praying away the very great pain. Tomorrow she would call
the church secretary and get Amy set up with Christian counseling. She wanted to do everything she could to help the girl process the unthinkable.

"What does God . . . want me to do?" She pulled away far
enough to search Ashley's face. Amy's eyes were red and swollen,
and her nose was completely stuffed. "You said I'm not in heaven
. . . because He still has something . . . for me to do."

"Lots of things." Ashley framed the child's face with her hand
and searched her eyes. "He gives us things to do every day. And
when we're done here, He takes us home."

She nodded, and it seemed like maybe she had turned a corner in this moment. But then a rush of tears came once more. "I
. . . just miss . . . them so much."

"I'm sorry, Amy." Ashley pulled her close again. "I'm so sorry."

Ten minutes passed while Amy clung to Ashley with her good
hand, as if by letting go she might drown. Gradually . . . probably
more because she was worn out than because the pain had lessened any, the sobs slowed and an afternoon breeze dried her face.
She sniffed and wiped her arm under her nose once more. "I'm
sorry, too."

"You're sorry?" Ashley would've hugged the girl all day if it
would've taken away even a fraction of her heartache. "Why are
you sorry?"

"Because you did a nice thing. You went to Texas and made it so I can live here." The corners of her lips lifted, and her swollen eyes all but disappeared. "That's what I want, Aunt Ashley. I want to live here with you. But then ..." her smile fell off. "I remembered that most of all I wanna live in heaven." She shrugged one shoulder. "And that made me sad." She tilted her head. "I wasn't sad to be here, okay?"

"Sweetie, I know that." Ashley kissed Amy's forehead. "And I want you to cry. Whenever you feel like crying or talking or asking questions, we can always come out here and you can do that."

"Okay." Amy yawned big. "I'm tired. Can I please go to sleep for a while?"

"Yes, honey. Let's go." She took Amy's hand and they walked into the living room, where the sofa still doubled as the child's bed. Ashley waited while Amy climbed up and sprawled out. The air conditioner was on, so Ashley grabbed a blanket from the back of the couch and spread it over her. "You okay?"

"Yes. I'm happy." Amy's eyelids already looked heavy. She reached for Ashley's hand. "Wanna know why?"

"Why?"

"Because until heaven, for now I'm home." Her smile was one of the sweetest Ashley had ever seen. "That makes me happy, Aunt Ashley."

"It makes me happy, too, honey." Ashley sat on the edge of the couch and rubbed Amy's back while she fell asleep. The whole time she marveled over the emotions of a child. How Amy could be sobbing one minute with no sign of comfort or relief, and then the next minute exhibit unhindered joy, her happiness sweet and genuine. It was that faith-like-a-child lesson her father had noticed at his barbecue birthday. The idea that kids held on more loosely. They might cry and grieve, but then just as easily they could transition to a happy thought or the chance to play with dolls.

Or, like for Amy Elizabeth, the joy in being home.

At least until heaven.

JOHN WAITED UNTIL THAT NIGHT TO slip away to his home office and open the package. Three months had passed since the accident, and summer was over. With the coming of fall the missing only grew worse, both the missing and the certainty that Erin and her family were safe and whole and happier than they'd ever been.

But sometime around the first of September, John wanted more than the hope of heaven to keep him company on the long winter days ahead. He wanted meaning and purpose, a glimpse of understanding into why Erin had to leave here so soon. And so he looked up the national registry for organ donors and wrote a letter. People met with the recipients of organ donations all the time these days. Hardly a month went by when John didn't hear about a talk show or news program featuring the reunion of organ donor families and the person who received the organ.

Just yesterday the news out of Indianapolis told the story of a teenage boy who died in an ATV accident, and his grieving mother getting the chance to hug the young father who received the boy's heart. The mother was quoted saying, "Just the chance to hug that man and hear my boy's heart beat one more time ... I felt like his life still mattered. It was the greatest feeling since the accident."

John wasn't sure about a reunion with the recipients. But stories like that one made him at least want a little information. Or maybe his being a doctor made him feel this way. After all, he'd only shared his curiosity with Brooke, out of all his kids. She didn't feel the need to know, but she understood his thoughts.

"It's not really a connection to them," Brooke had told him the last time they talked about it. "But if it brings meaning to the accident, then look into it, Dad."

So that's what he had done. His letter was a formality, a written request that the registry might give his name and address and some basic information about the Hogan family to any of the people given organs from Erin, Sam, or the girls. In case the recipients wanted to know more and in the hopes that they might contact him. That was all he could do. If the recipients wanted to stay anonymous, then that was that. But John had to try, and this morning when he brought in the mail there was a large manila envelope slipped in with the bills and advertising. The address at the top made him stop for several seconds, staring at it.

It was from the national registry.

Elaine was visiting her daughter across town. John had told her about the package, but he hadn't shared the news with any of the others. Elaine understood that he wanted to be alone to read whatever it held. There would be time to share the contents later. He opened his office window and sat in his leather computer chair. A cool bit of fresh air drifted through the screen and with it the hint of burning leaves from somewhere nearby.

Slowly, he slid his finger beneath the envelope flap and peered inside. As he did, his heartbeat sped up. It was like he thought. The package contained what looked like three separate sealed envelopes and a cover letter. He pulled that out first. It was addressed to him and it explained that enclosed were personal letters from three of the recipients. For his purpose, the registry had written on the envelopes of each of the letters which organ from which of his family members the recipient had been given.

John hesitated. He wasn't quite comfortable with this, as if by reading about the new location of one of their organs he was learning of their death all over again. But that thought was ridiculous, of course. Erin and her family weren't back in Texas, too busy to call. They were gone, and he wouldn't see them until heaven. He took a long, slow breath and slid the contents onto his desk.

Three letters.

Across the front of the first envelope it said: Verified by the Organ Donor Registry — Re: 13-year-old girl, lung recipient, lung donated by Clarissa Hogan.

John felt his own lungs tighten as he read the words again. His sweet granddaughter, so full of life and excitement about the future. And now … now her lungs lived inside another girl. John felt the tears in his eyes. He blinked them back so he could see, and without waiting another moment he opened the letter and pulled out two light blue lined pages from inside.

They were separate notes, and quickly John figured out that one was from the girl, the other from her mother. He read the latter first.

Dear Mr. Baxter,

Thank you for contacting us, and telling us a little about Clarissa Hogan, your granddaughter. The feelings this information stirs are strange and conflicting. We are so sorry about your loss, but so grateful for Clarissa's gift. Our daughter is bright and beautiful and very active. She is a soccer player, but she has been fighting a rare lung disease for the past four years.

Before the transplant, she'd been given only weeks to live. She was confined to a hospital bed and every breath was a gasp for life. Mr. Baxter, if you could see her now. She is completely healed from the transplant, and this fall she is playing soccer again. I can barely watch her run across the field without crying. The transplant was a tremendous success. We thought we were going to lose her, and now she has an unlimited future. Not only is she still with us, but she is more alive than ever before.

I wanted to tell you this so you would know a little of the good God has worked out of your loss. I haven't liked to think about Clarissa before this. The idea that another young girl had to give her life so that mine could live simply hurt too much to think about. But your letter gave me hope, Mr. Baxter. My husband and I can no longer be sad or guilt-ridden about the gift of life our daughter has been given. Instead, we will celebrate the fact that Clarissa has new life, also. New life in heaven.

Thank you again for reaching out, and thank you for your gift. Our daughter will take great care of her new lungs, but not a day will go by when we don't consider the cost of her restored life. The very great cost. Praying for you and your family always. Perhaps one day we will meet — we are open to the possibility. Thank you again. In Jesus' light, Beth Cooper

John set the piece of paper down and looked out the window at the night sky. His eyes were still damp, but he felt a sense of joy deep within, a joy he hadn't felt before. Rather than being sad over the reality of the girl walking around whole and healthy with Clarissa's lungs, John felt grateful. Like the Baxter family's tragic loss had a greater purpose because of this.

He picked up the second page, the one from the girl. This one figured to be more difficult, since the girl was only a little younger than Clarissa.

Dear Mr. Baxter,

My name is Sienna and I'm a soccer player. But four years ago I got sick, and starting last year I couldn't play soccer anymore. My lungs were so bad I would get out of breath just getting out of bed or walking into my little brother's room. The doctors said I was going to die if I didn't get a transplant.

But I'm old enough to understand how it works. Someone else would have to die for me to have life. So I had a talk with Jesus, and I told Him it was okay if He wanted to bring me home. I didn't want some other girl to die, and plus I knew I would go to heaven. Some other girl might not know about having Jesus as her Savior. So I asked God not to let me have a lung transplant unless it came from a girl who loved the Lord very much.

Your letter was an answer to my prayer. I'm so glad Clarissa is in heaven with most of her family. Since the operation I can run

*and play soccer and score goals like before, only now I can breathe.
Every day I thank God for my new lungs. But now I add something
else, too. I ask God to tell Clarissa hello for me. One day Clarissa
and I will be friends in heaven, I believe that.*

*If you ever want to come see one of my soccer games, that
would be great. I play harder now, because I have to try my best
every day. It works like that with second chances. Oh, and my coach
says maybe I can play in college. Please tell your whole family I said
thank you. Until next time, your friend, Sienna Cooper.*

John set the page down with the other one and covered his
face with his hands. This was exactly what he'd hoped to find
when he wrote to the registry. A reason to see good from the
devastating loss of his youngest daughter and her family. His tears
were happy ones, and he wiped his cheeks, breathing deep the
rich fall air. He hoped Sienna Cooper would win every game for
the rest of her life, and that God would use her very bright faith
and her beautiful testimony to change lives for Him.

The next letter was from the artist who lived at the south-
ernmost border of the state. She was only eight years old, and
she'd been given one of Clarissa's kidneys. The letter was from
her father, and it said that he'd found faith in God because of the
transplant. He was taking his family to church now. John let his
tears fall, let them clean out what remnants of doubt and hope-
lessness remained lodged in his heart. The picture of what God
had done and was still doing by bringing Erin and Sam and the
girls home to heaven was getting clearer with each letter.

Finally, he picked up the third envelope. This one was con-
cerning a mom with twin girls and a baby boy. The woman who
received Erin's heart. John didn't fight his tears as he read the letter from the woman's husband. His wife would be dead by now,
he said, if not for Erin's heart. He told a little about how the two
of them had fallen in love, and how at the right time the children

had come along. The next part of the man's letter was more difficult to read.

We aren't Christians, like you and your family. It's difficult to believe in a God who would allow tragedy and triumph indiscriminately. But I sense a change in my wife lately. Like she's searching for something. It makes me wonder about the connection she has to your daughter. Karma or something. Anyway ... since you are a religious person, I would ask you to pray for us. It can't hurt. Your daughter's precious gift to my wife has given all of us new life. Thank you seems inadequate, but still we are thankful with every minute, every day. Perhaps we will meet sometime. I have to wonder if my wife would feel connected to you in some way. Sincerely, Moe Bryant.

John's eyes were dry as he finished the letter. *Karma?* His stomach hurt as he looked over the man's words again. God working in the lives of His people indiscriminately? John wasn't sure what he expected, or if somehow he thought that everyone who received an organ donation must've been a praying believer, but this left him unsettled. Erin's heart beating in the chest of a person without faith?

But even before he could take the matter to God, a dawning of understanding began to come over him. Maybe receiving Erin's heart was only the beginning for Moe's wife. What had his letter said? John searched back to find the text. The man saw a change in his wife, like she was searching for something. Clearly that something was a faith in Christ — the way all people were designed with a desperate need for the Savior. Suddenly a smile came over him and he leaned back in his chair.

Erin would've loved this development. While she was alive, she was constantly involved in church ministry, serving one way or another. And she loved running into people who wanted to know about her faith. A memory flashed in his mind, a time when most of the Baxter family served dinner at the mission in downtown Bloomington. Erin and Sam lived nearby at the time, and they had brought their four girls to help serve.

"Jesus wants us to do this, right, Mommy?" Heidi Jo had asked the question in the moments before the doors opened. The little girl wore plastic gloves as she placed a cookie on each meal tray. John stood on one side of her, dishing out salad, and Erin stood on the other, lining up the first few trays in anticipation of the rush of people waiting outside.

Erin's answer stayed with John still. She looked at her daughter and smiled. "Loving people in the name of Jesus is the only reason we're alive. So, yes. Jesus wants us to do this."

John thought about the letter again, and the man's mention that perhaps they would meet sometime. He made a point of following up, making the visit happen. He had a feeling that the man was searching, too, and that in time John and Elaine could play an important role in helping the Bryant family find the faith they were missing.

A soft chuckle sounded in John's throat. Of course God had worked it out this way. The transplant recipient could've been handpicked by Erin. A new heart could only buy the woman a few decades of life. John smiled, grateful for the glimpse of what had to be God's plan in all this. Because now there was a possibility that Erin's heart might not only give the woman immediate life.

But life everlasting.

Twenty-Six

FOURTH OF JULY WEEKEND A YEAR AFTER THE ACCIDENT WAS A low-key affair, and Ashley was glad. A few of them headed down to the lake, and then back to the Baxter house. But now another summer had gone by and the Labor Day picnic was upon them. The one where they would all get together and stage the fishing derby.

The one where memories of a year ago wouldn't dominate the day, but rather they would be focused on the thing that had taken their place. The Baxter family's determination to live.

Ashley finished packing their picnic and a few bags of supplies. Then she called for the kids. "Cole ... make sure you grab the towels."

"Okay." He was seventeen that summer, driving and looking at colleges. For the most part he had decided on Indiana University—music to Ashley's ears, since he'd be close by. He started toward the stairs. "Want me to make sure the girls are ready?"

"Yes, thanks!" Ashley laughed.

He started to walk off, but then he stopped and turned back to her. "Remember last summer ... how I started talking about finding information about my birth dad?"

Ashley felt a flicker of the shock she'd felt that summer morning more than a year ago when he brought the subject up back then. This was the first time since then that he'd mentioned it. She nodded slowly. "I remember. Are you thinking about it again?"

"No." His smile came from the deepest, most tender place

in his heart. "This last year ... I learned something about family. Like it's not about blood alone. It's being connected ... it's growing up together and loving each other. It's believing in the same God and knowing you'd do anything for the person across from you at dinner. Like Amy."

"Cole." Ashley leaned against the kitchen counter and tried to catch her breath. She had never loved her oldest son more than now. "Wow ... that was beautiful."

He shrugged in the casual way he had about him. His eyes shone with a peace that hadn't been there a year ago. "It's true." He pointed toward the stairs. "I'll go get the girls."

The girls were never ready on time, but the reason was a good one. The two had become very close. They were nearly five years apart, but Amy seemed to have an extra sense of love and concern for her little cousin. Her little sister.

Devin came barreling down the stairs, a grin on his face. "Today's the day."

"Yes it is." Ashley crossed her arms and studied her younger son. Devin was growing again, and she knew it was only a matter of time before he caught up to her. "It's the day the Lord has made, for sure."

"Mom!" Devin erupted into a few seconds of giggling. "Not that." His eyes grew suddenly wide. "I mean, yes. It's the day the Lord has made definitely." He was clearly beyond happy, giddy from the excitement of the coming day. "I mean this is the day we win the fishing derby." He raised his fist in the air. "It's time for the Blake Boys to make a comeback."

Ashley smiled. "Okay, then today's the day for that, too."

He hurried off calling for Landon. "Dad ... you have the fishing gear and the tackle box?"

From somewhere in the garage came Landon's muffled response. Ashley breathed it in, the sounds and smells of a day like this. Every summer, every picnic at the lake with the whole family made her think they'd always have these special times. But that wasn't true. Erin's accident proved as much. Cole and Devin, Janessa and Amy ... they would all grow up and find their ways into families of their own.

Maybe their future families would have the chance to meet at Lake Monroe for Fourth of July or Labor Day celebrations. But maybe not. All they really had was this single, beautiful, sunny summer day. The end of another summer.

Ashley walked to the playroom and studied her newest painting, the one she had created in place of the one that used to hang here. Now the painting was more full. Her mother still sat in a rocking chair at the center of the piece of art, and baby Sarah was still in her arms. But now Erin stood beside her, one arm loosely placed around their mother's shoulders, her smile filling her face. Beside her was Sam and scattered all around them were the girls — Clarissa and Chloe and Heidi Jo — all of them alive and vibrant looking. She had painted Clarissa's face midlaugh — the way she still remembered her dear niece.

The painting had been a healing part of the past year. She finished it the day before Easter. *Appropriate*, she told herself. On the weekend most celebrated for new life, that she could provide for her family a picture straight from her heart. The picture she carried with her of those they loved, at home in heaven.

"Ashley?" Landon was looking for her.

She stepped out of the playroom and saw him headed her way. The sound of his voice, the look in his eyes still warmed her heart and made her marvel at the fact that he was really here, the man God had given her. As long as she drew breath she would be grateful for him. They came together in an easy hug, their eyes and hearts and souls connected. "Hey," his voice was low and marked by the passion between them. "You ready?"

"Mmmm. Not if you talk to me in that tone." She grinned, enjoying him. "We could always leave in half an hour."

He laughed. "How did I get so blessed? Marrying you, Ashley Baxter Blake?"

"The blessing has always ... always been mine." Her teasing tone gradually eased. "Thanks for staying ... thanks for loving me."

"Mom! Everyone's in the — " Cole jogged into view from the front door. He stopped when he saw them and his laughter joined Landon's. "Okay, you two. Are we leaving or what?"

"Leaving!" Landon grabbed his tackle box from the counter. He flashed Ashley a smile as he walked past her. "You're always distracting me." He winked at her. "You heard the boy, everyone's waiting."

THE PICNIC ENDED UP BEING ONE of their best yet. Ashley sat with Kari and Brooke at a table not too far from the water, watching the kids play Frisbee and football in the shallow water. Even the fishing derby had been the closest contest in years, and true to his prediction, the Blake men finally won. Twenty-one fish caught in thirty minutes. A new Baxter Fishing Derby record.

Like always, the Flanigan family joined them. Bailey and Brandon had been married for more than a year, their Christian theater business in town thriving beyond what they had dreamed. Dayne and Katy were expecting another baby — a brother for Egan, and they were talking about wrapping things up in LA and making their home base Bloomington once more.

Beside her, Brooke and Kari talked about the crisis pregnancy center, the one Brooke and Ashley had opened. Brooke and her teenage girls — Hayley and Maddie — had started a Bible study at the center every Saturday morning. It was an outreach to teens who had changed their minds about wanting an abortion. Brooke was going on, telling Kari about two new girls in the study and how they wanted to know more about God.

Ashley stopped listening. Her mind was too full of the wonder all around her, the way they had survived last year's loss. She spotted Amy playing with Devin and Malin and RJ — the cousins closest to her age. "Let's say you have to chase the girls first." Amy gave Malin a high five. "Because we're faster!"

"Okay," Devin looked at RJ. "Here we come!" The two boys set off after the girls, and against a backdrop of squealing and laughter the chase was on.

Amazing, Ashley thought. The resiliency of a child. The resiliency of all of them, really. She remembered watching a documentary once on Southern California wildfires, and being struck by the before and after pictures. After a fire swept through, the ground and everything in the path of the fire was charred black without any sign of life. But just a year later, fresh new grass lay thick across the place where once there had only been ashes. The trees held new buds and branches, and construction had replaced the burned-down buildings.

Beauty from ashes — much the way God had given it to them over the last fourteen months. Or like her father once said: *This too shall pass.* The heartache and grief and horror of the accident were something they would remember, but time had brought healing. She breathed in deep and surveyed the laughter and joy around her, their family gathered again. Survivors, all of them. A year later, life reigned.

Even for Amy.

At that moment, the child turned toward Ashley, almost as if she knew what her aunt was thinking. A smile lit up her tanned face and she raced up, her blonde hair flying behind her.

"Hi, Aunt Ashley. I love you." She gave Ashley a quick hug, her blue eyes shining with sparkles of joy and hope.

"I love you, too, little miss." She took Amy's small face gently in her hands and kissed her cheek. "Looks like you're having fun."

"I am." She was still breathless, her smile filling her face.

"But my hair's blowing in my eyes." She pulled a hair tie from her shorts pocket and handed it to Ashley. "Please, can you braid my hair? So it doesn't fly around?"

"Of course." Ashley felt a quick piercing of sorrow, the way she often felt it when Amy wanted her hair braided. This was how Erin had once connected with their father, and it was how the child had connected with Erin. It remained one way Ashley still felt her sister's presence, her memory here between them. She smiled and ran her hand over Amy's long hair. "Turn around, sweetie."

Over the past year, Ashley's dad had taught her how to French braid and now she was practically an expert. She ran her fingers through Amy's hair, layering it and twisting it and in no time she fastened the end with the tie. "There you go."

"Thanks." Amy flashed her a grin over her shoulder. "See ya!" And with that she ran back down the hill to join the others. Ashley wished for a few seconds that she could live here in this moment forever, when everyone was whole and happy and alive, when love reigned and God's goodness was evident with every breath. But that wasn't possible. Nothing stayed the same. Not last year's heartache and loss and devastation.

And not this.

She looked up the hill and smiled toward the place where her dad and Elaine sat together, holding hands. He was still healthy, still a strong fisherman. Still able to play with his grandkids on the beach. He had been in touch with the woman who had received Erin's heart, and he felt strongly that one day he would meet her. That in time the woman would give her life to Jesus. Nothing about Ashley's amazing father seemed seventy-one years old. But he was. And there were no guarantees about his health or the health of any of them.

Only when they all reached heaven would they have forever to enjoy each other the way they were enjoying each other here, one more time, on the shores of Lake Monroe. Ashley stood and dusted the sand off her shorts. Cole and Jessie and Maddie were tossing a football at the far end of the beach, and Ashley figured they needed one more person to keep the ball moving. She headed that way, her heart and mind filled with the voices and laughter around her.

This was what a family should be ... a family saved by redemption, one that could remember the good times and return to them whenever tragedy threatened to rock their foundation. A family that could rejoice together and celebrate reunions like this one at the lake. One where fame didn't touch it and where wrongs were quickly forgiven. Through the years, together they had found more than a strong faith in God, they had found a family ... one that would last forever. Through every sunrise and someday, every summer and sunset. Through it all they would always be this, the greatest family of all.

The Baxter Family.

FROM THE AUTHOR

Dear Friends,

When I thought about writing a final book on the Baxter Family, the task seemed daunting — both emotionally and logistically. The Baxters have lived and breathed in the pages of twenty-two books prior to this. Twenty-two pieces of their family story or the stories of people close to them. From *Redemption* to *Reunion*, *Fame* to *Forever*, *Sunrise* to *Sunset*, *Take One* to *Take Four*, and the Bailey Flanigan series *Leaving* to *Loving* ... through all of those books I've written about and fallen in love with the Baxter family.

If you ask me this very moment what each of them are doing, I will have an answer for you — further proof that my husband is right when he says I'll make an interesting old lady one day, when I can't tell my characters from my kids.

But still, I wasn't sure I could take the best of yesterday and wrap it into a compelling story for today, a story with enough detail to meet the needs of new readers and enough heart and reflection for the rest of you, my faithful reader friends who have journeyed with me from the beginning.

But I believe God gave me exactly what I was looking for when He gave me the story line for *Coming Home*. I cried often as I wrote this book, out of nostalgia for the way God had seen the Baxters through in the past and out of heartache for all they were going through this time around.

I didn't want to write the last paragraph.

But I can say this ... even as I finish up with these friends, the Baxter family, God is stirring new ideas in my heart and mind and soul. Some of them might connect back to Bloomington, and others will happen in new places, with new characters. I have a book coming out this fall called *The Bridge*. It's a book like that — new and full of fresh faces. A love story I felt privileged to write.

Still, as I look forward to all the exciting, emotional, life-changing books I've yet to bring you, it's been very important writing about the Baxters one more time, appreciating them and spending time with them. They are my first family of this Life-Changing Fiction™ God has given me to write. So if you're not familiar with the earlier books, this is your chance. Head to your local library or bookstore, or click the links on your e-reader and find your way back to *Redemption*, the first Baxter book.

You won't want to miss all that's happened before, everything that led us to this place. Either way, thanks for traveling the pages of this book with me. I pray God has used it to touch your heart, and that as you read the final lines you found a deeper appreciation for faith and family and finding your greatest life in Christ.

As always, I look forward to your feedback. Take a minute and find me on Facebook! I'm there at least once a day — hanging out with you in my virtual living room, praying for you, and answering as many questions as possible. On Facebook I have Latte Time, where I'll take a half hour or so, pour all of you a virtual latte or espresso or hot chocolate, and take questions live and in person. A couple hundred thousand of us hang out there and have a blast together. So come on over and "like" my Facebook Fan Page.

You all are very special to me.

Also follow me on Twitter, where I have an ongoing "Tweet a KK Quote" contest. You tweet a quote from one of my books and include my Twitter name — @KarenKingsbury. The first week of every month, if I retweet you, send your name and address to contests@karenkingsbury.com. I'll send you a free signed book!

Also visit my website at www.KarenKingsbury.com. There

you can find my contact information and my guestbook. Remember, if you post something on my Facebook or my website, it might help another reader, so thanks for stopping by. In addition, I love to hear how God is using these books in your life. He puts a story on my heart, but He has your heart in mind.

Only He could do that.

Also, on Facebook or my website, you can check out my upcoming events and find out about movies being made on my books. Post prayer requests on my website, or read those already posted and pray for those in need. If you'd like, you may send in a photo of your loved one serving our country in the armed services, or let us know of a fallen soldier we can honor on our Fallen Heroes page.

When you're finished with this book, pass it on to someone else. If you let me know, you will automatically be entered to win a signed novel through my "Shared a Book" contest. E-mail me at contest@KarenKingsbury.com and tell me the first name of the person you shared with! In addition, everyone who is signed up for my monthly newsletter through my website is automatically entered into an ongoing once-a-month drawing for a free, signed copy of my latest novel.

There are links on my website that will help you with matters that are important to you — faith and family, adoption and redemption. Of course, on my site you can also find out a little more about me, my faith and my family, the writing process, and the wonderful world of Life-Changing Fiction™.

Finally, if you gave your life over to God during the reading of this book, or if you found your way back to faith in Him, please know I'm praying for you. Tell me about your life change by sending me a letter to Office@KarenKingsbury.com. Write "New Life" in the subject line. If this is your situation, I encourage you to connect with a Bible-believing church in your area, pray for God's leading, and start reading the Bible.

But if you can't afford one and don't already have one, write "Bible" in the subject line. Tell me how God used this novel to change your life, and then include your address in your e-mail. If you are financially unable to find a Bible any other way, I will send you one.

One last thing. If you make an official request, I will donate a book to any high school or middle school librarian or to anyone staging a charitable auction. Check out my website for details.

Again, thanks for journeying with me through the pages of this book. I can't wait to hear your feedback on *Coming Home*! Oh, and look for my next love story — *The Bridge*, out this fall.

Until then, keep your eyes on the cross.

In His light and love,
Karen Kingsbury
www.KarenKingsbury.com

DISCUSSION QUESTIONS

1. What is the greatest lesson you learned while reading *Coming Home*? Why do you think you came away with that lesson?

2. Talk about a tragedy in your life. Recall the details and share how you felt at the time.

3. In the wake of that tragedy, how did you move on? What were some things that helped you?

4. Did the accident in *Coming Home* take you by surprise? How did the faith of the Baxter family help them deal with this tragedy?

5. There is a definite dynamic in the Baxter family. Which of the adult siblings can you most relate to? Why?

6. What did you think of Erin's vision of heaven? What is heaven like in your mind?

7. Erin and her family were coming home when the accident happened. Tell about a homecoming or reunion you were a part of.

8. Why are homecomings important? What good things have come from such times in your life?

9. What good came from the Baxters being together when the accident happened? How did they help each other?

10. The Baxters relied on their faith to survive the tragedy of Erin's accident. Explain how that came across in *Coming Home*.

11. Tell about how faith in God has helped you get through a tragedy or difficult time.

12. If you have never considered having faith in God, did this book make you think about the possibility? Why or why not?

13. If you have read about the Baxters in many books now, what lessons has this family taught you?

14. How have you applied what you've learned from the Baxter family in your own life? What have the results been?

15. Oftentimes, the Baxters would sing a favorite hymn of theirs — "Great Is Thy Faithfulness." What do the words to this song mean to you?

16. Organ donation is discussed in *Coming Home*. What do you think about organ donation and how has it affected your life or the life of someone you know?

17. Ashley has a revelation at the end of *Coming Home* — that life never stays the same. How have you seen this to be true in your life?

18. What is the greatest message of hope you'll take away after reading *Coming Home*?

19. Tell how your family is like the Baxter family.

20. In what ways do you wish your family were more like the Baxter family? What can you do to see that those changes happen?